PRAISE FOR
RACHAEL HERRON'S
WORK

"A poignant, profound ode to the enduring and
redemptive power of love."
— Library Journal

"A celebration of the power of love to heal even the most
broken of hearts."
- NYT Bestselling Author Susan Wiggs

"A heart-warming story of family, friendship and love in
a town you'll never want to leave."
— Barbara Freethy, USA Today Bestseller

ALSO BY RACHAEL HERRON

FICTION:

STANDALONE NOVELS:

THE ONES WHO MATTER MOST
SPLINTERS OF LIGHT
PACK UP THE MOON

THE DARLING BAY NOVELS
THE DARLING SONGBIRDS
THE SONGBIRD'S CALL
THE SONGBIRD'S HOME

CYPRESS HOLLOW NOVELS 1-5:

HOW TO KNIT A LOVE SONG
HOW TO KNIT A HEART BACK HOME
WISHES & STITCHES
CORA'S HEART
FIONA'S FLAME

MEMOIR:

A LIFE IN STITCHES

The Songbird's Call

by

RACHAEL HERRON

Publisher's Note: This is a work of fiction. Names, characters, places, and incidents are a product of the author's imagination. Locales and public names are sometimes used for atmospheric purposes. Any resemblance to actual people, living or dead, or to businesses, companies, events, institutions, or locales is completely coincidental.

The Songbird's Call / Rachael Herron. -- 1st ed.

HGA Publishing

ISBN-13: 978-1-940785-29-5

CHAPTER ONE

At one time in her life, Molly had liked a good old-fashioned country dive bar as much as the next singer-songwriter. Every honky-tonk smelled a little different, but they shared the same notes of pine dust and good tequila, of cowboy aftershave made of bay rum and cloves mixed with the scent of bitters and quinine. Each bar sounded the same, too – bottle caps snapping off, Hank Williams wailing on the jukebox, balls clacking on the pool table, men trying to impress women who were laughing and pretending to pay no attention.

Molly inhaled deeply and then wished she was back on the cruise ship. Even though she'd spent the last six years fighting mild seasickness, the ship had felt safe. She'd been anonymous there. The Golden Spike Saloon was packed with people, and all of them were smiling right at her. Faces. So many grinning faces. When had the world become so *friendly?* The floor pitched under her feet, a tiny swell that no one else seemed to notice.

That morning, so early the early-bird passengers hadn't yet made it to the breakfast buffet, Molly had hugged her friend Janette goodbye, bequeathing her two enormous bars of duty-free Toblerone from a grateful client. Molly had taken a plane that took off and landed uneventfully, then she'd taken a bus that had run fine and then one more bus that *hadn't* run fine at all. With an impressive explosion, it had blown some very important part of its engine an hour south of Darling Bay. She'd had to text her sister Adele's boyfriend, Nate – the one who'd helped her plot this surprise – to come get her, which wasn't her original plan. She'd wanted to arrive mid-afternoon. She'd wanted to find Adele and hug her to pieces, and then they'd walk down to the water's edge and watch the sun drip into the ocean.

Instead, Molly had arrived at the bar at its most crowded, and the patrons, most of them at least two drinks in, were elated to have *two* of their Darling Songbirds back in one room. Molly hadn't felt this famous in, well...it had been a little more than eleven years since the band had broken up and she hadn't been famous in about ten and a half. Fame had a short memory.

Nothing had changed about the old saloon, and yet everything had. The walls were still dark wood, the beams scarred overhead from being chopped and shaped by Molly's great-grandfather in the late 1800s. When she and her sisters were little, they'd hide in the storeroom at night and peek out at the bands playing on the small stage. Everything Molly knew about flirtation she'd learned from watching cowboys dance with girls in the half-light of neon beer signs.

But everything was different, too. Her sister, Adele, instead of being at her elbow in the storeroom, was next to her – they were full-grown women, standing at the bar instead of peeping out at it. Adele was *running* the place. Adele, her accomplished song-writing sister – the one Molly had been sure would never leave Nashville – was not only in charge of the bar their uncle had left to the three Darling sisters, but she was in love with the man who'd been running it when she'd arrived back in town. Like the bar itself, there was something more deeply changed in Adele – the jitteriness that seemed to have sometimes defined her older sister was gone. Adele had always been a fidgeter, unable to stand still, always *fixing* something. Now she seemed more...rooted.

Molly looked more closely at Adele. She followed her sister's happy gaze across the bar room and caught sight of Nate talking to an older woman wearing an ill-fitting Santa suit and a rope of flashing colored lights. "Oh, man. You have it so bad."

Adele shrugged guiltily. "*So* bad." Those honeyed locks waved gracefully around her face. Molly had always wished she had hair that looked like that. Instead, Molly had inherited their father's dark, straight, completely obstinate hair, and she could feel it was sticking up, out of control from the day's travel, and there was nothing she could do about it.

"You're so adorable I kind of want to hurl."

"I'm twitterpated. What can I say?"

Molly laughed even though it felt forced in her throat. "You're not even the kind to *say* twitterpated."

Adele closed her eyes. At one point, Molly would have known, automatically, what Adele was thinking. Their mother had always said it was like the three girls shared a brain, and even though it had just been a mother's gentle joke whenever they did something ill-advised (often involving an unbridled and "borrowed" horse), there was more to it than that. At one time, it had felt as if they really were inside each other's heads. Adele would know right before the younger Molly was about to cry and give her a peppermint purloined from the always full jar in Uncle Hugh's upstairs parlor. Molly would know right before their baby sister Lana was about to lose her temper and start yelling. Molly would slip her hand into Lana's and squeeze tight – Lana would grip her fingers so strongly that Molly would grimace, but sometimes the lightning wouldn't flash, and Molly would know that she had absorbed some of her sister's storminess. The three of them were stronger together. Better. When they'd shared a stage every night for those five years, their connection had been their magic. Even while playing to fifty thousand people – even while the rest of the brightly strobe-lit stage was full of other musicians and production crew and stage hands – in each other's eyes, there was only ever the three of them in the whole wide world.

Adele was the fixer.

Molly was the voice.

Lana was the artist.

It was always just the three of them, together, until they were so broken that they couldn't even bear being in the same state, let alone the same room.

Impulsively, Molly set down her vodka tonic on the time-worn bar. She turned and took Adele's face in her hands, one hand on either cheek. Adele had always been taller than she was, so Molly had to simultaneously pull down on Adele's head and stretch up on her own tiptoes to do it, but she managed to kiss Adele's forehead with a giant *smack*.

Adele looked stunned, her eyes wide. "I forgot."

Their father had always done that. If their mother's signature act of fondness was a soft hug and a light laugh, their father's had been this: the cheek grab, the kiss so hard it came across as an order of sorts, a demand to *love* and love hard.

"I know," said Molly. "I almost did, too. Can't forget this, though." She used her fingers to ruffle Adele's hair.

"God." Adele shook her hair forward and back. "I hated that part of it."

"What you should actually hate is the fact that you have pink ChapStick on your forehead."

"Oh, man." But Adele didn't seem to mind and only swiped at it haphazardly with a napkin.

"You're not getting it all." Molly took another napkin and rubbed harder at Adele's forehead. "There. That's better."

The rest of Christmas night passed in a blur of rum and eggnog and hot mulled cider in the saloon. Someone had brought a ham, and there were trays full of bacon wrapped appetizers. Molly had forgotten how busy the bar got during the holidays, everyone either celebrating with their families or desperately trying to get away from them. After an hour of the noise, Molly was exhausted but didn't want to go anywhere. Close to her sister. That was what she needed.

Adele seemed to be feeling it, too. "I'm so glad you're here. Have I said that already?"

Oh, no, it looked like tears were shimmering in Adele's eyes, and while Molly prided herself on being stronger than ever, she wasn't yet equipped to deal with her kryptonite. She smiled. "Maybe?"

"You and Nate. You both did all this. You *plotted*. Behind my back!"

Warmth rested in Molly's stomach. "And you love it."

"Best Christmas gift ever. You have to stay. You will, right?"

Molly *did* have to stay, but her sister didn't know that yet. The cruise ship's administration hadn't been willing to give her time onshore for the busy holiday season, but Molly had found herself unable to spend another New Year's Eve away from family. Lana was in Ontario for some unknown reason and, after the one single phone conversation Molly had had with her about the Golden Spike property, she was barely answering text messages. The only other place for Molly was here, with Adele, back in Darling Bay.

She watched as Adele darted Nate a private look that reminded her so sharply of the way their mother used to look at their father that it made her chest ache. One year, their father had bought a big box of maple candy. The candies were carved into tiny scenes – a man on a sleigh, a boy tapping a tree for sap – and they were made of nothing but maple syrup. The flavor was pure and sweet and couldn't be more mapley if it tried. They'd been the very essence of sugar, Molly had always thought.

That was the way Adele and Nate were looking at each other over the bar-patrons' heads.

It should be disgusting and sappy, as sickeningly sweet as the maple candy had been. Instead, the look warmed a place in Molly's chest she hadn't known had gone cold.

"Oh, Molly, isn't he great?" Adele didn't seem to have noticed that Molly hadn't answered whether or not she would stay.

"He's great." Molly had already been pretty sure that was the case after talking to Nate on the phone. He'd been friendly without being overly so. He'd offered to help in planning but hadn't assumed she'd needed it. He'd offered to pay for her flight but had attached no obligations to it. *I know you and your sister haven't seen each other in a long time. I'd love you to come to Darling Bay for the holidays. No problem if you can't, if you're already committed to doing something else. If you're free though, it'd be great to finally meet you.*

Molly had been in her small onboard office when she'd taken his first call. She'd stared at the calendar. Two weeks till Christmas. *Are you in love with my sister?* Although she'd already known the answer, she'd wanted to hear what length hesitation would be in his voice, like counting the seconds after the flash before the boom in a thunderstorm.

Completely. There had been no hesitation, not even half a second's worth. She'd let him buy her a ticket that very night. She would worry about how to pay him back later.

"He's so much..." Adele started.

"Yeah?"

"He's so much more than just great."

"Oh, Lord."

"It sounds clichéd to you."

"No." Molly didn't want to take away a single iota of Adele's happiness. "It's just that..."

"It sounds silly."

"It doesn't. It makes me wistful, that's all."

"And you? What about that guy you mentioned, the one in the laundry, right?"

"Oh, God. No. Jeremy didn't work out. Well, he worked *out*. That's about all he did."

"So you're saying he was strong."

Molly grinned. That had, in fact, been one of his best qualities, the way he could lift Molly and fling her around on the bed as if she weighed less than a bag of sheets. The cruise ship had a huge laundry room the size of three veranda suites put together, and Molly had experienced her fair share of being pressed up against the heated dryer drums as they had added to the ambient thumping noises. "Yeah, well." Jeremy had been fun – he'd been the one before Rick. And *Rick* was the one who'd left her broke and sad and angry, a terrible combination.

"You okay?"

Molly could almost feel the energy she'd conserved for this – the first meeting with her sister in three years – evaporate. "Yeah."

"You're tired. Look at you. Let's put you to bed. Come on."

"I thought you said we had to sing." It had almost been the first thing Adele had said after hooting with delight at the sight of her standing in the doorway.

Adele looked at her, her gaze soft. "There'll be time for that. Right?"

Maybe. If Molly didn't freak out and jump a Greyhound bus tomorrow. "Sure."

Someone had put "O Come All Ye Faithful" on the jukebox and half the bar was singing along. The older woman Nate was talking to had turned on the Christmas lights that draped around her neck, and she looked for all the world like a short, squat Christmas tree dressed in red cloth.

"Nate told me he put your bags in your room already."

Molly felt a wave of gratefulness sweep through her. "Upstairs? In Uncle Hugh's apartment?" That was, after all, where the whole family had stayed whenever they were in town visiting their dad's brother.

"Oh." Adele spread her fingers and looked down at them, as if she were holding something she wanted to show to Molly. "No. Not there. It's not quite ready for...guests."

Molly was a guest now?

"Do you mind very much? It's just been me and Nate there for the last couple of months, and I haven't fixed up the spare room, yet."

Molly straightened her spine. "I would never want to get in your way." Lovebirds, locked in love jail. What could be more irritating to be around, really? It would be better if she didn't have to avoid them and their inevitable kissy noises. Or worse.

"Crap, I'm sorry. I thought I could put you in room one. You'll like it."

Of course. Adele figured things out, and then Molly did what she was told. That's the way it had always been. "That's the only usable room, right?" She hadn't seen the damage yet, but Molly was the one Adele had called when she'd first arrived in Darling Bay after Uncle Hugh had died. The whole place had been a wreck. According to Adele, the twelve-room hotel that sat nestled up in the hillside behind the saloon was a trashed and unusable disaster. There had been no locusts, but that was about the only biblical disaster that hadn't befallen the rooms yet. From mold to fire damage, the rooms were uninhabitable except for one.

Adele nodded. "It's nice."

"You said the bed was hell on your back."

"I got used to it."

"You got used to being on your back?" Molly winked to take the sting out of her words. It would be fine. "Come on, show me."

"Okay...Oh, but *wait* till you see the courtyard." Adele pushed open the door and led Molly outside. "*Look.*"

CHAPTER TWO

O h," said Molly in a whisper. The space behind the bar used to hold one picnic table and one bench whose four feet never reached the ground at the same time. The only decoration had been a stockpile of old gas grills that Uncle Hugh had collected and never got around to fixing. It had been depressing, a place for the men to gather and smoke pipes while pulling on their beers, a place for the sisters to race through quickly on their way out to the beach or up to the oak trees in the hills beyond the hotel property.

Now, though, it was a twinkling paradise. Someone had built an arbor out of what looked like old driftwood. Grapevines twisted overhead, and on the sides, jasmine grew upwards. Smack-dab in the middle of winter, the jasmine shouldn't have had any flowers at all, but somehow, it was blooming shyly, releasing its heady perfume. Molly touched a tiny flower. "How . . .?"

"Ain't global warming great?" Adele tucked up an errant vine.

Twined through the arbor and vines were thousands of white lights that danced and swayed as the night breeze whispered through them. Sturdy-looking picnic tables provided plenty of seating. In the darkest corner, a young woman sat on a man's lap – she put on his cowboy hat and laughed and then leaned forward for a kiss. Molly, used to watching couples canoodle (and worse) on the cruise ship, suddenly felt embarrassed to be witnessing such a sweet embrace. She looked at her sister, who watched her expectantly.

"It's gorgeous."

"Nate did it all. Remember how Dad and Uncle Hugh used to sit out here for hours?"

Molly nodded. "Donna would be bartending and she'd yell dirty jokes to them."

"Oh, my God, I'd forgotten that part." Adele's eyes sparkled like the lights above. "Some of those jokes were so dirty I'm not sure I'd get them even now."

"Okay. Onwards!" Nerves shot through Molly's body, pulsing electricity to the tips of her fingers.

She followed Adele on the path that wound through the old rosebushes in the dark. Solar lights at ankle level lit their way, but they'd traversed this short route so many times as children, Molly was pretty sure she could have run up the paving stones with her eyes closed. Even though they'd only been in town on summer breaks and winter holidays, Darling Bay had always felt like home.

Their mother, dead for so long now, had planted some of these roses. They were thriving.

The hotel rooms were set back, built into the hill above the saloon in a half-circle. Rooms one through four were on the left, rooms five through eight were straight ahead, with the remaining four on the right-hand side. Shallow steps led up to the three sides, and a long porch ran right around. Somehow Molly had forgotten the porch swings, but as soon as she saw them – unmoving in darkness – the phantom sound of them filled her head like a melody she'd almost lost, all wooden creaks and happy groans.

As if reading her mind, Adele spoke over her shoulder, "Don't sit in any of them except this one here. I fixed it up after it fell with me still in it."

Of *course* she had. "I'm surprised you haven't fixed the others." Two hung sideways, their chains rusted, and one of the old swings was resting on the porch itself.

"Girl," Adele shook her head as she opened the door to the room, "you have *no* idea how much there is to fix. Come on in. It's safe in here, at least."

The bed had been moved, Molly thought, and the room felt smaller. The curtains were dingy off-white, but it smelled the same – of oak hardwood floors and something citrusy, and something that smelled exactly like Adele. "I'd forgotten you love orange-scented soap." Molly's two suitcases, battered by mileage and a thousand different cabins, had already been placed at the foot of the bed.

Adele patted a pillow, fluffing it. "Your detective nose. Yeah, when I was staying in here I used my own stuff instead of the old hotel soaps. You know there are about a million of them in the maid's closet? Like, he must have bought them at cost in the sixties or something. A gazillion tiny slivers of paper-wrapped soap. It doesn't go bad, right? If we ever open the hotel again, we could probably still use them, you think? Would antique soap add to the charm or take away from it?"

Molly shrugged. "I don't know much about hotel soap. Oh. Except for this one guy we had on an Aegean cruise. Or was it a Mediterranean one? Can't remember. He ate soap."

Adele pulled back a curtain. "See, I know most of the – wait, *what?*"

"Pica disorder. He came to see me on board because he wanted to make sure the housekeepers didn't put any in his room. He had a bottle of liquid soap that he wasn't tempted by. He just couldn't be in the same room as solid bars. He also ate paper. He had to buy a Kindle to keep himself from chewing pages as he read." She was busy sometimes, but not often. Being a nutritionist on a cruise ship was like being the ship's priest: only there in case of emergency. The onboard chaplain was just in case someone died. (Which people *had* done, actually, at a rate that had surprised Molly until she'd factored in the average cruiser's age along with their dietary habits. Young, healthy, active people tended to book trips to Nepal or Iceland or the Scottish Highlands – they didn't usually book all-you-can-eat week-long cruises to Mazatlán where the highlight was the early-bird tequila-fuelled bingo game.)

Adele laughed. "Let's hope he never comes here, then. He could be the one thing that would threaten our soap stash." She pointed out the window. "Look. Some of the path lighting still doesn't work, but that makes the saloon even prettier, I think."

"Oh, Adele." Another thing Molly had forgotten was this view down the low rise. The garden was mostly dark, but from here they could see the twinkle lights in the arbor. To the left side was the staircase that led up to Uncle Hugh's old apartment that made up the top floor of the saloon. White lights were strung around the railing, and multi-colored holiday lights blinked on and off around a sun umbrella. Tall, dark shapes made up the trees on the far side of the building.

Molly reached past Adele and slid the window open a crack. "There we go." The sound was barely audible, just loud enough to hear if she listened hard: a burst of music as someone opened the back door of the saloon, a clap of laughter, a woman's voice asking a question whose words they couldn't quite make out. Someone yelled, "Merry Christmas!" Other people might visit Darling Bay to hope for the sound of the ocean's waves. Instead, Molly had been longing for the sound of the saloon. "We fell asleep to that noise."

Adele looked so pleased. "We did. Our favorite lullaby."

Molly remembered what it felt like to make her sister happy, and she swallowed the lump that rested in her throat. "So." She sat on the bed, testing it with a small bounce. She flopped backwards. "Still a crappy mattress."

"I'm sorry. I know. It's on the list."

"Nah. I've slept on *way* crappier."

"I'm so glad you're –"

Molly cut her off. "So the hotel's closed except for this room."

Adele bit her bottom lip and nodded.

"And the café's closed. For how long?"

"Years now."

"Holy crap."

"But I thought, if you came home –"

"This is only a visit." Maybe. Probably. She wasn't willing to make a decision, not yet.

Adele nodded. "I know. But you're such a good cook. With your culinary-school experience, and you being a nutritionist, I can't imagine anyone more capable of taking over the café..."

Molly waited.

"I mean, I could show it to you. You could think about it."

Molly tried to keep her voice soft. "Don't push, Adele."

"I know, I know. But, really, how long can you stay? Give me a hint."

"A couple of weeks."

"Oh!" Adele's cheeks were so pink, exactly the same way Molly's got when she was excited. "That's *wonderful*. I can't wait to show you everything."

"From what you've said, it's a steaming pile of bull hooey." The vodka had made her limbs feel loose, and the half glass of mulled wine she'd sipped afterwards hadn't been a good idea.

"The saloon isn't bad. You saw that. And Uncle Hugh's apartment –"

"The love shack, you mean?"

Adele's cheeks were almost coral. "Did you really like him? Nate?"

Molly had spent exactly fifty-seven minutes in the guy's truck on the way into town. He'd been nice enough, and his excitement about their mutual surprise for Adele had been endearing. He was just a guy, though. Good-looking enough. He didn't smell bad. "Sure."

"I knew you would. I *knew* you'd like him. So." Adele brought her hands together, interlacing her fingers as if she were praying. "Do you want to, um, hang out? Or do you want to go to sleep? It's late, and I have no idea what time zone you're set to."

Molly had lost control of her internal time clock years ago. She knew she wasn't ready for sleep, though – not yet. Her nerves still felt electric, as if her body was set to a low buzz. "Yeah, I guess I'm pretty tired," she lied.

Her big sister had always been able to hear it in her voice when she was lying. Molly knew Adele would call her on it – she would go get a guitar and a couple of beers and then she'd insist that they sit around and talk till dawn. Molly wouldn't be able to get out of it even if she wanted to.

Instead, Adele just said, "Of course you are." Her words were bright. "I'll go. Sleep well."

Molly's disappointment was laced with sadness.

Everything had changed.

Including them.

CHAPTER THREE

Molly slept for a short while and woke up stone-cold sober with a headache. She stared at the ceiling until three in the morning, feeling the bed pitch and sway underneath her, a phantom leftover of being at sea for so long. Then she sat up. She wasn't going to sleep – she wasn't going to come anywhere *near* sleep as long as she was thinking about the old Golden Spike Café.

It had been her favorite place in Darling Bay as a kid. Lana had loved the beach, and it had been almost impossible to get her out of the sand dunes at the end of the night. Adele had just wanted to be wherever their mother was, sitting with her as she strummed a guitar on the porch overlooking the street below, singing in her sweet voice.

But Molly had loved being in the café. Uncle Hugh had employed cooks, of course. Arnie had been the breakfast and lunch guy, and he'd always liked his deep fryer more than most people. He used to growl as he worked, and the more the waitresses had yelled at him to speed it up, the slower he'd go. The night cook, Stew, had been the opposite, cheerful and so fast he'd sometimes drop the food on customers' tables because the waitresses couldn't keep up with him.

Then again, Uncle Hugh had loved cooking, too. He'd shove Arnie or Stew aside, ordering them to go get more oranges or sugar from the grocer, even though there was an orange tree in the back, even though Uncle Hugh stockpiled sugar like the next war was imminent.

One afternoon when Molly had been so bored she thought she might die (Adele and Lana were fighting, as usual, about something unimportant and annoying), she'd asked Uncle Hugh if she could help with the lunch service. She must have been no more than fourteen because they'd started the band when she was fifteen. Free time and boredom had disappeared then. "Please? I don't have anything to *do*."

He hadn't even blinked. "You wanna waitress or cook?"

"Cook, of course." Like him. That summer, Uncle Hugh had taught her everything he knew, and she'd spent almost every moment in the café, at his elbow. After she'd learned his repertoire of cooked items (chicken-fried steak, Joe's scramble and his famous bacon meatloaf), she'd branched out into fancier things, meals she insisted he put on the menu, treats the tourists had loved (custard blintzes, nectarine scones).

It had been her idea to move the old rusting caboose from the back of the property to the front, next to the café. "It would make a great coffee stand." An artifact from the defunct Central Pacific Line, the caboose had been left behind when the iron mine south of town had closed, leaving the Darling Bay spur unused. It had been good for nothing except fun for kids to climb on for more than seventy years. Uncle Hugh hadn't liked the idea at first. "I already sell coffee in the café. *And* in the bar."

"But it would be so *cute* to sell it "to go" in the caboose. Please?"

Uncle Hugh had listened to Molly, like her voice mattered to him. He'd hired a crew to move the twenty-five-ton caboose and they'd fixed it up together. It had grabbed the surfer crowd – they'd laughed and called the thick black coffee "caboose juice" and tried to talk Hugh into putting up a sign advertising it as such. Hugh had sensibly refused. The caboose and its line of surfers and tourists became as iconic as Skip's peppermint ice cream and the Christmas lights on the pier.

Now, as Molly walked past the caboose in the darkness, she could see it had become as rusted and derelict as it had been when she'd first climbed it at six years old. Poor old thing. Twice abandoned.

The front door of the café was locked. Of course.

Molly eased her way around the side of the building. Would she have to pick the lock of the side door? Did she remember how? When she'd been dating Joseph, he'd taught her as a bar trick, although he'd been pretty pissed off when she'd gotten a lot better at it than he had. When she started to be able to get into her own apartment with just a bobby pin, he'd broken up with her, which was really for the best, since he'd gone to prison the month afterwards for trying and failing to break into his cousin's safe, which happened to be inside his cousin's bank.

She didn't need the skill, though. The latch clicked under her hand, and the door opened with a groan into the dining room of the café.

The underlying smell – the smell deep, deep down – was familiar to her. Grease from the fries, milk from the shakes, wood from the old eaves overhead. No one could call it a *great* smell, but it stirred something sweet inside her.

The smell on top of *that* was stomach-churning. It was an odor of damp and mold, and something worse, acidic and putrid. Rotting meat, maybe, with a hint of rancid cheese. Molly covered her mouth. It didn't help.

Automatically, her hand went out to hit the light to the left of the door. Nothing.

She heard a rustling to the right and shivered. Uncle Hugh would have strangled a rat with his bare hands had one crept into his establishment (and then he would have cleaned the whole place meticulously—greasy food was one thing, actual dirt was another).

Fear froze her in place. This used to be home to her. She knew that the first table should be four paces directly in front of her. In her mind's eye, she knew that if she reached to the left, there used to be at least twelve freshly filled ketchup bottles always lined up on the rail.

If she were brave, she would put out her hand.

She wasn't.

Instead, she pulled out her phone. She snapped on the flashlight app. The beam of light was as shaky as her fingers, but it illuminated her immediate surroundings.

Broken. It was all broken. The chairs were tipped over, and two of the old tables looked as if something had been set alight on top of them. The floor – what she could see of it – was disgusting, black and sticky under her feet. Even prepared for the worst as she'd thought she'd been, this was horrifying.

She moved – carefully – behind the counter. The old black mats were cracked. Another rustle sounded in the kitchen to her right, and she swallowed a gasp. She imagined rats the size of dogs rummaging through the old cabinets. *Was* it rats? After years of being closed, what would rats still be doing in a place that didn't serve food? Had they just set up shop? Maybe they were working out of it, sending their little ratty kids into Darling Bay to hunt and gather before bringing the loot back to headquarters.

Holding her breath, she shined her light into the kitchen as quickly as she could. Something else moved, something that sounded as big as she was. Maybe bigger. Molly choked back the scream that rose in her throat and kept moving forward. Step by step. She knew every inch of this café, even better than she knew the pathway up to the hotel. She could close her eyes and walk into the kitchen and stop when she was a foot in front of the walk-in freezer.

But if she did that, she might get murdered by the horse-sized rats she could hear scraping themselves along the walls.

She straightened her spine. She was *imagining* hearing things, that was all. When she really listened, all she could hear was the thumping of her heart.

Another step. Then two. Then she was in the kitchen – and oh, no.

From the sweep of the light on her phone, it was even worse than the dining room. The walk-in didn't have a door – its cavernous depths held only empty, broken shelving. The industrial stove stood away from the wall at a cockeyed angle, as if it had taken one step forward to dance and then stopped, terrified. The grill was piled with old boxes, and the whole place looked like it hadn't been cleaned in centuries. She could feel rats—huge ones the size of small ponies—looking at her from holes in the wall, their beady eyes focused on her forehead, planning how they'd eat her when she fell over, dead from disgust –

Oh, she had to get out – now, she had to get out *now*.

She tried to spin on her heel, but her shoe stuck to the floor in something that felt like a combination of maple syrup and Krazy Glue. With a horrified squeak, she pulled her foot free and barreled back into the dining room.

"Freeze!" The shout was a low-pitched boom of noise to her left near the door. A floodlight shone on her, and she couldn't see past the sudden glare to what was behind it. "Hands up!"

Molly's brain went white with fear, a static buzz that filled her body. *Out,* all she knew was that she had to get out, and out was on the other side of that light, and she had to get around the person who filled the doorway.

She threw the only thing she had in her hand – her cell phone – at the person as hard as she could.

The light bobbled, and she could see the man blocking her exit put his hand to his head.

Molly had always had a good arm.

She bolted.

CHAPTER FOUR

The woman was fast, Sheriff Colin McMurtry would give her that. And she had an arm on her. That had been a solid blow to the skull.

But there was a reason every woman he'd ever dated had called him hard-headed. He shook his head once to clear it of the stars, and then sailed his body sideways, into the woman's frame as she tried to dart out the door he was blocking. He'd seen in the Maglite's beam that she was unarmed. It was a safe takedown. One he'd done a million times in his career, usually to furious men.

He thought taking the woman down would be easy.

Colin was wrong.

She roiled under him like an angry cat coming up out of a barrel of water. If she'd known any self-defense moves, Colin would have laid good odds that she might have gotten away from him – she was as strong as sin and pissed as hell. She didn't land any solid blows, though, and every time she jerked an arm free, he tightened his hold. They were half in the doorway, half out of it, and Colin had the first half of a thought about how funny they must look to someone standing in the street, and then her left leg got free, and he had to stop imagining how they would appear to an onlooker. He rolled her from her side to her stomach, pinning her arms behind her back. She gave an *oomph* and then stayed still. He could feel her energy coiling itself, but he also knew he had the upper hand and he could wait her out if he had to.

"You're under arrest," he said.

Her body went still under him. He had the unwelcome thought that her light, sweet perfume was the only pleasant thing in the disgusting café.

"You're a cop?" Her voice was low.

"What did you think I was?"

"A robber? A rapist?" Her words were breathy and, he realized, terrified. Fear rose from her body in waves, and Colin suddenly felt sick.

He stood, slowly, ready to relaunch at her if he needed to. "Who the hell else yells *freeze*? Of course I'm a cop. Stand up. Slowly. Keep your hands behind your back and turn to face me."

She stood, her hands shaking. Her head remained high as she turned. Improbably, she was wearing a pair of yellow pajamas covered with Kermit the Frog playing the banjo. What kind of burglar wore pajamas? On her feet were silver flip-flops. Also not the best bet for a criminal getaway. There was something going on here that Colin didn't understand, and he *hated* not understanding things.

"Back out slowly into the parking lot," he said. The faster they got out of the café, the better. Besides the light floral fragrance he'd caught on the woman, the rest of the smell was made of old grease and something that reminded him of boiled cabbage, except less pleasant. He should snap the flex-cuffs on her, he knew he should. One dangled from his fingers – he'd grabbed it automatically as he'd stood up. Something had stopped him, though. Maybe it was the look on her face. She had the look Nikki got sometimes – utter surprise that something could go so wrong, so quickly. "Move slowly. Don't run."

The woman took ten paces backwards. Her face remained implacable. Colin pretended to himself that he couldn't notice how pretty she was, with her dark-brown hair falling just to her shoulders, and her curves that made her flannel pajamas look almost indecent. God, she was familiar. Did he know her? She wasn't a local, but...

"There. That's far enough. Sit down." The direction was automatic. He didn't really think she'd run – she didn't have the look anymore. It was better to have her seated. Safer.

She sat on the curb at the edge of the small parking lot and drew her knees up, wrapping her arms around them.

"Now. Name." He wasn't in uniform – he'd been on his way home after finishing the three reports he'd been behind in when he'd seen the bouncing light inside the defunct café – but he always had a citation pad inside his jacket pocket. You never knew.

"Molly."

"You got a last name?"

"Darling." She stuck out her chin as she said it.

Oh, crap. "*That's* it. I *knew* I recognized you."

She nodded, her nose now as high as if she were the queen. As if she expected him to apologize.

Which he wasn't going to do. "You shouldn't have been in there."

"I wasn't trespassing."

"How the hell was I supposed to know that in the pitch dark?"

"Maybe by asking." Her eyes were dark in the dim streetlight, but the anger in them sparked so hot he could feel it in his gut.

"I told you to freeze. The next step would have been to establish your identity." Colin rubbed his cheekbone. "I'm probably going to have a black eye tomorrow."

Her frosty expression melted. "No. Really? My dad taught me how to throw. I didn't mean to –"

Colin sat on the curb next to her. "It'll be fine. Not like I haven't had black eyes before. Lots of 'em." He put his palms on the sidewalk and leaned back. "You're not under arrest anymore, by the way."

"Oh, good."

"You weren't worried." She'd known she'd been allowed to be in the café – it was *her* café, after all.

"I wasn't worried about the burglary rap, no. But apparently I also just assaulted a police officer."

"Eh." Colin rubbed at his cheekbone again. He could use an ice pack, that was for sure. "Welcome home," he said.

"Thanks."

"Don't think I heard you were coming back. Surprise visit?"

In the corner of his eye, he saw her stiffen.

"We know each other?"

"Colin McMurtry." He waited for her to remember.

It took a moment. Then, there it was. "Oh, no." She leaned forward, her elbows on her knees, her head in her hands.

"Yep."

"I hit you with my car."

"You did." Colin pushed back the unexpected laugh that built in his chest.

"It was more like a tap, really," she said.

"That's what you said then, too."

"But it *was*. You had time to jump onto the hood of my car."

She'd turned right at a stop sign without checking the crosswalk first. He'd been in it and in order to keep from getting more injured, he'd thrown himself onto the car to avoid getting dragged underneath it. "I think my jumping was precipitated by your hitting."

"I didn't actually *hurt* you. And your cousin agreed with me."

God, Donnie had been with him that day. He'd forgotten. That was right before Donnie got put away for aggravated burglary. McMurtrys were always on one side of the bars or another, usually the wrong side. "But I'll always be able to say a Darling Songbird hit me with her car."

She slid him a glance he couldn't interpret. "I bet you don't have call to brag on that often."

"In Darling Bay? Sure I do. Your albums are still on repeat in half the businesses in town."

"Oh, God. Why am I here?" She looked up into the foggy night sky.

"That's a big question. I'm a cop, not a priest." Like any of his family could have made *that* cut.

She sighed, continuing to gaze upwards.

It was quiet, the only sound was an owl on the hill behind them and the constant low whoosh of the ocean just out of sight, at the bend of the road.

"It's so silent here," she said. "Does anything ever change?"

"All the time. I can barely keep up."

At that, she smiled. Lord, have mercy on a man. Molly had always been his favorite Darling Songbird. Colin would bet every man in town had one that suited his preference, from the fairer and thin Adele to the jet-black-haired bad girl Lana. But his preference had always run to healthy-looking women, and Molly, the lead singer with the voice of a fallen angel and the curves to match, had always been the one he couldn't take his eyes off.

"Like what?"

Colin strained to remember what she'd said before he'd started comparing her to the other Darling girls. "Changes. Well. You heard about the fire at Skip's Ice Cream."

"I did, actually."

"They're in a new spot. Along with the bagel place."

"Woo." Her voice was dry.

"I hear Dot Rillo at the post office is thinking of painting the inside again."

"What color is it now?"

"Off-white, I think. I heard a rumor she's thinking about eggshell, but a neutral taupe was also mentioned." Colin wished he was making it up. He could give a rat's ass about the color of the walls inside the post office, even though it was the talk of the town. Literally. He'd heard about it at the bagel shop in the morning and in the Golden Spike at night. Once, Dot had proposed a pale eggshell blue at one of the town hall meetings, and the place had exploded. Terry Dunlap had ended up punching Herbie Sanchez over the paint-chip samples and Mabel Mellor had gone into hysterics. Colin had had to shut down the meeting for the citizens' safety.

"So that's the biggest news in Darling Bay."

Well. There was darker news, too. There had been a meth-house bust just the week before and two out-oftowners were going to prison for at least the next seven years. No one wanted to hear about that. No one wanted to talk about the four men who had been arrested in the last five months for beating their wives. A kid had tried to kill himself with a shotgun and instead had shot off his ear, but the only rumor he'd heard about it was that it had been a gun-cleaning accident. Darling Bay protected its own. Nothing changed, and the town was always idyllic. That was the way it had to be.

"Yep. Painting the inside of the post office. Next year they're talking about repainting the outside of the police department. I can't get too excited about that or I won't sleep a wink from now till then."

"I'm sorry that I hit you with my car."

He shrugged, and the night owl hooted again behind him. His mother had thought hearing an owl was good luck, but then again, she had heard them a lot, and she'd had some really rotten luck in her life, so he didn't put much stock in it. "You were sixteen."

"I think my driver's license was still wet from being printed."

"Have you hit anyone since?"

"No."

"Then I think you're doing okay."

"Thanks."

He should stand. He should get in his patrol car and drive out of town to the cliff-side house that would be dark and cold, having been empty all day and night. Like usual.

But something about this felt good. Sitting on the concrete with someone he'd tackled as a suspect. He would do his damnedest to forget how very, very soft she'd felt underneath his body. That was unprofessional, and he was a good cop, not a bad one.

"So, are you here to stay?"

"Nah."

Her answer came too fast. "Really? Seems like your sister's here for the long haul."

"Adele's in love."

"Happens to the best of us."

"Doesn't it, though?" Molly sounded wistful, and Colin wondered who the lucky guy was. He must be something, to have caught her eye.

"So, you're sticking around for the new year?"

"Yeah. Probably."

"You girls going to reopen the café?"

"No way. Did you see what was in there?"

Really, he'd only seen her. "Yeah."

"It's horrible. We should burn it down and collect the insurance." She met his eye for a split second. "Whoops. Sorry. I forgot I was talking to a lawman. Just kidding?"

"Check with your sister before you get too carried away. I don't think she has insurance on it yet."

"You're joking."

"Nate told me she got the hotel and the bar insured, but I think the underwriter balked when they saw the state of the café."

"I don't blame them."

His cheekbone throbbed. There was a pause that he didn't know how to fill. He'd been seventeen when she'd smacked him with her new, bright-blue Nissan. The Darling Songbirds were just getting hot then, and there had been a glow of imminent fame surrounding the girls like pink, sparkly halos. Colin had thought Molly was so pretty he wouldn't mind her knocking him down every day in crosswalks all over town as long as he remained mostly uninjured.

He'd gone to see the girls sing once when he'd been about nineteen. She'd talked to some friends of his after the concert, and hadn't ever looked his way. He'd thought maybe she'd been embarrassed about hitting him with her car, but it had always struck him as all too possible that she just hadn't remembered him. Just another McMurtry no-nothing.

"You should go back to bed." He gestured at her pajamas. "Assuming that's where you came from."

Molly arched an eyebrow, then she stood slowly. One of her silvery flip-flops had slipped off, and she put her foot back into it. Her toenails were dark red, and the gleam of the polish made him feel like he was looking at something intimate. "Not a bad idea."

"Morning's going to come too early." His mom used to say it when she'd tucked him in at night. Funny, he hadn't said that phrase in years.

"Sure you don't need to arrest me or anything?"

He dipped his head, wishing he was wearing his old, battered cowboy hat that he wore on weekends. He felt the need to touch the brim. Instead, he touched the star-shaped badge he kept clipped on his jeans when he was off duty. "Not tonight, I guess. We'll see how it goes tomorrow."

"I expect I'll rob the bank in the morning."

"I'll tell Jessie Huss to watch out for you."

"Good idea."

Both of them were stalling. He could feel it. "Are you staying here? At the hotel?"

"Yeah. I'm in the one room that probably won't come down around my ears overnight."

"You want me to walk you there?" Colin had an image fill his mind – her standing with her back to her door, him dipping his head until his mouth reached those full lips of hers. Oh, man, he was losing his damn mind.

"No," she said. "I think I'm brave enough to make it there myself. As long as no cops jump out of the bushes at me."

"Here. I have something for you." He pulled a plastic star-shaped badge out of his pocket, a replica of his own, and handed it to her.

She held it sideways so she could read it by the streetlight. "Junior Deputy? You just happen to have this on you?"

"For kids." The heat of embarrassment climbed up his chest. "You know, for bravery."

Her right eyebrow lifted, but then she smiled, and it was like the streetlight's wattage suddenly surged. "Yeah, well. I could use a little of that."

"Good night, then."

"Yes. Okay." She turned and was through the parking lot and up the hill through the garden so fast it was as if she hadn't been there at all.

Like she was a ghost of Christmas past. Like she'd come to tell him something important.

He wanted to listen.

CHAPTER FIVE

Molly woke to Adele pounding on the door. "Up and at 'em! Things to do! I need your help!"

Molly groaned and pulled the covers over her face. Then Adele used her master key.

"Unfair."

"You can't keep me out!" Adele pulled back the curtains to let in the winter sun and then handed her a key ring. "Use my car. Go get bagels and lots of cream cheese. I'll take two everything bagels. Nate wants one blueberry and one onion. Here's money, get what you want."

Molly's head felt full, her thoughts thickened. The tipsiest she'd felt was in that dang parking lot with Sheriff McMurtry, and by then the Christmas wine had worn off. "You can't eat two bagels *each*." It wasn't a question.

"I didn't think I could, but then Nate bet me I couldn't and now it's our Saturday-morning tradition. Oh, and get the paper, too, huh? Meet us in the saloon? Nate's working on a new garbage disposal, and I'm helping by telling him he's doing it wrong every few minutes." Adele gave Molly a quick hit-and-run hug and then left.

The bagel place was mobbed. Darling Bay seemed to have gotten the message that Molly was back in town and *everyone* seemed to know her. They exclaimed. They hugged. Two old ladies kissed her cheeks, and one old man tried to kiss her on the lips, but she'd been dodging overly friendly elderly men on the cruise liners for a long time, and she easily slipped his grasp. Fifteen minutes later, she was back in the car, panting with the *overwhelmingness* of it all.

Darling Bay.

Growing up spending summers and holidays in a town named by their great-grandfather had always made it sound like they'd had money, like it was *their* town. But they hadn't, and it wasn't. Molly's parents had been mostly broke all their lives, struggling to make it big in Nashville. They had come to visit Uncle Hugh every summer, still broke. Even poor, however, they'd always been treated well on account of nothing more than their name. It had loaned them status. The three girls had been the tiny coastal town's mascots, and that had been multiplied a hundred times over after they'd started the band. The Darling Songbirds' rise to fame had been swift and sure, taking them to the top of the country charts.

Until it had all fallen apart.

Fitful rain spattered the windshield. Dark clouds over the marina scudded in rapidly, and she watched the man at the newsstand pull his racks of papers inside.

There had been a time when being in Darling Bay during a rain storm had been Molly's favorite place in the whole world.

Maybe it still was. A feeling that was almost happiness crept up her spine. She wished for lots of rain. She wished hard for *buckets* of it. She wanted to sit with her sister on the front porch of the Golden Spike Saloon in that old porch swing and watch heavy, fat drops hit the sidewalk. She wanted to watch people walk past carrying umbrellas, and she wanted Adele to tell her the name of each kid who splashed in the puddles. Molly had been working on board for so long, she couldn't remember the last time she'd *had* neighbors let alone known their names. That's what Darling Bay was all about. Knowing your neighbors and then gossiping about them.

Several blocks before the Golden Spike, she passed a police car. She couldn't tell who was sitting in it and she tried not to be too conspicuous about peering into it as she drove past.

Even with his head down, looking at something he held in his hands, she could tell it was Colin McMurtry. The guy she'd hit with her car, so long ago. He had a wider jaw now. Last night she'd noticed his chest had broadened, too, and in the dimness of the street light, she'd been able to see he had a few crow's feet around his eyes.

Something fast and grey streaked in front of the car.

Molly screamed.

She jerked the wheel to the right, and swerved hard. The car fishtailed a little, and she held the wheel tight. Too small to be a dog, maybe it had been a cat? Surely it was too small to be a cat. Could it have been a rat, like the one she'd imagined she'd heard early that morning in the darkened café? Was the whole town *full* of rats? It was a wharf town, after all.

But she'd heard no thump and felt no jolt. Maybe she'd missed it, then, whatever it was. She looked in the rear-view mirror to see if she could spot something dead in the road. All she saw were flashing lights.

Yep. He was pulling her over.

Fantastic.

She bumped the side of the curb with the front tire. *Dang it.* He was going to think she was drunk at nine in the morning.

The clouds picked that moment to burst. Well, if Molly was going to get a ticket, maybe the buckets of water being dumped from the sky would speed up the process. She tried not to think about the fact that she barely had enough in the bank to cover a parking ticket, let alone a moving violation.

"Hi," she said, as the sheriff came to her window. Rain drenched him, and as he glanced upwards, she noticed again how firm and wide his jaw was. "Going to arrest me again?"

She could tell he was trying to swallow a smile. "Depends. Are you drunk?"

"No, sir." His hair was thick and black, and a wet lock fell over his eye. His eyes were as dark as his hair, and his lashes were long and already misted. He looked as if he should be striding a highland in a kilt, not wearing a cop's uniform.

"Sir? Come on, now. Do you know why I pulled you over?"

"Because I swerved back there like a maniac?"

He nodded. Rivulets of rain ran down his face and into the neckline of his shirt. There was a slight bruise over his brow, but he didn't have a black eye. Thank God.

"That would be why. Is everything okay?"

"I didn't hit one single person."

"Good for you!"

"Hey." Her stomach tightened. "You're getting soaked." A gust of wind pushed rain into the car's open window. "And so am I."

"*Why* did you swerve?"

"I think a baby mongoose ran in front of my car."

"A mongoose, huh? I wasn't aware we had a problem with those in town."

Something about the grey skies above and the water coursing down his head and shoulders made him look like a block of granite, carved by wind and weather.

"Baby possum?"

He shook his head and water fell from his cheekbones. "Not at this time of day."

Was he going to cite her? Or were they just going to keep talking in the middle of a downpour? "So what do *you* think it was, then?"

"Probably one of those kittens I saw last week."

"*Kittens?*"

He nodded. "There were a couple of them just up the block, but when I went to search the bushes for them I couldn't find them or their mother."

"Poor things." She looked out the window at the rain that lashed down. "In this weather."

"I'll go look for it."

Molly had the car door open before she even knew what she was doing. "I'll help."

"It's pouring."

"All right, master of the obvious. Let's do this."

And something sparked in his eye that made Molly feel so warm that for a moment, she didn't feel the freezing rain even in the slightest.

CHAPTER SIX

For fifteen minutes, they searched for the cat that might not even be a cat. Colin went farther into the bushes than she did. He climbed easily over logs, while Molly searched under them. She lifted low branches, and called softly, in case the kitten heard and came out.

They found nothing.

Colin said, "You're freezing."

Molly's teeth chattered. "I'm fine."

"You're not fine. Get in the car."

Molly wanted to tell him he was wrong, that he didn't know what he was talking about. The only problem was that she was starting to shake all over. "Fine. But you get in, too."

And then she saw it. A little grey bedraggled kitten, huddled under the edge of the curb, next to a storm drain. One more surge of rain water might drag the wee thing underground. "There!" She pointed.

As Colin approached, the kitten shrank low. "We need something to lure her out."

"Cream cheese! For the bagels. Hang on." She grabbed the container from the car and opened it for him. "Here."

Colin moved slowly, looking for all the world like he didn't care that he was soaked, kneeling in the gutter, extending a fistful of cheese. The kitten, distressed, opened its mouth, but Molly was too far away to hear it. If Colin moved too quickly, it might go into the drain, or run out into the traffic lanes.

Then the kitten walked towards him, and licked his fingers, tentatively at first, then with some conviction. Molly would have swooped up the cat then, but Colin gave the little thing an extra few seconds before moving in slowly. Rain ran across his back and his hatless head. It dripped from the gun that hung at his hip.

He stood, a smile breaking across his wide jaw. "Look what I got here," he said.

Inside the car, Molly started the engine. She turned on both of the seat heaters as Colin moved the passenger seat back to accommodate his long legs. She turned the blowers on hot. "Let me see her."

"It's a her?"

"Sure." Molly didn't know how to tell the difference, but she gave the cat's behind a quick peek. "Maybe." She held her up to the blower and rubbed her with the pile of napkins that had come with the bagels. "What are you going to name her?"

"Me?"

"I live in a hotel room, remember. And only temporarily."

"I don't need a cat."

"No one does. They just happen to you."

"To *you*, maybe."

"Congratulations. You now have a kitten."

He shook his head. Water drops flew. "I have a critter I need to take to the pound."

And then the kitten leaped from her hands into Colin's lap. She velcroed herself to his shirt and opened her mouth in what looked like it would be a wide meow but delivered only a squeak.

Molly repeated herself, sure this time. "You now have a kitten."

"Well, *hell*."

Molly laughed, and the feeling was warmer than the seat heater under her thighs.

Colin craned his head. "Those bagels smell amazing."

"Are you trying to change the subject?"

"Nah. Just thinking of a name." He reached back to open the lid of the box, keeping his other hand firmly around the kitten. "Blueberry? Onion? I don't think so."

"Will you really keep her?" He was probably pulling Molly's leg. He was a police officer – he couldn't keep every stray that crossed his path.

"Asiago. That's it." He held up the kitten and looked into her face. "Hello, Asiago."

The warm place inside Molly melted even more. Drenched cop, tiny drenched kitten. She felt her face flame. "What a *brute* you are."

He looked startled. "What?"

"Brute." She pointed. "That kitten has her claws in you, you big softie."

Colin McMurtry didn't look soft. His jaw was square and hard. His hands were wide and his profile was as rugged as the coastline south of town.

And he held the kitten like she was made of something precious and breakable.

"Yeah." He touched the kitten's nose to his. "Who likes a little nuzzle? Does Asiago like a nuzzle?"

"Brute, like I said." Good grief, it felt like flirting. Flustered, she said, "Want a bagel?"

"Sure. This day keeps getting better and better. You have enough to spare one?"

"They're for my sister and Nate, but there are at least a couple extra in there."

"What, are you one of those who won't eat gluten unless it has all the carbohydrates sucked out somehow?"

Molly didn't answer him. Yeah, she was one of those people. She cared about what went into her body. She'd finally gained some semblance of control over her carb intake, and she didn't want to lose that.

"They're for Adele and Nate."

The kitten was gnawing on the tip of his thumb. "But you *would* eat one, right?"

"I'm a nutritionist. Those things are empty carbs, all white flour." Why was he pressing this? Did he want her to say it? Did he want her to admit that she knew she was a bigger girl, and should be watching every calorie that went into her mouth? It was a sudden jolt of surprise, a twist in the pit of her belly, that Colin might be just another guy who thought all women should be the perfect size.

She pulled out a blueberry bagel. Water dripped from her hair down her neck. She put the bagel in his hands. "Take it. Please. And I'm so sorry, but I just realized I have to go."

"Wait, what —"

"Are you going to write me a ticket?"

"Of course not." Colin looked astonished, as if he'd forgotten what kind of uniform he was wearing.

"Adele and Nate are waiting. Go dry yourself and that little thing off. You don't have to keep her. I was just being silly." Ridiculous, really. "She'll be fine at the pound. Someone will adopt her."

"I'll see you later, maybe?"

"Sure," she said. Whatever.

Colin placed the bagel in his pocket and then got out of the car. He held the kitten under his jacket, and his expression had gone stony. He walked back to his patrol car briskly, and it was raining so hard she couldn't see him in the rear-view mirror. He pulled out, giving her a crisp *whoop* of the siren as he passed her.

Yeah, she'd blown that.

They'd been having a surprisingly...delightful time.

Molly almost regretted the tone she'd had in her voice. But her sharpness had equaled the level of disappointment that coursed through her, a sudden, unpleasant shock. She was done with men telling her what to eat.

Or really, ordering her to do anything at all.

God, she wanted a bagel.

CHAPTER SEVEN

Her heated seats had been nice, Colin thought. He pulled the patrol car up to the front of the police station, shut off the vents that were only blowing cold air anyway, and turned off the engine. He looked up at the two-story building for the millionth time, as the kitten wrestled her way closer to his ribs under his jacket.

The building was so depressing-looking. Someday he'd paint it under cover of night. Blue, maybe. Or a bright, cheery yellow. That would shake up the town, wouldn't it?

His old man would roll over in his grave if he knew the police station had gone canary yellow.

Inside, Marsha gave him a stack of Post-its. She knew she was supposed to use the computer to send him information, but Marsha was old-school. Sometimes he thought the office supplies were the only reason she did the job.

"Dirk Whitey called again. He says that if Barbara Dow doesn't stop parking her school bus in front of his house, he's going to, and I quote, "light it up"."

"I don't even know what that means, do you?" Would he shoot the school bus? Set it on fire? Whatever it was, it didn't sound good.

"No clue." Marsha was on the far side of sixty, with bright silver hair she kept in a short bob. She'd been an administrative assistant at the sheriff's office for a lot of those sixty-plus years, and it was no secret she'd always wanted to be a police officer. She would've made a good one, too. She was detail oriented, liked order in all things, and brooked no nonsense. Back in the day, though, female police officers just hadn't been an accepted thing. Every day she wore a dark-blue button-down shirt tucked crisply into dark-navy pants – her version of a uniform. "But he said he'll only talk to you. *Is that a kitten?*"

"It is. And I'll give Dirk a call." Not like he didn't have deputies who could handle this kind of thing. He had six of them. Two were off on medical, though, two were mostly worthless and taking up space until retirement, and that left him with two good ones, which wasn't near enough, even in a town as small as Darling Bay. As the sheriff, Colin should have been tied to his desk. He shouldn't have to sit in a patrol car and clock speeders. Last week he'd had to pull crossing-guard duty when

Brad was in court. That had made the mothers laugh, all right. The sheriff, wearing a bright-yellow vest, holding the stop sign and directing seven-year-olds across streets that were never busy. "Anything else?"

"*Kitten.*"

He just gave her a cheery nod of agreement and then shut his office door. He stripped off his jacket and shirt, and used the spare towel he kept in his desk to dry off with. The kitten, now mostly dry, scampered across the papers on his desk.

Molly.

He touched his brow bone gingerly. The swelling was down, he knew, but it still looked bad. Probably good for another week. He hadn't been able to sleep in the wee hours, and every time he'd rolled onto that side of his face, he'd thought of Molly again.

She did something to him.

That whole bagel thing, though...He'd had a girlfriend once who'd worked at a gym. Every single thing Jamie did all day was geared around what she could do to earn the food she put in her mouth. An hour on the treadmill meant a piece of pizza. Half an hour of running earned her another frozen yoghurt. Luckily for him, two hours of sex earned a bowl of ice cream, both things he had been very much in favor of. But it had been exhausting, watching her worry over every piece of food she put in her mouth.

He wouldn't have thought Molly would be like that. She was a curvy girl, after all. Always had been. He vaguely remembered tabloids that had printed unflattering pictures of her, back when the Darling Songbirds were on top of the charts. Then again, they'd printed a lot of crap about Molly, since she'd been the mouthpiece of the band. The voice. They'd been political, hadn't they? Something about vegetarianism and pissing off the country station's advertising sponsors? Had that criticism gone along with the unflattering snapshots in the tabloids? He hadn't spent any time thinking about it back then, but he guessed it could do a number on a woman's self-confidence.

Not that Molly should ever worry about anything like that. She looked amazing, if a little on the thin side for her. He remembered her a touch heavier, slightly thicker in the waist. He liked that memory.

Her eyes. The memory of them had kept him awake last night, too. Her, sitting next to him in the dark on the sidewalk, after having beaned him with a cell phone. Something had moved between them, like static electricity. He'd had a dream about her, nothing special, just that she was looking in his eyes and laughing at something he'd said. He'd woken up smiling.

His desk phone rang, and the kitten jumped almost straight up in the air. Litter box. He'd have to get one of those. And cat food.

He reached for the phone, already dreading whatever was waiting for him on the other end. It was never a friend calling to see how he was. It was never someone wondering if he could meet them for a drink, or stop by for dinner. The work phone was the work phone for a reason. Being the sheriff came with a bunch of bullshit, and a lot of it came right down the phone line.

"Hi, big brother," Nikki said. "You're so handsome and wonderful."

"What now?"

"I'm behind on my rent."

"You called my work phone for that?"

"I know you hate answering it. I figured I'd give you a good reason."

Colin tried to keep the sigh inaudible. He knew he probably failed. "How much?"

"Six hundred?"

"Is that a question?"

"Well, I only owe four hundred as my portion, but I'm pretty close to losing my cell phone, too."

She didn't even sound apologetic about it. Not that Colin wanted her to grovel. That wasn't the point. God knew if he'd ever had to ask for money, he would've had a hard time doing it. Nikki didn't seem to. Then again, she was used to it.

"What happened to your job?"

"You hated me working at the laundromat."

It was true. He had. But at least it was a job. "Did you get fired?"

She ignored him. "You said that only lowlifes hung out at the laundromat. You said that I'd get in trouble if I worked there."

Oh, God. "Did you?"

"And by lowlifes, you meant poor people. Did you ever think of that?"

That was a typical Nikki move. Shifting the blame on to him "I have no problem with poor people."

"Of course you do. You're a cop. That's practically your job. Poverty breeds crime, isn't that what Dad always said?"

"I don't give a damn what Dad said."

"Big words."

Colin used the damp towel to scrub at his still wet hair. The kitten leaped for the leg he'd leaned against the desk and just made it, clinging to him with tiny claws. "Did you call just to argue with me?"

Her laugh came over the line. "Well, to argue and ask you for money."

"How are you?" Colin meant it. He wanted to know.

And Nikki knew just how to dodge the question. "Someone told me you had a bruise on your forehead."

"This town, man."

"Did you get into a fight?"

He almost made a joke about walking into a door, and then stopped himself. "Molly Darling is back in town. I thought she was a burglar at the old Golden Spike Café, and when I startled her, she threw her cell phone at my face."

"Oh, that's *awesome!*"

"I knew you would say something like that."

"She was the big one in the band, right?"

Colin bristled. "If by big you mean the pretty one, yeah."

"I *loved* them. So, anyway, do you think I can borrow the money?"

"What about going on unemployment? Didn't we talk about that?" He hated that he had to say that to her. No one in his life should be on unemployment. But Nikki just didn't seem to be able to stick with a job for more than a few weeks. She'd never been able to.

"I checked. Unemployment will pay me $200 a month. There's no way in hell anyone can live on that."

He stayed quiet and pressed his thumb into the kitten's forehead. She purred so loud she sounded like a tin can full of quarters.

"So, come on. Can I borrow it?"

Borrow. As if she'd ever paid back a dime in her whole life.

As if he needed her to. He didn't. But a little gratitude would go a long way. "Fine. I'm at work, though. I'll get it to you later today."

"You mean you'll come over here?"

The hope in her voice drove a nail of heat into his already painful eye. He couldn't go to her place and not lose his cool. She knew that. "Meet me at the Golden Spike at five."

"You'll buy me a drink?"

"What are big brothers for?" Big brothers were for pushing their little sisters, for making them do more, *be* more. This was his fault for not encouraging her to do better in the past. For not making her be the person he knew she was.

Colin sat in his chair and lifted Asiago to eye level. Such a cute little thing. A bright spot in the day. Just like Molly had been.

"Sweet!"

With a click, Nikki hung up, leaving Colin to wonder as he always did what more he could have done. And what more he would have to do.

Asiago opened her mouth and again nothing but a squeak came out.

"Yeah, well." Colin rubbed her forehead once more. "Sometimes the words just don't come out right, huh?"

CHAPTER EIGHT

*You love me like a rock
You got me on a roll,
I never saw you comin'
But I got you in my soul.*

Molly and Adele perched on the edge of the rickety old stage in the saloon, a perfect place to sing and play. In fact, it was *where* Molly had learned to play guitar, she remembered. There used to always be someone propped there, shaping chords and singing songs. It felt like coming home, sitting next to her sister in the not-busy bar. Three guys playing cards in the corner ignored them completely, and Norma – the one who'd been draped in Christmas lights the night before – was the only one sitting on a barstool. She still had the lights around her neck, but they remained unlit. She herself seemed *quite* lit and tossed back shots with alarming alacrity.

Adele had asked Molly to listen to a song she was finishing, one that was due to her producer in Nashville by the end of the week. Adele had looked almost nervous when she'd asked her, and that had broken down Molly's defenses. It had only taken Adele less than ten minutes to convince Molly to sing along on the chorus. Ten more minutes and Molly was adding a second line to the third verse. It felt good, being with her sister like this, drawn back into that sisterhood of music, that relationship made of sweet harmonies and rhymes.

Adele strummed through the chorus one more time, quickly. "There's something not quite right." She rubbed her nose.

Oh, Molly had *missed* watching Adele think. The way her eyes unfocused, staring softly into the distance. Their mother had had that look when she was writing songs, too. That's where Adele got it from, the love of putting words and music together. Adele and Katie Darling, as close as any mother and daughter could be. Molly, always closer to her father, had just been the lead voice, and only because they'd made her.

"It's perfect. There's nothing missing."

Adele glanced at her quickly. "Something. I'm telling you."

Molly leaned back and stretched, feeling the rough wooden stage under her fingertips. "It's a country song about love. You don't need more than a guy, a girl, and a misunderstanding solved by a kiss."

"It'd be nice if life worked like that. Although I do think many things can be solved by a kiss." Adele's cheeks went prettily pink.

"You have it bad."

"I do."

"Are all these songs about him, then?"

"What else am I supposed to write about? He's all I think about. It's ridiculous." Adele feigned a deep interest in the G string's tuner key. "I did have to write a heartbreak song for Jason Aldean, and he sent it back saying it was way too chipper and I should send it to Taylor Swift."

"Ouch."

"Right?"

The song they'd just been singing was stuck in Molly's head now. It was catchy. It would do well. "So, are you going to keep writing songs, even though you're not in Nashville anymore?"

"They seem to be letting me do the job remotely. I guess I have some credit finally built up in that town."

"Finally. And now you've got the media trailing you again, huh?"

Adele's popularity had been enjoying a resurgence since a California lifestyle magazine had printed a picture of her and Nate singing to each other in the bar. The tabloids had jumped on it, and now she and Nate were also known as the Darling Lovebirds, Adele had told Molly. *I haven't bought a single copy of any of those magazines – I wouldn't – but people keep tagging me on Facebook with their posts.*

No one tagged Molly in Facebook posts.

"Yeah, they've been around. I guess it's good for business. You know," Adele said slowly, "if you stayed, we could do more of this."

Molly looked down at her cowboy boots. She hadn't worn them in years, but she'd packed them to come back here. They still fit right. "How do you like living with Nate?"

"Way to change the subject. What did you think about my idea to split the property?"

Molly had hoped that the subject wouldn't come up for a few days, till after the new year, maybe. She'd hoped she would have an answer prepared. And she didn't.

Adele seemed to take her pause as a bad thing. "I *know* it's not fair, me wanting to keep the saloon open. I know the two of you probably want to sell. But there are three properties, right? The saloon, the café and the hotel. If we divvied them up, we could each do what we wanted with them. And I know me taking over the saloon, which was the only thing up and running, is actually worth more money, so I'd be willing to adjust the terms for that..."

"Oh, stop. We think it's fine to do it that way."

Adele jerked as if someone had tugged her upwards. "You talked to Lana?"

Molly kept her eyes on the toe of her boot. "Yeah."

"When?"

"Before I came."

"What did she *say*?" Adele's tone was ragged.

This. *This* was what Molly wasn't going to do. She wasn't going to be the one in the middle, not anymore. She wasn't responsible for making either of her sisters happy. Not anymore. This was the time she was going to think about herself. For once. But she supposed she did owe Adele a little bit more in the way of explanation. "She said it was fine if you want the saloon." What Lana had actually said was, *Are you serious? Why she thinks I'd want any part of that property is beyond me. She can do whatever the hell she wants to.*

"Seriously? Does she want the hotel? I thought the café would be perfect for you, since you're a nutritionist, and you know about food, and you used to love being there with Uncle Hugh –"

"Slow down there, tiger."

"Does she need money?"

"I don't know." That was the truth.

Adele propped the guitar against the edge of the stage and turned to sit facing Molly. "And you told me on the phone you need money. Are you okay?"

She didn't want to go into this. Not now, not here, in the place that was making her feel at home in an almost startling way. "I'm thinking about things, okay?"

"Let me help." Adele's face was all concern, her brows drawing together, her eyes worried.

"There's nothing for you to fix. I'm okay. Lana is okay."

"There's *nothing* I want more than for you to stay."

The thing Adele didn't say, that she also wanted Lana to come home, hung in the air between them as clearly as if she'd said it.

"I know."

"But..." Adele bit her bottom lip briefly, and Molly felt it – she knew what was coming. "What about your money?"

And there it was. Molly drew her legs up under her to sit cross-legged. She folded her arms. She'd *had* money, yes. All three girls, when the band broke up, had split with the same amount of cash. Molly knew Adele had made good investments. She also knew that Lana had blown her entire wad within the first six months. She herself had held on tightly to the money, waiting for exactly the right thing to come along to invest in. And it had. She'd let Rick persuade her that the kelp health smoothie would be the future wave of healthy eating. It had science behind it. It was actual vitamins and minerals, in an almost undetectable flavorless liquid. It had been the first thing Rick had bullied her about. *Health made easy. Even you could lose weight on this stuff.*

Her daddy would've been disappointed in her. He'd always said that if you bought into something (or someone) like that, you deserved what you got.

So yeah, she had deserved to lose all that cash. "I invested in a boyfriend's stupid pyramid scheme."

"Oh, no."

"Lost it all."

Adele put her hand over Molly's. "How's your heart?"

Molly looked at her fingertips, which were dented from the guitar strings. Her calluses were long gone. "Fine. Mostly." Rick had been exciting, with his big plans and charisma. She'd loved him, and she'd had dreams of their future. Then he'd gotten verbally mean. She'd stuck around way longer than she should have. It had all made her feel so *stupid*.

"Do you really have to go back to the ship?"

She still hadn't told Adele she'd quit. Maybe she hadn't really admitted it to herself. And the last thing Molly wanted to think about was getting back on board any sea vessel, even a new one. The funny thing was that she'd always been prone to seasickness. She'd drugged herself with non-drowsy Dramamine during the day, and slept fitfully at night. She never got to go into town when the boat docked, because she'd been so busy with appointments. She'd been to a hundred dream destinations without ever getting a chance to see the sights. The benefits had been good, that was true. Free room and board. The food wasn't even that bad. She had helped co-workers cobble together meals that wouldn't kill them, nothing like the luxurious, fattening fare of the regular passengers. There was no lobster or all-you-can-eat buffet for staff, although there was always plain chicken and good salad. When they'd hit more tropical destinations, there was beautiful fresh fruit. It didn't make up for the loneliness. New crew members came aboard and left, kids taking a break between college years. At thirty-one, Molly had sometimes been the oldest one in the staff dining room, something she had tried not to think about too hard.

"More. I demand *more* time with you."

Adele, demanding. She'd always demanded and bossed and pushed (so had Lana, come to think of it). But it was done in love, and Molly knew that. "Demand all you want. I'm tougher now. I can stand up to you." She didn't mention that she'd been googling nutritionist jobs in California. She'd even researched nutritionist jobs in Darling Bay. She'd come up with a big fat zero, of course. No surprise there. Molly smiled and leaned sideways to nudge her sister's shoulder with her own. "Besides, I went in there already. Into the café. It's a complete nightmare."

"You did? Today?"

"Last night. Well, really early this morning."

"But the power isn't on."

Molly laughed. "And that was *terrifying*. I used my cellphone light to look around."

"You shouldn't have gone there in the dark. I should've gone with you. Oh, my God, you could have *died*. There are probably three or four different ways to perish painfully in there."

"Are there rats? Because I swear I heard something that sounded like rodents in the walls or under the appliances."

Adele blew a breath of air out through her lips. "I have no idea. I went in there once to look around, tripped over some piece of metal on the ground and hit my head on the old stainless-steel sink. I got a small cut, and pretty much decided I was going to die from some terrible disease. I haven't been back since. I guess I'm trying to pretend it doesn't exist."

"You haven't heard the best part yet. The local sheriff thought I was a burglar, and I was briefly arrested. It's just my fast talking and sexy Kermit pajamas that got you out of having to bail me out this morning."

"Colin McMurtry?"

"I threw my cell phone at him in the dark. He has a bruise over his eye today."

Adele nodded while looking over Molly's shoulder. "I can see that."

Molly's throat clenched. "No."

"He just walked in."

"Oh, my God."

Adele narrowed her eyes suspiciously. "Wait, your back is to him. How did you know he has a bruise? It wouldn't have come up that fast, would it?"

Her sister never missed a thing. "Saw it when he pulled me over this morning."

"Damn, girl. You know how to make an entrance."

"What? I didn't get a ticket."

Adele laughed but Molly stayed frozen, unable to turn around. For a moment, she let herself remember how Colin had looked sitting in her car, water streaming down his face, his eyes so dark the pupils disappeared. Her stomach tensed at the thought.

"See. There are many reasons you should stay. A good-looking man who bruises easily."

Molly shook her head. "I can buy an apple if that's what I want."

"Okay, a man who's in charge of things. Cops are hot, right? Even if his family is…"

"What?"

"Oh, nothing, really. Don't you remember his cousins, though? Those four guys who raised hell?"

Molly had a vague memory of thin boys with dirty faces, the kind of boys who had thrown mud clods and sold weed in high school. "What happened to them?"

"All in jail, I think. Along with their dad. Colin's dad did okay – you know he was the sheriff before him?"

It sounded familiar. "Kind of." She wanted to look – she wanted *so* badly to look behind her.

"Anyway. He looks good in uniform."

Molly couldn't help it – she twisted her head the slightest bit, shooting the quickest glance she could.

Colin was *not* in uniform. He wore the same blue denim jacket he'd been wearing early this morning when she'd assaulted him. His dark-brown hair was standing on end as if he'd been dragging his fingers through it. The woman across the small table from him was young. And blonde. And beautiful.

Crap on a biscuit. She turned back to Adele. "I wouldn't stay in town if you paid me."

"Okay, so what if I paid you?"

Molly gave an exaggerated sigh and slid lower in her chair. "Stop."

"Seriously. I could put you on the payroll."

"I'm not taking your money. Period."

Adele crossed her arms. "Then I'll loan you enough to help you open the café."

"I'm not looking for a new job." She wasn't. No way. Maybe if she told herself that long enough, she'd believe herself. "And you're not going to boss me into it." She felt the shape of her pocket – that silly plastic Junior Deputy badge dug into her thigh. She liked it. It reminded her she used to be braver. "No more bossing, from anyone."

"We never bossed you!"

Molly just stared.

"Okay. We bossed you constantly."

"Between Dad telling me what to eat, and you making me sing louder and Lana making me do any harebrained scheme she couldn't talk you into –"

"Come on, Molly." Adele's voice was pleading. "I miss you so much."

"Guilting me will make me feel worse, but it won't make me stay." *It might.*

"Oh, *fine*. More in a couple of minutes." Adele stood. "Nate is in the back, I think – I need to get Colin and Nikki drinks."

Colin was on a date. It made sense; Colin was a handsome man. And of course he'd be dating someone adorable, someone named *Nikki*. Just one more quick glance. They wouldn't notice.

Molly craned her head.

They were laughing together, their heads bending close to each other. Then, horrifyingly, Colin caught her looking and gave her a cheeky wink.

Molly gasped and dropped her eyes, mortified.

Wait. Why was she the embarrassed one? How could he *do* that in front of another woman? How completely and utterly rude. Molly tried to feel a pang of pity for the gorgeous blonde across the table from him but failed miserably.

Yeah.

Heaven help her and her sainted mother forgive her, for one hot second, Molly wished *she* were the skinny blonde.

CHAPTER NINE

Molly Darling was in the bar.

Colin should have known she would be.

Okay, if he had searched his heart, he might've been able to admit that it was why he had suggested meeting his sister at the Golden Spike.

He wasn't going to look at his motivation that closely, though. He would save the scrutiny for her.

Molly Darling – with those curves that went on forever– wasn't even pretty. She was beyond that. Colin's father had had a word for a girl like her: a *beaut*. "What a beaut," he'd trumpet loudly, turning his head to follow with his eyes the woman they'd just passed on the sidewalk. There had been nothing more embarrassing to Colin, but often, if his father was in uniform, the woman in question wouldn't seem to mind the comment. She would blush prettily and maybe toss his father a saucy glance. Colin had noticed the same thing happening when he himself was in uniform, of course. Women were more attentive. Waitresses smiled more, filling his cup of coffee more often than anyone else's. There was something about the badge, it was true. Something it was possible he had profited from – hook-up wise – in the past.

But that was in the past.

He would never be his father.

"What are you looking at?" Nikki's look was dagger sharp. "That girl? She's cute."

"No." His protestation was too quick. Obvious.

"Oooh. You *are*. Okay, she looks really familiar."

"*Psst.*" Colin smacked her hand. "Stop staring."

"Me? That's you. Who is she?"

"No one." What a lie. Molly was someone, all right.

"A Songbird. *That's* who it is. That's Molly Darling."

"Nikki..." Collin's voice was a warning.

But it was too late. Nikki was waving her hand and already hollering, "Molly! Molly Darling!"

Molly, of course, looked horrified at his sister's bellowing. She glanced behind her, as if there were another Molly to be found that she could throw into the fray. Then she gave a half-smile and waggled her fingers. It looked as if she were on a float at a parade.

Nikki glanced at him sharply. "Do you know her? She's looking at you, not me."

"Leave her alone. She probably gets that all the time."

"Then she's used to it."

Colin leaned forward on his elbows. "Quit trying to dodge my question. What's the next job you're going to apply for?" She'd wriggle out of answering, he knew that. She would try to bounce her way right out the front door in T-minus-three seconds or so. He'd given her cash, and now there was no reason for her to stay.

And right on cue, Nikki looked down at her phone. She pushed a button. "Oh, crap."

"Come on." Colin was tired of it. "Don't try to –"

Nikki stood. "I'll just be a minute."

"Wait –"

"He's just outside. One sec."

Colin didn't have to ask who *he* was. Todd Meyers. Todd came with a shit-ton of natural charisma, and a rap sheet as tall as he was, which was considerable at six foot two. He liked old Camaros, evading police at high speed, and Colin's sister. He'd been bad for her for the last three years, and Colin worried he'd be bad for her until something terrible happened, something he couldn't bear to think about. There was no evidence Todd had ever laid a hand on his sister, but Colin and Nikki had been raised in the same household. You learned what you learned at a young age, which was the whole damn problem. Dad was dead, the rest of his side of the family was in jail – wasn't that enough bad influence out of her life?

Colin followed Nikki outside. He stood on the porch, three feet above sidewalk level, and listened to Todd rev the engine, gunning it as if he were about to tear off at a hundred miles an hour. Nikki was leaning in through the passenger side saying something animatedly he couldn't quite hear. She threw a glance over her shoulder at Colin, and her face was as guilty as it had been the year he caught her polishing off the very last of his Halloween candy when he was nine and she was five.

He opened his mouth to shout, but then closed it again. Anything he yelled at this point would be too little, too late. He knew what would happen next.

Then it did. Nikki tossed an apologetic look his way, and tucked herself into the roaring Camaro. They blew the stop sign three seconds later.

"Fuck."

From behind him, a woman's voice said, "I've had bad dates that I thought would win awards, but that was seriously Olympic-worthy. I think you just got the gold."

Colin turned. Molly covered the smile on her lips with her fingers, as if she was worried she'd said too much.

"Wasn't a date. But I was about to take her out to eat because I'm starving. You hungry?" His own words surprised him.

"Yes."

Her answer startled him, too. In a good way. "Fancy or plain?"

She shook her head. "Not fancy."

"Hot dogs?"

"Hell, yeah."

And just like that, his frustration turned into a warmth he hadn't seen coming, winter sun breaking through the fog.

CHAPTER TEN

She'd said yes. That was the funny thing. Colin made her nervous. He made Molly conscious of the way her body moved, and the way her clothes hung on her frame. She pulled at her black top, making sure it wasn't clinging to her. She thought about changing her answer.

And then Colin shot her a dark, sideways glance, and she actually felt something burble in her chest, a cross between a giggle and a squeak.

Awesome. Currently acting like a fourteen-year-old girl, check.

The owner of Darling Dogs, Waylon Dunning, took their order with a pen that only worked intermittently. He'd opened the place in 1947 and hadn't missed a day at work since the Nixon administration, and it took so long for him to write their order down that a line built up behind them. "I don't get it," he said. "With no *bun*? What kind of a hot dog has no bun?"

"It's just a little healthier."

Waylon looked at her blankly.

"Fine, I'll take the bun." It wasn't worth arguing about.

They stepped aside to wait. The sun was setting over the ocean rather unspectacularly. The fog bank was swallowing its last rays, and the pinks and purples were muddy, like old watercolors on a plastic tray. The roar of the ocean was muted, just a low whoosh.

Colin said, "So you haven't gotten arrested today."

She liked the way his voice sounded rough and low, but with smoothed edges, like a river-tumbled stone. "So far so good."

"Nice job."

"Excuse me, can you hand me a napkin?" The voice was thin yet familiar. "Thanks, honey."

Eva Doyle. She hadn't aged a day. Well, that wasn't true – the lines that had always been there were deeper now next to her lips and under her eyes and perhaps she was a little more stooped, but Eva had always carried her years well. Molly figured she had to be in her mid-seventies by now. She could have passed for ten sun-kissed years younger.

Eva's face broke into an enormous smile as she wiped a bit of mustard off her top lip. "Molly Darling! Is that *you*? Oh my very goodness, it is. You sweet girl."

Molly was folded into a hug that was tight and soft at the same time. "How are you, Eva?"

"Oh, you know, I'm doing the same as I always have. Just chugging along. Are you here to help your sister?"

"I – "

"I just *knew* you girls would all come home eventually. Birds migrate away, but they always come home to roost. Seems like your sister Adele has a good hand on that saloon of hers. And that man, come to think of it. She's a strong one. All of you are. Tell me you're going to reopen the café. You *have* to tell me that." Although Eva's eyes had always been a light blue, they were paler now, as if worn away by ocean waves. "I can't keep eating these hot dogs every night."

Molly laughed. "You don't eat them every night."

Eva stood taller by a fraction of an inch. "You think I don't, girl? I'm a cleaner."

Molly glanced at Colin. He was biting his bottom lip, as if he was trying not to laugh.

"Sorry?" Of course Eva was a cleaner, Molly knew that. Eva had been the head maid at the Golden Spike Hotel years ago. There had been no one better in the industry, Molly's Uncle Hugh always said. Eva could walk into a dirty hotel room, spin around while tossing sheets into the air and, Mary Poppins-like, the room would be cleaned, straightened, and perfect in what seemed like seconds. Molly had worked one summer helping in the laundry, and she knew this was no small feat.

Eva nodded hard. "You come into this world either a cleaner or a cooker. If you accidentally get born as both, never admit it. I can boil water, make eggs, and I'm pretty good at making s'mores in the fireplace. But other than that I've never cooked, and I don't mean to start now. I miss my job at the hotel, I tell you what."

Molly had forgotten that employees used to eat for free in the café. That had been one of the perks, along with steep discounts on liquor in the saloon. And sure enough she could still picture Eva sitting on one of the café stools, a carton of fries at her left hand, a *People* magazine at her right. "You loved the garlic fries. I remember that."

Eva laughed. "That I did. *Tell* me you're reopening the café. You always loved being back there with Hugh."

Molly shook her head. "No way. I don't have the time or the money."

"You're breaking my heart, and eating this way can't be good for it, right?"

Waylon poked his head out the order window. "Every night. She's here every damn night."

"Eva! You can't say that to a board-certified nutritionist. I can give you some easy recipes – things that you can make with as few as three ingredients –"

"No, honey. You can give me as many recipes as you want, and I'm never going to try them. If I did, I'd burn the house down. I *like* a good hot dog. It fits in my budget, too. I ate at the Golden Spike Café almost every day of my adult life, and until it reopens, this is all I can afford. You'd be surprised how many pensioners hang out here."

Molly had a terrible vision in her head of rows and rows of elderly men and women getting all their protein from *hot dogs*, their vegetable intake from sauerkraut.

And in the next moment, she saw those same people in her mind's eye clustered into the old red booths, lined up along the café counter. The Golden Spike Café had been a gathering point, a place for the whole town to get together. Now that she thought about it, there was no other place like it in town. There was the bagel shop, but that had standing room for no more than two at a time. There was the pizza place, but that was small and dark. There were two fancy night-time-date restaurants, but they were expensive.

A town like Darling Bay *needed* a place like the Golden Spike Café.

As if reading her mind, Eva said to her clearly, "It's not the same here without it. It's like we lost the heart of us."

Something small and cramped inside Molly's chest unfolded the slightest bit. What if . . .?

Eva tucked her napkin into a pocket as if it might come in handy later. "Well, sugar, I'm so glad you're back. No matter what you end up doing. You come see me. I'll tell you everything Rosamunde is up to, and you can give me the Darling-girl gossip." Eva lifted herself to tiptoes to give Molly a kiss on the cheek.

And she was gone, a short, solid, sailboat chugging down the sidewalk on her way home.

"Oh, no."

Colin shot her a grin. "You have that look on your face like Nikki gets right before she does something stupid."

Molly blinked. Now he was calling his girlfriend stupid? Because *that* wasn't okay.

Colin seemed to realize his words might have been just shy of polite. "I mean not really *stupid*. What I mean is –"

"No, I think you're right, though. I'm going to do something incredibly stupid." She took a quick sip of her soda. The bubbles burned her tongue. "I think I'm going to reopen the café."

CHAPTER ELEVEN

Colin's heart leaped. It actually moved in his chest, like a marlin soaring up out of the ocean and flipping in the sunlight. She might *stay*.

Then someone hooked him in the gills, and he was suddenly flopping on dry land.

If she stayed? She might be trouble.

If she was only in town a short while, they could have a good time together. He would try to, at least. Not like he could predict his success with a woman like her – God knew she could have her pick of men – but he could try his damnedest.

She was hot. And smart. And funny. Basically, she was his kryptonite.

Why did that scare him so much? It wasn't like he didn't have company sometimes, and some women had stuck. He'd almost bought Rosa a ring, until she'd suddenly left town with Cobb, his undercover deputy who'd taken his job so seriously he'd gotten under *her* covers.

Might be nice to ask Molly out on a real date. One that didn't involve hot dogs.

But a woman like her had a man waiting somewhere, surely. Even though her hands were ringless, that didn't mean her heart wasn't already spoken for. And then there was the whole fact that she was a *Darling*, town royalty, and he was the only male McMurtry not sitting in a jail cell at the moment.

This all coursed through his brain in what felt like half an hour but was probably more like two seconds. "So you would stay."

Molly looked astonished by his words. "I guess *so*."

"We weren't in the same café the other night?"

"Yeah, I think we were."

Overhead, a seagull wheeled and cried. "Because the one I was in looked like a nuclear bomb had gone off inside."

Molly gave a small, unconvincing laugh. "Nah, it was practically ready to reopen."

Colin nodded. "Sure, all you need is a new blender for the milkshakes. Good to go."

"Yep."

Waylon called their order, and they took their dogs back to the table they'd been at. Two bites, then three. They ate in silence. He could almost feel the heat created by her brain spinning, turning the idea over and over.

Finally, he finished his last bite and said, "You really think that's a good idea?" Why was he still talking? This wasn't his business. If she stayed in town, so be it.

"I have no idea." Molly's eyes sparkled as she bit into her hot dog. And sparkling wasn't a euphemism – in the increasing darkness, her eyes literally lit up. He'd never seen anything like it. Some late nights, when he was sick of paperwork and people altogether, there was a spot in the marina he liked to pull his patrol car into. It was a good hiding spot, good for thinking. It had a great view of three fishing boats, part of the old oil dock, and the water was always bright from the lights of the pier. In those lights, the water always sparkled. To him, it was prettier than any jewels could ever be. Diamonds didn't hold a candle to the way the tops of the small waves shone at night.

Her eyes, though? They were giving both waves and diamonds a run for their money.

"What about your job?"

"I hated my job." She popped the last bite in her mouth and chased it with a long pull on her Diet Coke.

"You get to travel." His brain stalled. "Wait, did you say hated? Past tense?"

"I travelled the world, and I got to see no part of it. I was queasy every single day. Every once in a while, I got off the ship long enough to get some kind of coffee drink in whatever port we were in. Every place sells the same tchotchkes. Every port has the same hucksters, the same wide-eyed tourists, the same people who want to make a quick buck off a rich tourist. A poor working girl can't have much fun in a place like that, unless she wants to dance on table tops after imbibing gallons of cheap rum."

"I've known a lot of people who think that would be a great vacation." Colin tried to make his voice light. He tried to look over her shoulder, past her, out to the darkening water, but those eyes of hers kept catching his like criminals caught bad raps.

"It's not my idea of fun." She leaned forward. Colin could almost see her excitement in the air, a static electricity of sorts. "Eva doesn't have a place to *eat*."

"Good God, if that's what this is about, I'll make her a sandwich!"

"She needs a place to go." Molly spoke as if he hadn't said a word.

She wasn't listening to him. If a car crashed into the pier next to them, which one actually had not long ago, she probably wouldn't notice. She had been pretty when they got here, and now she was edging close to glorious. "So, what, did you quit or something?"

"Eva needs a place to go where she can eat something healthy. Something that isn't a hot dog. And something that she can afford. That's *exactly* my skill set. My thesis was affordable nutrition. I researched how families can live on ten dollars a day and still meet their nutritional requirements. And yeah, I lost my damn mind and quit."

Colin tried for a laugh to cover his shock. "Darling Bay? This town has no interest in nutrition. If you offered anything that wasn't a greasy hamburger, fries and a beer, you'd be held in contempt of the town municipal code. I'm pretty sure of it."

"No, it could be amazing. Buckwheat pancakes with honey-maple butter. Sustainably caught seafood, from right *there*." She pointed out towards the fishing boats. "I could *do* this."

"You have the cash for that?" Something flickered in the back of her eyes. No, she didn't have it. "I guess you could always get a loan from the bank. The rates are pretty low right now, and if you turned a profit quickly, you could probably get away with not going in more than one or two hundred K in debt."

"Two hundred *thousand*?" The worry was there, deepening the brown of her eyes, and she laced her fingers in front of her on the tabletop. "It couldn't be that much."

Ridiculously, Colin wanted to stand, lean over the table, and catch her mouth with his. He wanted to wrap his hand around the back of her neck and draw her in close to him. Tightly. He wanted to taste her.

"Sounds like a great idea for a multimillionaire to invest in. You know any?"

Molly nodded. She wasn't listening again. This non-date, and he knew it hadn't been one, was over. Fine. He needed to get back to his office, away from the confusion this woman stirred in him, like static on a police channel.

He chucked his bottle in the direction of the recycling bin and missed by a mile. "Well, I guess I'm done."

She looked surprised but not upset. Not even a little bit. "Thanks," she said. "I can walk myself back in a little while."

Colin wasn't the kind of man to let a woman walk home in the dark. Even in Darling Bay, things could happen. "I'll go with you."

Molly shook her head. "No, I'm going to sit here a bit longer. Don't worry." She grinned at him. "I have my badge. I'll be safe." She took out her phone and looked down at it. "I'm going to make some notes. I have a million ideas swimming around in my brain, and I want to catch some of them before they get away. And I have *you* to thank for this. If we hadn't got hot dogs together, if I hadn't seen Eva, I'd probably be leaving in a few days."

Colin gave a nod. Good, it was established it was definitely his fault. Nothing better than that. "I'll see you."

God, he hoped he would. At the same time, he was scared he might.

CHAPTER TWELVE

The next morning, Adele was at Molly's hotel-room door at eight. She let herself in, of course. A quick knock, a twist of the key in the lock, and a bright voice, "I'm so excited! I still can't believe it!"

Molly groaned and pulled the covers over her head, then peeked out. "It's too early for this."

"If you're going to run the café, you're going to have to get used to early mornings. Up and at 'em, sunshine! Let's get down there and throw stuff around and figure out how to *do* this!" Adele twirled.

"Does Nate ever want to kill you?"

"Never. I'm everything he ever wanted. I'm the light of his life."

"So the answer is yes. Daily."

"*Oh*, yeah."

Molly struggled into a sitting position, rubbing her eyes. The idea, which had seemed so incredibly brilliant last night, had dimmed. "I've got no clue where to start."

"I don't either. We'll figure it out."

And here, already, was the sticking point. That *we*.

Molly wanted to do this on her own. If – and it was still a big if – she decided that this was actually a good idea, she wanted it to be *hers*. Not yet another Darling Songbird collaboration. When the band broke up eleven years before, the split had crushed all of their hearts, leaving the girls scattered, alone, each of them homeless without her sisters.

But Molly had taken one worthwhile thing from it – it felt good to stand on her own two feet, without propping herself up on her sisters' shoulders.

And she wanted the café to be hers. Not Adele's.

Molly cleared her throat, hoping the nerves she felt were just because she needed coffee. "I'll figure it out." She was correcting Adele's last words. Only she didn't want to have to spell it out. She didn't want to hurt her sister.

"You'll let me help?"

Adele's help. That was the thing. Adele was wonderful, a marvel. She was a force of nature. She could get more things done by noon than most people did in a weekend. But Molly didn't feel like being bossed. Not anymore.

"Absolutely. When I figure out what you can do."

"But –"

"Let me at least start this by myself. I'm going to the bank on Monday."

"But you'll..."

Molly waited for Adele to finish her sentence. Molly would what? Screw it up? Get it all wrong? Adele had always been the one to get things right. She was the one to fix things that broke, the one who had cleaned up their messes for a long time. She was good at it. Only Molly had grown up. "I'll be fine."

Adel nodded sharply. She got it. "I guess I'll leave you to it. Let me know if you need anything." She didn't meet Molly's eyes.

That was fine. Adele's feelings could be hurt for a while. She'd get over it. "I do need cleaning supplies. I'll buy stuff like Clorox and 409, but can I borrow the mop and bucket from the bar?"

Adele's voice was curt as she said, "Whatever you need. Just take it."

"Thank you." But Adele had already closed the door behind her.

Molly showered and put on her oldest T-shirt and jeans. The shirt had a gigantic blue kitten face on the front, and was ripped in three places at the hem. It was tighter than she usually liked to wear in public, but it was just for cleaning. A nutrition bar for breakfast, a cup of coffee reheated in the hotel-room microwave and she was ready. Armed with rags, cleaning liquids and a pair of bright-pink rubber gloves, Molly let herself into the café.

And her heart fell to the filthy floor.

It was even worse than she'd remembered. If a fire had ravaged the place, leaving nothing but black char in its wake, it might have looked more attractive than what she was staring at now. In the darkness of night, the dirt had been hidden. Now, in the light, everything was visible. Grime covered every surface, every counter, every chair, every table. For a brief second, Molly considered crying. Then she considered running away, leaving town, a note for her sister pinned to the hotel-room door.

She shook herself. Enough. She stuck in the ear buds of her phone, cued up her favorite dance list, and started moving.

First things first. Today was for the dining room. Everything had to come out. She wouldn't even set foot in the kitchen yet. That would come later, when she had a better idea of all there was to do.

One by one, she lugged each heavy wooden chair outside, singing as she moved. Then she wrestled each table into the parking lot. An hour later, the parking lot looked as if she were about to host a dinner in an open-air dining room for people who didn't mind a dark dose of depression served with their meal.

The lamps that stood in the corners came out and leaned crookedly against the tables. She set the heavy Victrola just outside the door. Molly remembered winding it as a child, playing records on the nights – not infrequent – when the power went out due to storms or high winds.

Then the dining room was empty. It echoed dully, her footsteps ringing hollow, the mop and bucket making an unholy racket as she pushed them forward. The scent of bleach in the hot water stung her nose. She was already sweating her ass off, and the cleaning was just getting started. Molly cranked her tunes louder.

She dragged the mop forward and back, scrubbing as hard as she could. She sang out loud, coughing every once in a while in the foul-smelling air. She didn't even care when one of the poppiest Darling Songbirds songs was played. Usually, unable to listen, she hit the forward button. But today, it felt right, singing along to "Honey and Honky-tonk" at the top of her lungs.

She dumped the mop bucket and its disgusting contents down the outside drain and refilled with what felt like her tenth bucket of hot water. Thank God for the outside fish-cleaning sink. The cool morning air felt good on her wet skin, and she closed her eyes for a moment, stretching.

Then she felt a tap on her shoulder. Molly screamed, and whirled, wielding the mop as a weapon.

"Whoa, there! Sorry! I didn't know you were armed!"

It was the beautiful blonde she'd seen Colin with the night before. Nikki.

CHAPTER THIRTEEN

Nikki was the date he'd said wasn't a date, the woman who'd gotten into the car with the other man and left Colin standing alone on the front porch of the Golden Spike.

Molly jerked out the ear buds. "Can I help you?"

"I just wanted to know what you were doing."

Oh, Darling Bay. Molly had forgotten how everyone in a small town was nosy, as if just living there gave them that right. "Cleaning." Her voice was flat.

"Sorry, but didn't I see you at the bar last night?"

"Maybe?" Molly was a ball of sweat. She could feel it trickling down her forehead and running into her eyes. She felt as grimy as the furniture she'd pulled into the parking lot. The gorgeous blonde standing in front of her wasn't making her feel any better. She wore a button-down blue blouse, a dark-blue skirt, and blue flats that looked new. Not a scuff on them. She was the stark opposite of Molly, before and after in the flesh.

"No, I *know* I saw you. You're a Darling Songbird. You're Molly. Am I right? Oh, I know I'm right!"

Oh, Lord. Was this really the time she had to run into a fan? Molly bumped into fans just about never, nowadays. The band had been forgotten for the most part, save in this little corner of the world. Here they were big fish in a pond the size of an mason jar. It wasn't something to be proud of.

"You'll forgive my not shaking hands. They're covered with things you don't want to touch, trust me."

The woman bounced on the tips of her toes. "Oh, my goodness. I'm just so excited, you don't even know. I think I might be your biggest fan."

That was *entirely* possible. "How nice." Molly shoved a sweat-soaked lock of hair out of her eyes, knowing as she did so, she was probably dragging another dark smear across her face.

"I'm Nikki. Nikki McMurtry."

Oh. Something bright glinted across the street, blinding Molly momentarily. "You're his *wife?*"

"Whose wife? Oh, ew, Colin's? No! I'm his sister!"

"Oh." The idea of Colin *not* having been on a date last night was entirely too welcome.

"Did you think I was his girlfriend or something last night? That's horrible. You mean he didn't correct you?"

It wasn't like Molly had asked. It had been none of her business.

"I'll never forgive him for not introducing me to you. We met, once, a long time ago. I'm sure you don't remember. But you helped me. You helped me a lot."

"I'm sorry, I don't..."

"I was leaving summer camp at the youth center, and Cortez Burdass started chasing me, yelling that he was going to throw me into traffic."

Oh. Molly remembered the bully, his bellowing voice, his empty threat (there was almost never traffic in Darling Bay, after all). And she knew she had yelled something at him, but it was so long ago now. She didn't know what she said.

"You yelled at him that if he put a finger on me you would punch him in the balls."

Laughter jolted her. How could she have forgotten that? In a house with two sisters, she'd been late to even hearing about the concept of balls – how they could hurt a boy if smacked the right way. And the right way seemed to be any way at all. That day had been the first time she'd ever said the words out loud, and they had felt powerful. Her father had been right – he'd been telling her she had to speak up, like her sisters did, if she saw something that needed to change. *Use that voice of yours. Yell when you need to, Molly.* So she had yelled at Cortez. It had been the first time she'd heard the power of her own voice. Just her words, yelled, had had a very real, physical effect. Cortez had given a squeak and then he'd run away like a little girl, leaving the actual little girl gaping at

Molly in awe. It had been extremely satisfying even if she'd been shaking a little.

And as far as Molly knew, it was the first and last time she had ever had any dealings with this Nikki McMurtry. "I'm glad it helped. That guy was a little jerk."

"Now he runs the second-best fishing tackle shop in town, and he's still an ass. In fact, if you wanted to go threaten his balls, I'd like to watch."

"Noted." Molly turned back to finish filling the bucket with hot water. She added the last slug of her second bottle of Lysol to it. With a heave and a sigh, she lifted it down to the concrete.

"Can I help?"

Molly shook her head quickly, automatically. "I got it."

"You're...cleaning?" Nikki made it sound as if cleaning the café was the worst idea she'd ever heard, or at least the most ridiculous. She peered inside as she held open the glass door for Molly to roll back into the dining room. "Because I gotta tell you, this looks like a lost cause."

"Yeah, it might be."

Nikki tilted her head. "But you're going to punch it in the balls?"

That was it, actually. "Yes! I'm going to punch it so hard it sings like a canary."

"Let me help."

Propping herself on the long handle of the mop, Molly took another look at Nikki. Her pink lipstick was recently freshened. Her eyeliner was perfect. Every strand of hair was in place in that artfully waved way women wore their hair on Thursday-night television. She looked like a model. "You're not exactly dressed for it."

"I don't care. I just had the most awful interview of my life. I hate the clothes I'm wearing, these shoes are pinching my feet, and I'm in the worst mood ever. I need to attack something."

"And you don't have a house to clean? A car? You actually feel like scrubbing down the dirtiest diner in the history of the western world?"

"Believe me, my house is as clean as it's going to get."

There was something in the woman's face that Molly liked. An openness. Her eyes looked sad, and at the same time Molly thought she could read something hopeful in them. Nikki's shoulders were bowed just enough that it looked like yes, she'd had a bad interview. And maybe it *would* be good for her to scrub something. "I can't pay you."

"I don't care."

Molly shook her head. "No, I really mean it. I have no money. I have no idea why I'm cleaning this shithole, and I can't guarantee that you won't get some kind of tropical disease from what you touch in there."

"I said I don't care. I *really* don't. I just need to make something look better. You ever get that feeling?"

"Yeah. I do. All right, then. There's a box of rubber gloves on the picnic table in the front."

And then, strangely, Molly cleaned side by side with Colin's sister. Molly cued up her dance playlist on her phone, and turned up the speaker so that the music filled the dining room, the sound quality thin but audible. Nikki knew the words as well as Molly did, and they both sang along. Nikki managed to unstick most of the windows with a putty knife, and the scent of salt air filled the dining room, christening it, chasing out the smell of mildew and bleach.

After two hours, three-quarters of the floor space had a natural sparkle. Some of the old linoleum would have to be pulled up and replaced – there was no saving it. The northern wall, the one with the fewest windows, had obvious water damage, and when they tried to wash it, the paint peeled off in long, thin strips.

They went outside and attacked the tables and chairs. Molly was grateful they were in the parking lot and not set up on the main sidewalk. As it was, four or five residents peered over the low white fence to ask what they were doing. Molly answered politely twice. To the third resident, Nikki put her hands on her hips, and said, "We're building an airplane."

The man huffed. "I thought you were having a garage sale or something."

"A garage sale?" Nikki flapped a Windex-soaked rag in his direction. "Do you see a garage here? Do you think we're having a gigantic tag sale on old tables? Are you an antiques dealer?"

The man backed off, still puffing out his cheeks.

"Because if these are antiques, sir, we can give you a fair price! Each piece, just a thousand dollars!" She turned to face Molly. "Sorry. That wasn't very polite."

"It was wonderful." Molly meant it. "I'm starving. Let's eat."

They scrubbed their hands raw, and over two sub sandwiches as big as Molly could talk the deli guy into making them, they ate.

"This is amazing." Nikki spoke around a mouthful.

Molly chewed appreciatively. "The best part is this." She rapped the plastic deli table with her knuckles. "So clean. If I had any cash at all, I'd order fifteen of these and throw out the café tables. No, I'd burn them. Only that might put too many toxins into the environment."

"Nah, that furniture will be beautiful when we're done with it. Just a little more elbow grease and some Murphy's wood soap, followed by a good oiling. Worst-case scenario, we re-stain them. That stuff was made to last. You're lucky."

"You really think so?" Lucky. Molly didn't know how much luck had to do with anything. The reason she was broke wasn't about luck – that was all her, all the time.

"Come on. Think about that old café. Isn't it literally sitting on top of a gold mine?"

"Maybe a mineshaft? One that's about to collapse?"

"No, really, didn't your family mine gold?"

"Oh, lordy." Molly laughed. "No. There was gold up in the valley, but it was never ours. Some of that gold ended up in the Golden Spike that joined the

Transcontinental Railroad in 1869. But my great-grandfather just named the town after himself and opened a saloon called the Golden Spike. That's as close as we ever got to a precious metal, unless you count the Golden Spikes they serve at the bar."

"Oh, man, I had one of those once. That's all it took. What was in that thing?"

Funny. Molly hadn't thought of that drink for so many years. The tourists had always loved it – probably still did. "Bourbon, Goldschläger, Angostura bitters, hot apple cider, and a lemon wedge. So yeah, with the Goldschläger, you're really drinking gold."

"That's so weird. And awesome. I wish I had something like that. Something that meant something to me, that had been in my family a long time."

Molly stabbed her ice with a straw. "Do you and Colin have family here?" Oh, dang it. They were all in jail. She shouldn't have mentioned it.

"Me and Colin are the two who are left, that's all." For one short second pain shone in Nikki's eyes. "Been that way for a long time."

"Are both your parents gone?"

Nikki stared. "Really? You don't know?"

Molly shook her head. "It's been a while since I knew any Darling Bay gossip. But you don't have to tell me a thing." She hated it when people pried. She didn't need to do it herself.

Nikki just blinked. "My mama died of a stroke, and then my daddy, who was the sheriff just like Colin, ate a bullet. On the sidewalk in front of the police department." Her gaze was blank.

Molly sat in silence. She didn't know what to say. Was there any condolence big enough? Instead, she just said, "Me and my sisters are orphans, too."

"I know."

Something lurched inside Molly's chest. She had two options. She could stand up and leave the deli with Nikki, thank her politely, give her a California hug, and hope that she saw her in the new future. Maybe they'd exchange cell-phone numbers.

Colin's sister.

She ignored the voice inside her that asked if she was actually being selfish, not altruistic.

Screw that. Of course she was being selfish. Nikki liked cleaning. She was a hard worker. "You want a job?"

The change in Nikki's face was instant. "But..."

Molly leaned forward in her eagerness. "*But* is everything. All I have for you is a but. But I have no money right now. But I don't know what I'm doing. But I know I need help. And somehow, someway, I will figure out how to get you on the payroll. That is..."

"What?"

"That is even if you wanted to go into this with me."

"I'm loving where you're going, but as what? What are you looking for?"

"I'm looking for a hard worker. Someone who will help me manage the place. My right-hand woman. Someone to help me hire and train the new staff." Molly groaned. "God, I feel so stupid. I can't believe I just asked you that. As if a normal brain and human being would accept a job I couldn't pay them for until the restaurant opens." Molly herself could get by on the little cash she had left in her last savings account, and a third of the royalties still trickled in, drop by tiny drop. The fact that she had had the gall to ask someone else to work for free made her cheeks flame so pink her face actually hurt. "I'm sorry, what a terrible idea. I do this thing sometimes where I have a feeling and I act on it and, I swear to God, it's the thing that has got me into the biggest scrapes in my life."

But Nikki was still sitting there. Still listening. "So you're *not* rich like all of us thought you were?"

Molly gave a soft laugh. "Hell, no. I've been working on board cruise ships for the last six years. I'm a nutritionist."

"*Seriously?*"

"Every once in a while I got to meet someone famous and look at the plates of baby-bird food they ate. Most of the time I just got paid to counsel people who would listen politely, show me their Lean Cuisines, and then proceed to ravage the seafood buffet. I *had* some money, yes. And a guy I worked with had a fantastic idea for a protein smoothie made with seaweed. I swear, the second I met Rick, I swung into full-blown crush, and by the time I'd given him seed money for the venture, I was in love. I'd already imagined the beautiful children we'd have together." Wee little Della with the pink ribbons tied in her blonde hair, Rick Junior pumping his sturdy legs until his swing went highest of all. She'd gone so far as to worry about Rick Jr.'s temper—whether he'd inherit, whether it was something they could prevent a child from getting. *So stupid of her.* "He and I went into business. He really thought he was going to make a million dollars, and I just wanted to be near him. Instead, the FDA came after him, something about the kelp that he sourced having some kind of small biotoxin."

Nikki snorted.

"Yep." Molly had managed to blow her portion of the band breakup money on one guy, one bad idea, one damn heartbreak. It was so like her that the most surprising part was that she had been surprised. "Anyway, I know you probably can't afford such a crazy idea of a job, and I don't blame you. I'm embarrassed I asked you."

From behind her and over her head, came a voice. "Asked her what?"

Molly spun. She felt a completely inappropriate gut punch of lust to see Colin in his crisp blue uniform, the star on his chest so shiny it winked in the sun, smaller pins and chevrons attached to the cloth, symbolizing things she didn't understand.

He looked like a strong man. A man who would protect his own. She might be in trouble. And not just because he was a law man.

CHAPTER FOURTEEN

N o." This wasn't going to happen. Working in the café was *not* the job his sister would take.

"Yes." Nikki crossed her arms.

"I won't let you." Shit, it was the wrong thing to say. It was the exact opposite of what he would need to say to dissuade his sister from taking yet another dead-end job she would eventually get fired ignominiously from, probably because of her deadbeat boyfriend. "I mean, obviously, do whatever the hell you want. But it's a bad idea."

How Nikki could make a nod look sarcastic was beyond him.

Molly – who was wearing a dirty T-shirt that was snug around her curves, and jeans that fit her just right – looked like she was getting the gist of his meaning.

"You can't mean that you don't want her to work with me?"

"I don't mean –"

"Why not?"

"There's not a –"

Nikki nodded, her eyes looking viciously pleased. "Yeah, tell us."

"You think working in the café isn't good enough for her?" Molly sounded incredulous.

Colin was a smart man – he knew he should back away slowly, keeping his eyes on them, the way he would from a junkie holding a knife.

But he wasn't that smart. "I don't."

He swore Molly's spine grew at least an inch taller, and she was still seated. "Excuse me?"

"I can see how that might offend you, but the thing you have to remember is that my sister is smart." Oh, crap. This could not end well.

"Ah. Okay. A smart person couldn't possibly work in a little old place like the Golden Spike Café. That must be why I'm doing it."

Here we go.

"I'm just a singer. And you know us Songbirds, we're flighty as all get out. Anyone who makes a country record doesn't have an IQ more than twenty. Never been sure mine even made it to double digits, actually."

"Molly –"

"Is this the way you always talk to your sister?"

Colin didn't feel like he was talking to anyone but Molly at this point. "I talk to her the way she needs to be talked to."

"Well, *that's* the most chauvinistic thing I've ever heard."

If a man could produce steam, Colin could feel it rising from the back of his neck. "I feel like maybe this isn't any of your business." He turned to look at Nikki, who still had her arms folded tightly, and her lips even more so. "Come by the station when you're done here."

In a cheerful, fake voice, Nikki said, "An order? Lovely. No, thanks."

Fine. They would do it here. Molly opened her mouth to say something else, but he shot her the look he'd given Jimmy the crackhead that time he'd tried to charge at him with the blowtorch. "This is *Todd's* fault. That asshole has kept you under his thumb for long enough. You've got to get out of there. Come live with me. You can have the spare room. I've told you that a million times, but you have to *do* it this time."

"This has nothing to do with him. You're just mad because I'm not getting the job you think I should get. And you know what the truth is, Colin? The truth is this – no one thinks I'm good enough. And they're right. I'm not."

"That's bullshit!"

"Is it? I'm a McMurtry, just like you. I'm never going to be good enough for this town. You might have risen to the top of the sheriff's department, but that has nothing to do with me. You're his son, yeah, but I'm *her* daughter. I had an interview at the Frostee Freeze up the coast today, and I was told I was under qualified. *Sixteen* year olds aren't told that. No one expects a damn thing from me, and they're right not to. The only one who does is you, and you have to get over it. I'm never going to be the person you want me to be." Nikki said to Molly, "I'll take the job. We'll work out the pay later. What time do you want me at the café tomorrow?"

Molly's eyes were wide. "Eight."

"See you then." His sister spun and paced away. She couldn't be going far – he didn't see her car parked anywhere close by. Colin didn't want to watch Todd scream up in his Camaro to pick her up. Colin never had the desire to illegally discharge his weapon as much as he did when Todd's ride was in his line of sight.

He glanced at Molly. With good reason, she looked confused. "I don't boss her around like that all the time." He scrubbed his face with his hand, hard. "*God*. The damn *Frostee* Freeze. I have a friend at the golf course, a guy who's married to one of the instructors who owes me a favor. I could've pulled some strings and she knows that. Not that that makes it a sure thing. She's damn right no one in this town would ever let a McMurtry girl rise any little bit higher than her means."

"I'm well aware that this is a gold rush town, but are we in eighteen fifty-three now?"

His temper was still frayed, but it didn't mean he had to be an ass to Molly. "I'm sorry. There's nothing wrong with working at a café."

"Well, yeah."

"It's just that...well, my dad met my mom in a diner."

She tugged on the hem of her dirty blue shirt. She was a wreck – sweaty and filthy – and still managed to be adorable. "And?"

"He married her because he thought she was beautiful. He hated her because he thought she was worthless."

Molly stared. "Oh."

What the hell was he *thinking*, opening up to a perfect stranger like this? A hot one, yeah. But still a stranger. "Everyone thinks Nikki's the same. Beautiful and worthless. Useless."

"Then they're all idiots."

He cracked his neck and grazed his holster with the heel of his right hand. "Yeah, well, those idiots are my job security."

"If it helps, I have no money and she probably won't work for me for long."

"Good."

Molly blinked. "Yeah, that still sounds condescending. You get a lot of action with that attitude?"

"I do all right." He pushed out his chest. "I can show you if you want." It was a rebellious, stupid thing to say. It wasn't even flirting, it was grandstanding, a rooster move.

"No thanks. I'll stick with your sister."

"She can do better."

Carefully, coolly, Molly's eyes swept his body, all the way down to his boots and then back up again. "So can I." She swept into the café, closing the door behind her.

Shit. Colin often had women ticked off at him, for a lot of reasons that were usually purely professional. But not these women.

He stalked back to his patrol car and then, closing the door like he did a million times a day, slammed it on his thumb.

The pain felt earned.

CHAPTER FIFTEEN

The wind was strong on the side of the hill. Molly had forgotten how mournful it could sound up here, a low moan of air that felt like an ache to listen to.

Ahead of her, Adele's strong legs pumped resolutely as she hiked smoothly and quickly. Molly had lost her breath five minutes up the trail and hadn't gotten it back yet.

"Wait up!" How many times had she called that out in her life? Adele, always out in front because she wanted to get there first to suss out whatever situation it was (a playground, a sound stage) so she could fix problems before they even arose. Lana lagging far behind because she was so lost in her own world she never cared enough to keep up. Molly almost followed up with her old secondary cry: "Wait for us!" But Lana wasn't behind her.

Molly wouldn't have admitted that she looked over her shoulder. When she did, her heart fell.

The three of them might never climb to the cliff together again.

"Come on!" Adele's customary response. Always.

Even with the pang she felt missing Lana, Molly's spirits rose as they crested the second-highest rise and caught their first view of the ocean. It was dark blue today, with tall whitecaps portending the late-winter storm heading in. The sky blended into the edge of the horizon, where a dark haze hung heavily.

Adele slowed enough that Molly caught up. She gestured up towards where the sun would have been if it had been allowed to break through the thick fog. "No groundhog today, huh?"

Molly shook her head. "Six more weeks of winter, I guess." It was really February? "I can't *believe* I've already been here that long." She broke off – Adele was already ten paces away, and the wind caught her words and blew them back inland. One more rise of the hill and they'd be there, and then Molly could catch her breath. You'd think all the physical labor she'd been doing in the café would have paid off, but apparently that was strength training, not this kind of cardio.

Six *weeks*. It had flown by in a blur of work. Molly had been sleeping better than she ever had before, falling into bed at the end of long days spent clearing out the old, bringing in the new. The barely new, that was. Adele had co-signed on the loan, which had hurt, Molly could admit. She wasn't doing it alone, like she'd wanted to. But the look on her sister's face had made it worth it. The bank had given Molly a loan big enough to pay Nikki (way too little—if Nikki stayed, she'd give her a raise the second they made a dime) and to buy the equipment she needed if she remained a cutthroat second-hand shopper. She'd gotten a walk-in freezer from a fish grocer who was retiring, and an industrial stove (twelve burners!) from a restaurant supply store that had turned out to be a guy named Neddo who rolled up a metal door on a huge storage unit. He promised none of the stoves were hot and then he'd laughed himself silly at the dismayed look on her face.

And the café still wasn't open.

It was close, though. Another week and Molly *swore* they'd be ready, if they had the staff in place and trained. They had interviews the next day, then two more inspections, a test run of the menu, a new sink in the back bathroom and new glass in the front two windows, and they'd be good to go.

Oh, and a door-opening bell. Molly wanted the kind that chimed cheerfully as people entered – a tinkled chime, not the buzzers which were the only things she'd been able to find, even after making the long trip down to San Francisco in the rented van.

And new silverware.

And maybe a few more bread baskets.

Oh. Candles? Did they need candles? They were getting paper menus printed (cheaper to change out while still working on the menu) and Molly herself had started a small blaze at a romantic restaurant years ago when she hadn't noticed she was holding the menu over the flame – and how long was training going to take, anyway?

"Watch yourself!" Adele's voice was sharp.

"Oh!" Molly leaped away from the edge.

"Just because the trail leads to the brink of danger doesn't mean you follow it! It's an old trail." Adele put her hands on her hips. "Do I need to leash you to me like Mom used to do with Lana at airports?"

"Sorry." Molly followed carefully behind Adele, trying to keep her mind off the café.

But the café was all she'd been thinking about.

She had definitely *not* been thinking about Colin McMurtry. Almost never, that was. Not that often.

Okay, except for the time he'd been at Martha's Market. He'd turned onto the row where she was – the tampon aisle, as luck would have it – holding his basket like it was a weapon. She'd hurled herself through the nearest door she saw and ended up nose-to-nose with Benny the butcher. She'd fanned herself. *Hot out there. Just cooling off for a minute. This is refrigerated, yes?* Benny, not used to people in his area, had just blinked slowly and then gone back to cutting pork shoulder.

After she'd bought her tampons and yoghurts, he'd been chatting on the front sidewalk with an old woman who had bright-purple hair. Colin had smiled broadly at Molly.

Like Molly was just another citizen in his jurisdiction. As if she were a vote he needed to win.

She'd smiled back as cheerfully as possible. She didn't have a problem with him, no siree.

They'd repeated the scene at least four more times – at the library where he'd been talking animatedly to an old cowboy holding a stack of paperback westerns; at the post office where he'd chatted so long to Dot Rillo about the upcoming postal increase that Molly had almost been unable to return his smile. At the drugstore. At the bagel shop.

Every time, he'd been nothing but friendly. Each time, he'd smiled. Friendliest sheriff west of the Mississippi, no doubt. People seemed to love him.

No. The sheriff hadn't been on her mind.

Not at all.

It didn't help that he kept dropping off goodies, invisibly, leaving things on one of the tables out front. A bag of warm cookies from Josie's, two fresh cups of coffee. Once he'd left a whole pizza. Nikki's phone would chime her brother's text noise (a siren) and she'd grin and run outside to wave at him as he pulled away in his patrol car.

It didn't help that Nikki didn't seem to notice that Molly was actively trying to avoid thinking of him. As they worked together, she chirped all the time about her brother. *He's so driven, you know? He works so hard. He's supposed to have weekends off but he never takes them. He ends up in the office anyway, doing paperwork, or helping his officers*

with stuff. Investigating. He'll come around, you know. He won't
mind me working here forever. We'll serve him a bleu burger and
he'll just die, I know it.

Molly hadn't asked one question — not one. Still, she
now knew that Colin's favorite meal was mac'n'cheese,
and that he'd gotten an MBA before getting a job at the
department and rising to take his father's place. She
knew that he liked dogs but he liked cats better, even
though he hadn't had one in a while, since old Sammy
Joe'd died.

She did her damnedest not to wonder what he'd done
with the kitten, Asiago. He'd probably just dropped her
off at the pound. She would have been adopted in a
heartbeat.

Nikki filled the air with talk as they worked. When
Nikki mentioned her father, her voice tightened. Molly
and her sisters had had a terrible time recovering from
their parents' deaths, and they'd died of natural causes.
How much harder would it be to heal from a suicide?

And besides, she was learning plenty just by keeping
her mouth shut and her ears open. Now she knew
Colin's favorite color was dark blue, though his personal
car was gold. It was an old Chevelle that he didn't drive
much since the department provided his take-home
patrol car and gas, but that he loved.

Molly knew that his last girlfriend, Maggie, had been
an accountant with tiny boobs. (Of course.)

Molly knew that he hadn't dated anyone seriously in
at least a year, maybe two.

Nikki talked. Molly just listened.

Now, up almost to the end of the clifftop pathway, she pushed the thought of him out of her mind yet again. In front of her, Adele took the last few steps with an enthusiastic stride. Molly followed more slowly, each step deliberate. She leaned carefully against the cold metal railing. "You trust this thing?" Its legs appeared to be sunk into rock, but the metal didn't feel heavy enough under her fingers.

"The fire department tested it with something like a thousand pounds of pressure. It'll hold. Hey, you okay?"

Molly took a short, sharp breath and tightened her grip on the railing. Below them, the Pacific pounded the coast. It was deep blue today, with a lighter strip of cobalt close to shore. Four pelicans flew above the water, appearing to be swimming through the air, the slow strokes of their wings almost touching the surface.

To the left, they could almost see the old folly on the shore. Built with leftover iron from when the rail was constructed, the decrepit, open-air structure had been the site of the Darling Songbirds' first concert for Darling Bay.

"Molly's Folly," said Adele, pointing. "That way."

"You're never going to let that go, are you? She'd been fifteen then, and had kissed a thirteen-year-old boy because her sisters had tricked her into it

Adele laughed so hard she choked. "We told you he was seventeen."

"You two *bossed* me into kissing him. You made us go on that walk."

"You could have said no!"

"It's funny now, yeah. It wasn't then. His breath tasted like corn nuts." She'd wanted to kiss the boy, though. He'd been a tourist from Eureka. She couldn't remember his name, but she remembered he had bright-blue eyes and freckles. He'd been her first kiss. She hadn't known both her sisters *and* her parents were watching, that she would never live down the way she'd moved her head back and forth, swiveling it as she'd seen people do on TV. At least she'd kept her tongue in her mouth, which was more than she could say for the boy.

Adele leaned forward, too, her hair lifting in the wind.

Molly tried to catch her breath. "Man, I was in better shape last year, I swear to God. I weighed twenty pounds more but I was doing yoga every day. I had stamina. Now I'm skinnier but weaker."

"Well. You look great."

She made a face. "Thanks."

"What?"

Molly's hair thwapped her in the face, and she pulled it back and tied it with a rubber band. "Nothing."

"No, what? You have that voice."

Sisters. Molly did have the voice – she *knew* she had it. And she couldn't help it.

Molly turned her back on the view of the water and faced the hillside stretching far into the distance. The way the oaks and eucalyptus swayed, hundreds of yards in the distance, was comforting to her. The air smelled of salt water and, distantly, of cattle. "It's just that – you always say I look great when I've lost weight."

"I didn't mean it that way." Adele looked stricken.

"I know."

"I didn't. You look good no matter what."

"Not true."

"It's just that now you look so healthy –"

"Dude, I just said I was healthier when I was heavier. I'm skinnier because I've been stressed and not eating. *This* isn't healthy." Her sister wouldn't get it. Adele had been thin her whole life. Perfect body. Perfect face. She'd never kept a food journal. She'd never gone to a food counselor. She'd never been called country-fried anything by the media.

"I'm sorry."

A wave of cold air slapped Molly in the face and she shivered. "What are you sorry for?"

"For making you feel like..." Adele's voice trailed off.

That was the trouble. Adele knew the topic was fraught, that there were things she should understand about how Molly felt, but she didn't know what the *exact* problem was. Molly would never be just right, just as she was, for anyone. If she was thin, she felt weaker. If she was heavier and stronger, people called her fat. On national media. Okay, that hadn't happened in a long time, but once it did, it was practically impossible to get over.

It wasn't worth explaining. "It's fine."

"No, tell me."

"Really. I'm fine. Look at that." Molly turned back and pointed down the hill. "Frankie Stunenberg's roof is still covered with blue tarps, see? How long have they been up there?" The Stunenberg house was a sprawling property, big enough to see clearly even from this far away. They were known as the reclusive millionaires who never spent a dime on anything, including roof repair.

Adele's smile was thin – her nervous smile – but Molly watched her decide to go along with it. "Since dinosaurs splashed in Lathrop Creek. Before I mock him too mercilessly, where else can you see that particular color of plastic-tarp blue?"

Molly scanned the town – there. The hotel. Of course. "Whoa. That's a lot of tarp."

"Six rooms."

Molly took a breath, held it, and then said, "What are we going to do about that?"

Adele's shoulders relaxed – Molly could see them drop the slightest bit. "I don't know," her sister said. "Get Lana to come help?"

"Never going to happen." But the mood was broken, the string that always ran invisibly between them smooth and untangled again.

"I'm still going to hope."

Molly leaned against her sister's shoulder briefly. "You've always had altogether too much of that going for you."

"No such thing. Hey. Remember that time we came up here to do that photo shoot?"

"Oh, man. For some glossy magazine." Molly wished she *couldn't* remember that. But she did, clearly.

"*Vogue* or something awful like that. Maybe *Elle* or *Glamour*." Adele's eyes crinkled at the corners as she smiled, and Molly wondered when she'd gotten those tiny, almost invisible lines. Smile lines. They made her sister even prettier. "That was a terrible shoot."

Molly leaned on the railing. "They made us put on our first performance outfits. The ones Mama sewed for us." The magazine had thought it would be a cute call-back to the way they'd gotten started, and they'd worn the outdated, old-fashioned clothes on the cover of their first album. They were ridiculous: button-down western shirts, the kind with the heavy embroidery over the breast pockets, wide red skirts over crinolines, and pink cowboy hats.

Adele nodded. "Lana had outgrown her dress and it was just awful, remember? They had to cut up the back of her shirt and safety pin it together so that it looked normal in the back? And it was about this cold and windy and we lost at least two spare cowboy hats before they came up with the idea of tying them into our stupid braids –"

"It was me."

"What?"

"Who outgrew the shirt."

"Oh, honey, it wasn't." Adele looked desperate. "It couldn't have been."

"Of course it was." How could her sister have forgotten that? Molly was the big one. Molly had always been the big one. If anyone was going to rip her pants, if anyone would be embarrassed by the media, it would be Molly. Never Lana, never Adele. Always Molly.

"I'm so sorry."

"Well, I'm ready to go whenever you are." She wouldn't meet Adele's eyes. Molly *should* be a grown-up and realize that things had changed, they weren't kids anymore, and God knew they weren't teenagers, either. They'd been so naïve when they had been in the band, all of them. Everything had changed.

Especially Molly.

"It's fine, it really is. I don't want to talk about it. I've got a ton more work to do in the café before it gets dark."

Adele gave a quick nod. "Promise me you'll come to the bar tonight."

The bar was the last place Molly wanted to be. Surrounded by loud, happy people who had money to burn buying drinks didn't sound like her idea of a good time tonight. "Can I give you a firm maybe?" She smiled to soften the words.

"No, it's important."

Since when was it ever important to hang out in a bar? Fun, sometimes. Important? Just about never.

"I've been so exhausted every night. I'm not good company, I swear. And I don't want you buying me any more drinks. I can buy my own." There was pique in Molly's voice, she could hear it. She felt twenty-two again, when she was trying to make her own way in the world, never able to quite afford the essentials, even with the royalty money that used to come in a lot more regularly than it did now.

"You have a loan from the bank. That's for fixing up the café. I'm not letting you buy your own drinks, don't be ridiculous. Just promise me. Tonight is going to be something different, and I think you'll like it."

Awesome. Adele was probably going to sing with hunky Nate, and everyone in town would swoon when they looked at each other with stars in their eyes. It would be some brilliant song that Adele had probably dreamed up in her sleep, and Molly would watch, impressed and loving her sister hard while hating every second of it at the same time, and despising herself for feeling that way.

When was she finally going to grow up? Why was this so hard?

"Honestly, it's a surprise especially for you."

Her sister would sing a genius song, and the everyone would swoon. Adele was their darling, that was already obvious. People grinned like idiots when she walked into a room. It was like the band had been reimagined as Adele and her Darling Sister Songbirds. No one remembered Molly. That's how it felt, at least. Not that she *wanted* them to remember her – the fact that people's eyes skittered over her was a good thing. She didn't want to sing for Darling Bay, God, no.

As if Adele could hear her thoughts, she said, "Sing with me?"

"On stage? No way."

"No. Here." Adele's voice was so soft the wind carried it partially away, and Molly could only hear the echo, feel the shape of it.

"Adele."

"Please? Remember how Mama would ask us to sing right here when we were little?"

That was the problem. Molly did remember. And it hurt to feel those memories so close to her skin again. "Yeah."

"Just a few verses. For old time's sake."

Molly didn't answer. She looked down at the toe of her orange canvas sneaker. She nudged a rock so that it touched the one next to it, and then she gave her ankle a quick snap, sending the rock over the edge in a silent low arc. She was literally contributing to the downfall of this cliff. Someday it would collapse and she would be partially to blame, for hastening its subsidence.

"Please? For me?"

When had Molly ever been able to say no to Adele? Almost never. And this wasn't going to be the time to begin, obviously. "You start."

They talk about the rainbow

Like we could fly above,
But those who always say that,
Don't know anything 'bout love.

Fly, fly, fly...
Till none are in the sky.

The wind stopped, as if it were listening. A murmuration of starlings blossomed in front of them, then parted, wheeling lower, diving down below the cliff's edge so that the collection of birds was actually lower than they were. They spiraled back up again as if lifted by the sisters' voices.

As you rise a little higher,
The air, it gets real thin,
The thing that brings a bird down
Is a little piece of sin.

Fly, fly, fly...
Till none are in the sky.

Molly had always sung lead on it, with Adele's sweet harmony twisted around the edges of the verses. Adele's voice was exactly the same, in perfect pitch and tone, clear as a bell. Molly couldn't quite hear what her own voice was doing, but it *felt* right, like her pitch was in just the right place.

As they reached the last verse, Molly stretched out her hand and took Adele's.

They didn't look at each other.

That was good because Molly was one hundred per cent certain that if she'd seen her sister's face, she would have cried.

They sang the last verse.

When you fly above us,
And look down at what you lost,
Remember when we fell to earth.
We're love's true cost.

The only thing missing was Lana, holding Molly's other hand.

Fly, fly, fly...
Till none are in the sky.

CHAPTER SIXTEEN

Colin entered the Golden Spike, glad to be out of uniform for once. He spent too much time in this bar helping Nate clear it of rowdies while wearing his badge, and it felt good to be in old jeans and a black T-shirt. He would never completely fit in – everyone knew the sheriff always had his badge in his pocket. Even in plain clothes, he could feel people reacting to him. The men hunched over their poker game sat up almost imperceptibly, while the cash that had been on the table disappeared as if the players were magicians. Scott Tinker punched in songs at the jukebox. He turned and looked over his shoulder as if he'd heard Colin enter the bar. Yeah, he knew about Scott's outstanding warrant, but it was for two hundred and fourteen dollars on a parking fine he hadn't taken care of, and while the guy was a jerk, Colin was off duty. He didn't give a crap about the warrant.

He said hello to the mayor's daughter and the head librarian, and he gave a brief wave to the brother of one of his deputies. What would it be like to police a different, bigger city? What would it feel like to be able to go to a bar and simply be a regular person? People knew he wasn't on duty, but if the shit hit the fan, they'd be looking to him. Just like a paramedic had to spring into service if someone stopped breathing, a member of the police force had to jump in when bad things happened whether he was on or off the clock.

Maybe soon he'd take a vacation somewhere. He couldn't remember the last time he'd gone out of town for more than a weekend. The last time he'd done that, it had been with Maggie, and she'd complained the whole way to Monterey. She'd picked a fight with him on the journey home. It hadn't been awesome.

He could go to Oahu for a week and dip his toes into the sand. Or somewhere else warm. Cabo? Spring Break was coming, and a couple of his deputies liked to go ogle the girls on display. They'd been trying to talk him into going, too. But while Colin liked to ogle a girl as much as anyone else, the idea of eyeing women so recently out of their teen years made him more than a little uncomfortable. He liked a woman who was ripe.

For a second he imagined the way Molly filled out the back of her jeans. That was a prettier sight than any twenty-one-year-old in a bikini by about a mile.

The Golden Spike was packed, a great crowd for a Thursday night. There had to be twenty people lined up at the bar, and five or six couples already dancing to Lizard Lips. A local cover band, they reliably played the old country tunes people wanted to hear. They used to have a pretty solid repertoire of Darling Songbird tunes, but Adele had put a stop to that shortly after coming to town. Nate's band, Dust & Rusty, was always fun to watch, and a long time ago Colin used to sing more regularly with them. For a short time, he'd considered even joining the band when Nate had asked him, but one night he'd had to jump off the stage to arrest the guy who had punched out a man who'd just kissed the arrestee's wife. Again, the sheriff wasn't welcome at every party in town.

It took him six tries to make his way to the bar as he said hello and exchanged pleasantries with half the town. One of the two Homeless Petes shook his hand and wanted to chat about the stock market, and then the other Homeless Pete started jabbing in his ear about how he was going to build a tiny home behind City Hall if Colin would allow it. "Sure, let's talk this week." Finally, he made it to a miraculously available stool and sat next to Norma.

"How you doing, young lady?"

Norma grinned like she was seventeen. She always lapped up his flattery like a cat with milk. And that made it fun. "Doing great, Sheriff."

"You know that I can't handle it when pretty girls call me anything other than Colin."

Norma batted her eyelashes at him and shook her head, a waterfall of necklaces tinkling as she did. Norma always looked like a short, round hot-tub in whatever full muumuu-like dress she wore, and with her jewelry, she usually sounded like a beaded curtain as she moved. "You're a terrible flirt."

Colin doffed an imaginary hat at her. "I do my best. You seen Nate? He wanted to talk to me."

"He's around but he's got a terrible cold. Shouldn't be here at all but he's a stubborn cuss, ain't he?"

"The worst." He gave a short wave at Dixie, Nate's busy-night bartender.

"Oh, yeah?" Dixie, her short curls bouncing as much as her breasts did in her red half-shirt, leaned up and over the bar. "A wave isn't good enough. Kiss."

He kissed her cheek with a big, wet noise, and Dixie gave a whoop. "That's more like it! What can I get you?"

"Johnnie Walker, Coke back."

Dixie gave her patented grin, the one that would have won her all the male attention in town if that had been the way she went, which wasn't. "Oooh, left the badge at home, huh?"

It burned in his pocket. "Yep. Know where Nate is? He said he needed a favor." Colin didn't mention he hoped the favor had something to do with Adele's sister Molly. He stood up to look over the crowd. Nate was nowhere to be seen.

"He's in the back with Adele. I'd get him, but I'm always a little bit scared to sneak up on them, you know what I mean?"

"I do. But you know what? I ain't scared."

"Oh, God. At least knock first."

Colin knocked on the door of the back room, just once. He pushed it open with a roar. "*Fire exit!* I'm here to check your emergency fire exit!"

And sure enough, Nate and Adele had been locked together head to knee. They sprung apart rapidly.

"What the *hell*, dude?" Nate tugged down the edge of his T-shirt. "Last I checked, you don't work for the fire department." His voice was a low rasp.

"Why're you croaking like a bullfrog, huh? That what passion does to a guy?"

Adele wiped the back of her mouth and grinned. "You're a terrible friend."

"I'm a great friend. Look at me." Colin bent and retrieved Nate's ball cap from where it was lying next to the ice machine. "Picking up your clothes."

"You're lucky that's all the clothing of mine you get to pick up." Nate jammed the cap on backwards and looked as annoyed as his frog voice sounded.

Dixie yelled something Colin didn't catch. Adele called back, "I'll be right there!"

Colin watched Adele hurry out of the storeroom and make her way into the bar. Funny, he'd never taken much time to really look at Adele, not until recently. Adele's and Molly's figures were totally different – Adele had long limbs and a thin face, while Molly was more compact. Shorter. Rounder. *Softer.*

He wondered if she'd be in tonight.

He wanted her to be. Maybe this time he'd get a chance to apologize for being so short with her those weeks ago, when he'd been startled by the thought of his sister working in a café. Since then every time he'd bumped into her in town, he'd been hemmed in by a chattering citizen. He'd hoped the coffees and treats he'd been dropping off on his way to work were going towards his forgiveness. Molly smiled a tight, polite smile at him every time they passed in public.

He didn't want polite from her, even though he *really* didn't need a complication that came in a package like Molly. Especially when that complication happened to be paying Nikki cash under the table.

"Did you hear me?"

Colin shook his head. "Who's going to be able to hear a word you say croaking like a drunk burro like that? You really think you'll be able to sing tonight?"

"That's why you're here, smart-ass."

Colin stepped backwards. "You said you were going to buy me a drink."

"I am. I'll buy all your drinks." The hoarseness of Nate's voice sounded painful. "I need you to sing. I'll still play guitar."

Nerves in his fingertips zinged. "No way." He played okay, he knew that, but his voice was only serviceable.

"Scrug will still be lead. I need you to sing my two songs. You know all the words."

"What, and just stand there empty-handed like a jackass?" That would make it even worse, crooning into a microphone like some cabaret lounge singer. "Is Adele's sister going to be here?" He didn't even want to say her name – his stomach was jumping enough already.

"You can play the Martin. No such thing as too many guitars, right? And nah, Molly never comes in. She works with your sister inside the café all day and then works into the night by herself. Probably in there sanding something right now. When she's done, she nukes a frozen dinner, and then she goes to bed. Sometimes she and Adele sit on the porch with a beer, but that's all the socializing she's been doing lately."

"You said you needed a favor. You didn't say you needed a big one."

"Thanks," Nate croaked. "What would I do without you, pal?"

CHAPTER SEVENTEEN

Molly spent five extra minutes on her appearance before going downstairs to the bar, cursing herself as she did so. She put on eyeliner, thickly lining her upper lid, something she hadn't done in a long time. She put on dark-red lipstick. She curled the ends of her hair so that it wasn't such a haystack mess.

Then she took out the one shirt that fit her, that actually showed the curves of her body. It was a long-sleeved green shirt made of soft rayon, and in the past it had made her feel lumpy. But sometimes, just sometimes, putting it on and looking at herself in the mirror made her feel like she...well, like maybe her curves were just right.

She stood in front of the mirror in the hotel-room bathroom. It was old glass, and wavered slightly in the middle like a funhouse mirror.

And sure enough, the shirt clung too tightly to her breasts, hugging her soft belly.

No way in hell would she go downstairs like this.

You used to be braver.

Yeah, well, she used to be famous and richer, too. Now she was just a girl. She pulled on a loose blue sweater over her blue jeans, and tugged on her orange sneakers. She didn't need to impress a single person down there.

Unless Colin was there.

No. She wouldn't go.

But crap on a biscuit, she'd *promised* Adele she'd be there.

So Molly marched downstairs, feeling as if she were signing in for jury duty. It was a task she just had to get through, then she could be done with it. There was a couple canoodling in the dim white lights on the back porch under the arbor, and Molly was annoyed by the very look of them. The woman was twined around the guy as if she were the plastic wrapping to his candy bar. Molly cleared her throat roughly, but they didn't stop sucking face. Honestly, if people were going to make those kinds of noises, why couldn't they take it somewhere else? A car? Their own homes? A cemetery?

She ignored the logical part of her brain that reminded her people had been kissing behind bars since liquor was invented. If there *wasn't* a couple kissing behind a bar, it just meant the night was still young.

Sighing, she pulled open the back door. A blast of music hit her, lively drumming mixed with a less ambitious bass line. Must be Lizard Lips. They were all about expression and heart, and not always about the musicality.

She stopped in the darkness in the tiny hallway. It felt like she was trying to shrug herself into clothing that used to fit, that she used to be comfortable in. The music wound around her, and she placed her hands carefully on her belly. The amp squealed with that feedback particular to small clubs, and she had a visceral memory of playing the dive-bar circuit as they had tried to attract attention in Nashville. Music with the overlay of laughter. It was the soundtrack of her adolescence. Playing in bars full of people made happy by drink and friends and kissing and laughter – she'd loved the distinct sound of bars even before she could legally drink in them.

But now, standing in the hallway, she felt twenty again. Scared.

She could still turn around. She could still go back upstairs, carefully treading the broken steps in the dark, back to the one room in the hotel that still had a bed that was worth sleeping in. She could apologize tomorrow to Adele, plead a headache.

When it was really just a heartache.

She missed that time with her sisters. Back then. When everything had been so exciting, before they broke out big, before Mama had died, and then Daddy. Back when they were still playing bars that smelled like this, of old wood and peanut shells and dusty rafters and hopeful cologne.

Molly turned to leave. It was too much, and she was too tired.

Then a tall man carrying a guitar tumbled through the swinging door into the small hallway, lurching into her in the dark.

"Careful!"

"Damn, I'm sorry, I didn't see you there." Colin – because of course it was Colin, it would *have* to be him – yanked the guitar out of the way.

Molly hated how her pulse sped up. "It's fine. I've been jabbed in the belly by a headstock before." *Awesome.* Way to bring her belly into it.

"I was just trying to get this string changed, and I thought it might be brighter back here, but it's actually darker. Goddammit. Sorry again."

His words were choppy, and in the dimness, she could see that his eyes were wide. He was in the grip of stage fright – she'd recognize it anywhere. "You're playing tonight? I didn't know you were in a band." Oh, crap. That sounded like she was admitting she *did* know things about him. Which she did. She knew a lot of things.

"I'm not." He was struggling with a tuner key.

"Here," she said. "Can I?" She reached for the guitar's strap.

"God, yes. You kidding me? I haven't changed a guitar string in five years. Maybe more."

It had been closer to ten for her, but she didn't need to tell him that. And she'd be willing to bet she'd changed more guitar strings in the dark than anyone else currently standing inside the Golden Spike, except maybe Adele.

It wasn't until his arms stretched to put the guitar's strap around her neck that she realized exactly how close they were standing. She turned slightly, and her hip brushed his thigh. "Sorry," she said. "I'll just..." She anchored the string with the bridge pin. "It only takes a second, really, once you get it down."

"Yeah, well. I've forgotten everything I ever knew, apparently." He paused. "I'm sorry, you know."

"Nothing to be sorry for." She kept her eyes on the string.

"There is. I'm sorry for not wanting Nikki to work in the café. I was an ass. She seems happy. I've been trying to run into you to say so, but every time I've seen you, someone's been yammering in my ear. And I was a little bit scared that if I actually came into the café, she'd throw me out *on* my ear. Or you would."

Molly adjusted the tuning peg and tried to ignore the thrill that ran along her arms. "It's totally fine. And Nikki likes the presents you leave her. Us. Thank you, by the way. So what are you doing holding this gorgeous Martin?"

"Oh, no. In the light, you'll be able to see that Nate's lending me the beater of the bunch. It's so old it groans when you pick it up."

He was exaggerating. She could feel it humming in her hands. This beautiful old thing wanted to be played. Bowed freeboard, cracked soundboard and all, it was still a Martin. "There. Better than new."

"I appreciate it."

"No problem."

Their words were light, but there was something under their tone that was deeper – she couldn't tell quite where he was looking as he took the guitar from her. She thought that his gaze was locked onto her mouth – or maybe he was looking behind her, to the right of her.

"You look nice."

He could barely see her. She knew that. They were standing in a dark hallway. He might be able to make out her red lipstick and that was about it.

"Yeah." The word was sarcastic even though she didn't mean it to be.

"Why do you say that?"

A thin tremor rocked her. "It's fine. Here's your guitar. Go play."

"You staying?"

She shook her head.

"Why not?"

All Molly could do was shake her head. Her lips felt frozen even though her body was overheating like she was standing too close to an open oven.

With the hand that wasn't supporting the guitar, Colin took her hand.

"What are you doing?"

"You should stay." His hand was firm and callused, as if he worked outside in his free time. A brief but incredibly clear picture made its way into her mind: Colin with an axe in his hands, chopping wood, sweating through a thin T-shirt, pausing at the end of a swing of the axe to look at her. Right in the eye.

The way he was doing now. His thumb stroked the back of her hand.

As if he knew what he was doing, which was the opposite of what she knew. She knew nothing. She felt like she never had, not until the moment he touched her. Molly's breath caught in the middle of her chest as if she were the one who was chopping wood. "You're that good?"

"I'm that bad."

He was talking about the band. Of course. But the other meaning that was laid underneath those words sent a shiver rocketing down her spine. "Mmmm." How could a thumb be that sensual? She was melting inside – if she leaned against the wall she would slide right down to the floor.

"Please stay. I'll buy you a drink."

She was already drunk, couldn't he tell? She hadn't had a drop, but her knees felt loose and her cheeks blazed like they did after two glasses of wine.

Her mouth formed the word without her brain's permission. "Okay."

"Okay." In the dimness, Colin's grin split his face wide.

Molly wanted to kiss him.

She wanted to sway her body into his, and she wanted him to catch her, and she wanted him to put those hot, hard lips against hers. She wanted to lose her breath in his mouth and not be able to find it until next week, when she finally had to rise, gasping to the surface.

Instead, she pulled her hand back as if he'd burned her (and he had – she hadn't seen it coming at all) and spun, heading into the bar, knowing she should already regret the decision to stay and listen.

But she didn't.

Not even one little bit.

CHAPTER EIGHTEEN

Colin regretted touching her almost instantly. He wasn't sorry for asking Molly to stay. He wanted her in the bar in his line of vision, naturally. Any man would want to look at her, to feast on the way her curves moved under that thin blue sweater.

But he wished like hell he hadn't touched her. It was a fuse that, once lit, couldn't be easily extinguished. He knew that.

He pretended he was fine. He played the guitar with Dust & Rusty and backed up Scrug on vocals, while Nate played guitar behind him. Helping out the band was easy – he knew the songs, and his wrist moved to make the chord shapes without him having to think much about it. The harmonies were easy, as in all good country songs. The words were simple, the rhymes solid with just enough unpredictability to keep them interesting.

Just enough unpredictability.

While the band swung into a slowed-down version of "Walking the Floor over You," he watched Benny Simmons ask Molly to dance. She'd been sitting at the bar, laughing with Dixie like they were old friends, even though Dixie was a relative newcomer. Molly toyed with the stir stick on her drink, biting it absentmindedly. It was a Manhattan. He knew because he'd bought it for her. He'd stood at the bar, smiling politely at Dixie, rigidly holding out his twenty.

He should have been chatting Molly up instead of clutching the bill like Norma was going to snake it from his grasp. Colin had no problem flirting with women. None. He'd always considered himself kind of smooth, if it came right down to it. He knew how to meet a woman's eyes and plant in her the suggestion of how he would follow up. What he might do to her. What she might want to do to him.

With Molly, though, his brain went on the fritz, all static and buzz.

When he and Nikki were kids, there'd been a TV in every room, usually a junky one dragged home by his father from the dump. Chuck McMurtry's off-shift hobby was electronics, even though he wasn't very good at it. He'd have a few drinks and then open the back of whichever TV it was, pulling tubes and moving wires. Colin had a recurring dream in which his father jolted backwards suddenly, electrocuted with a terrible *zzzzzztt*. He never knew if it was a wish or a nightmare. Maybe a little of both. But it never happened, and every TV their father had ever fixed up had remained terrible – the antennae trailing up the wall, out the window, and over the highest branch he could talk his kids into climbing. In the middle of any *Star Trek* rerun, Colin could be sure that the image would shut off at least once, sometimes every minute, frizzling and shorting out, over and over.

That's what Colin's brain felt like when his eyes landed on Molly.

His hand fumbled at the G chord as she slipped from her bar stool and smiled up at Benny. She offered him her hand.

As the band moved into an original, "Love Me Sweet," he tried to counsel his brain into paying attention to the music. He was singing this one, and it was a good one, romantic. Colin knew Nate had written it shortly after he'd hooked up with his Songbird.

Lord, what love could do to a guy who used to be normal.

The first verse started, and Colin stepped up to the mic.

I know I did some good things
Once upon a time,
I killed a dragon, saved some men,
Raised the sun in wintertime.

But none of that means a damn
When I look at what I got,
I'm a country boy with you, my love

In our country Camelot.

Benny swung Molly out with a wide swoop, and she spun. Even in her jeans, she managed to look like she was a princess at the county fair. Her cheeks were pink, and her eyes sparkled.

Colin wanted nothing more than to stop singing, prop the Martin on its stand, and haul Molly out of Benny's arms. Benny Simmons was a nice enough guy for a retired game warden who yodeled professionally, but he was a couple of decades too old for her, at least.

I'm a country boy with you, my love
In our country Camelot.

In the hallway, Colin had taken Molly's hand. And she hadn't pulled away. Okay, she had, but not for several long, wonderful seconds, seconds in which she was either electrified in the same way he'd been or...

Had she followed the way his eyes had moved to her mouth, again and again? Had it been her instinct to say yes to his drink or had she just been polite? Had she regretted it when they'd bellied to the bar and he'd suddenly lost all ability to speak English to a beautiful woman?

And why the *hell* did just looking at her make him feel like he was in danger of revisiting his teen years, a confused sixteen-year-old with a boner in the swimming pool, too hard to get out without humiliating himself in front of the whole school?

The song wound down, and the pairs of dancers slowed. They clapped.

Molly looked at him.

She looked right at him, her eyes locked on his. His heart rate increased like he was chasing a suspect through a backyard.

Then Scott Tinker, drunk as a skunk and twice as odorous, lumbered in front of the stage. Beer sloshed out of his pint glass, froth and liquid landing on his boots. "Holy *shit*." His voice was as bleary as his eyes. "Is that..."

Tinker stared at Molly. A grin wobbled across his wet lips. "Oh, shit, you're a Songbird. Right?" He jabbed a knuckle in her direction. She appeared frozen, two paces from Benny. She glanced at Colin and then back at Tinker.

In one fluid motion, without ever taking his eyes off Tinker, Colin lifted the guitar strap from around his neck and put the guitar in its stand.

"You're the fat Darling Songbird. You're the one with the tits!" He made the universal *badaboom* signal with his hands, moving them towards and away from his own fleshy pecs. "I *love* the fat one!"

Heat swept up the back of Colin's neck like someone had thrown lit kerosene on him. He leaped down from the stage and grabbed the man's left arm. "Scott Tinker – "

Tinker swore viciously. He jerked hard and swung with his other arm at Colin.

And it was just what Colin needed. With one leg sweep, Tinker went down, hitting the floor with a thud that echoed to the beams overhead. "You're under arrest."

Tinker's wet groan sounded like a wounded, very drunk bear. "For wha-aaa-aat?"

"Outstanding warrant. Resisting arrest." *And for being a goddamned asshole.* The just-in-case disposable restraint he always carried in his back pocket was around Scott's wrists in less than a breath.

Colin jerked Tinker up to standing. "Let's go."

"But she's the –"

Colin leaned forward as he marched him out. "You say the word *fat* one more time and you'll be in my cell till you come out skinny." He looked over his shoulder at the only important person in the room.

Molly didn't look at him as she ran out the back door, her head tucked, her stricken-looking sister right behind her.

CHAPTER NINETEEN

Adele could knock all night, but Molly wasn't opening the door. Maybe ever.

"Go away!" she yelled.

"Open!"

Molly slid farther into the bed. She'd barely managed to take off her sneakers before she'd tunneled under the covers.

"Molly! I *order* you to open the door!"

That tone of voice had *always* worked on Molly in the past. But not anymore.

Another hard knock. "Molly!" A pause. "I'm going to get the master key. You have to talk about this."

Molly sat bolt upright and yelled at the door, "I will punch you right in the nose you if you come in here! *Leave me alone!*" She meant it. She'd never hit another person, but a girl could start.

"Honey." Her sister's voice was softer. "He was a drunk idiot. That's all."

It would be nice if that had been the only problem. Just a drunk. Molly had run into her fair share of them in bars over the years, both when she was playing and when she wasn't. She didn't give a shit if an old alcoholic thought she was fat.

She really didn't. Screw that guy.

The problem was that Colin had been there. Colin, the guy she'd been both sort of avoiding and also hoping she'd run into every day for the last six weeks.

He'd watched her be humiliated. His face had twisted with something, instantly, something Molly didn't know how to define. Rage? Disgust?

Then he'd chosen to make sure no one would ever forget what the asshat had said. If Molly had been the only one to hear it, she could have ignored it. She used to ignore it on a daily basis, after all, and she'd been so much younger then, so much weaker.

She knew Darling Bay. This would be all the town talked about for at least a week, and if it was a slow month (and it probably would be), it would be gossip fodder even longer.

She listened to her sister's footsteps go down the stairs – she could almost hear the sadness in them, the way Adele scuffed her heels on the ground.

Comforting Adele wasn't what she wanted to do right now. Adele would think *she* was helping Molly, but she'd be wrong. Molly would be the one doing the heavy lifting. *I'm fine. I don't mind. I know you think I'm pretty. Yes, I know I'm pretty, too. I sure do. I absolutely trust you. I have confidence, don't you worry.*

The weird thing was that she did have confidence these days.

Or at least, she usually did.

When she'd been on board the cruise liners, she'd felt great. Of course, it hadn't hurt that she had been the nutritionist. It had said that, right there on her door. On each of the three ships she'd been on over the last six years, she'd had her own office, and the last two had had tiny portholes. Between clients, she could stand and look out over the water. Sometimes, if they were a day or less out from port, birds would swoop along the sides. She would routinely watch dolphins joyfully flip themselves out and back into the water. The way they raced alongside was so gleeful that even after Molly had gotten used to them, she still couldn't take her eyes off them. The only onboard marine life lectures she'd ever gone to had been about the dolphin pods.

Dolphins were so graceful.

And *they* weren't thin.

The dolphins were *strong*. They had wide deltoids and broad external obliques. Their flippers were thick and useful. They had layers of fat to protect them from the cold and to be used as energy. They were robust – maybe the healthiest things Molly had ever seen.

Sometimes, on board, she'd felt like them. She swam in the Olympic-sized pool every morning at six, and no matter where they were, there would always be a couple or three older guests, pulling themselves through the water. All of them had a bit of fat, too.

Solidity was good.

Molly had liked the way she'd stood on the ships, her feet firmly planted hip-distance apart. The huge cruise liners barely rolled except in the biggest of storms, but she'd been always ready for the surge, ready to steady herself.

When she'd fallen for Rick, he'd loved that about her. He'd been such a small man, barely five foot four, and she'd been two inches taller and forty pounds heavier than him. Even his T-shirts had looked like they belonged to a child. But he would confidently wrap his arms around her and say he adored her just the way she was, even though his whole reason for being on the boat was exactly the opposite of hers. He was the bariatric expert, the second nutritionist. She was the counselor. She talked to people who wanted to talk about their struggles with eating, with their weight. She helped them draft plans to get healthy when they reached dry land again. And while she was the therapy, Rick was the science. He made the liquid shakes for their guests on restricted diets. He measured things, locked away their treats, and praised them for bypassing the lobster rolls.

One client had said that during an offshore excursion, Rick had sold her uppers to help burn off extra fat.

Molly had chosen not to ask him about it. Before she'd taken the job, she would have thought that a person on a liquid weight-loss diet prescribed by the doctors would want to be anywhere but at a floating buffet table.

Rick had said it was the opposite. "It's about the cheating, babe. It's about the fact that someone like me can oversee what they're supposed to be eating, and then they can sneak away from me and eat three pieces of cheesecake. Then they go to you to confess. You're good cop. I'm bad cop. I tell them what they're really supposed to eat or drink, and then they go screw it all up again." He'd wrapped his arms and legs around her. She'd always had the feeling that he would have climbed her like a tree if she'd let him.

"Why do they even take a cruise, if that's the plan?"

When she'd asked him that, he'd stuck a knuckle softly into her side. "Is there ever a plan? I mean, come on."

Dread had filled her, thick and cold like one of his disgusting shakes. "What do you mean?"

"They listen to you. They *love* you, they tell me that all the time. But you could stand to lose a few pounds."

"I'm healthy." Molly's heart had hammered in her chest, and she'd wanted nothing more than to get away from him, to get out of his cabin, to get back to her own, where she could close the door and never come out again. "You *know* I am." Her heels could hit the mat in a downward dog. She could plank for three minutes before her arms started shaking. She'd been taking a Jump'n'Pump class at the onboard gym for employees and she was getting good at lifting the small weights while dancing to a beat. Sometimes it reminded her of the choreography she'd done on stage with her sisters years before.

"You're sturdy. Like a fat peasant." He'd thumped her belly like he was testing a watermelon.

And she'd *let* him, that was the worst part.

"You really think I'd look better thinner?" She'd lost weight. She'd been fifteen pounds heavier the year before. He didn't know that – he hadn't known her then.

"No girl actually looks *good* with a belly." He'd spun sideways on the bed so that he could put his mouth on her belly button. Instead of kissing it, he blew a raspberry that made her breasts jiggle. "If you worked harder, you'd be a lot prettier. Not like you're not fuckable now—you are. You're not a total fat cow. Yet, anyway. But you'd be more fuckable skinnier."

He'd been doing her a *favor*, saying that.

Months. For months she'd let him tell her how she wasn't good enough. She'd listened. She'd believed him.

Then he'd jiggled her belly in the staff dining room with a derisive laugh after she finished eating a bowl of oatmeal – *as wobbly as your breakfast, huh?* Molly had caught the look that flew between Janette and Chase.

Abusive.

How had she not seen that was what he was immediately? Why had she put up with it? She'd thought he'd been bossy, maybe a bit demanding. How had she let herself get in this situation? It wasn't like he was physically abusive with her, of course.

They were just words.

But goddamn, they were enough.

With Janette's urging and Chase's encouragement, Molly had broken up with Rick for good by the time they'd docked in Cabo, just as the FDA had come asking questions about the kelp smoothies. He transferred to another ship, taking her seed money with him. She knew she'd never see the cash, or him, again. Her heart had *ached* for him – traitorous, stupid heart – and she'd worked out like a mad woman. She'd taken her own nutrition advice and lost another ten pounds, then she'd looked in the mirror and she'd seen herself as she was – a plump girl who, no matter what, would always be a little heavy. Big, double-D breasts. A softness at her chin. A belly that wanted to spread into a muffin top if she wore too small a belt.

And maybe, just maybe, that was okay.

As an experiment, she'd refused the lure of the scale on board the next three-week journey. She didn't count calories. She did yoga when it felt good, and she ran a few laps around the boat's track, but only when she could honestly say it was what *she* wanted to do. She watched her body get firmer. Not smaller, healthier. For the first time since tabloids used to trumpet their guesses for her weight, she didn't care what the scale said or how her skinny(est) jeans fit. She thought about how she *felt*.

And with the assistance of three self-help books, four onboard counseling sessions, an online message board, and a couple of affirmations that made her cheeks flame with embarrassment when she said them out loud to herself in the mirror, she'd gotten comfortable with her body.

Well.

She'd *thought* she had.

Molly groaned and rolled over in the bed. There was only one working lamp in the small rose garden outside the window, but since she hadn't shut the curtains all the way, a thin line of light crept up to the ceiling. If she closed her eyes and imagined hard, she could hear the ocean's *shuuush* a block away.

The most difficult part wasn't just the fact that the guy in the bar had said it. It wasn't hearing that she was *totally* the fat one.

It was the way a woman had laughed. While the people closest to the stage had just blinked silently, one woman's laugh had cracked through the air from near the door. Loudly. Of course, it was absolutely possible the woman hadn't even heard the guy's comment and had been reacting to something Norma or Dixie had said. But if she *had* been laughing about the man's comment...oh, it would hurt. Molly couldn't say it wouldn't.

And Colin – the way he'd been so embarrassed for her that he'd had to *arrest* the guy. Sure, he'd mentioned a warrant. But he'd leaped off the stage in one bound to seize the bastard because he'd felt her shame. Because he'd felt badly for her.

Molly was mortified.

She put her hands over her face and listened, pretended she could hear ocean air out the window. Six years on the water – she felt lost without it. She'd been too far from the ocean for the last six weeks, even if it was never more than a few blocks away. If she pulled open the hotel-room door and walked briskly, she could be touching the water in less than four minutes.

Well, why the hell didn't she do that? Molly sat up resolutely.

She pulled on a thick cream sweater over her thin blue one. She slipped her feet into her orange sneakers. She tucked her phone and room key into her jeans pocket.

A knock came again at the door.

Crap.

Adele had probably been sitting out there on the porch steps since the last time she'd knocked, just waiting to hear her move around again. But Molly had meant it – she would *not* deal with Adele and her feelings. She swung the door open hard and fast.

"I'm sorry if you feel hurt, but –"

Colin stood in front of her, his hands jammed into his pockets.

Umph. "You are *so* not my sister."

Colin looked down and then back up, as if to check. "I'm not."

An open pit emptied in Molly's midsection. "Why are you here?"

He parried, jerking his chin towards her. "You're dressed to go out."

"Is there a law against that, officer?"

He rubbed his chin with his hand, hard. "Mind if I join you?"

Molly sighed. "I was just going to the beach."

"Let me come with you."

It was an order.

It was bossy.

She hated bossiness, so she opened her mouth to say *No* again, but what came out of her mouth was, "Okay." And even more strangely, she wanted to say it.

"Okay," he repeated.

She bobbled on the soles of her feet.

He swayed, too.

Then, out of nowhere, the sheriff kissed her.

CHAPTER TWENTY

C olin didn't mean to kiss her. He'd knocked on her door meaning to apologize quickly and leave just as rapidly.

But Molly had opened the door expecting her sister and instead got him, and something about the vulnerability in her eyes mixed with the way her cheeks had flared with color had made him move forward, put one hand behind her neck, and draw her to him.

Her lips were as soft as they looked, and her breath, as she'd gasped, was hot and sweet.

And that would have been enough. More than enough. He wanted nothing more than to make her feel better. He wanted the kiss to help.

A simple, sweet kiss.

Then the kiss changed.

Instead of pulling back and smiling at him, Molly Darling kissed him back.

Sometimes, when Colin took the Chevelle out for a spin, he'd punch the gas with his foot and open her up, just to feel the speed push him backwards, to feel the *change*, the rush.

That was how Molly kissed him. Like she was opening the throttle, ready for speed. She kissed him harder, this time with *her* hand behind his neck. She met his intensity and matched it, raising the heat until he thought the core of him would turn into molten steel. Her tongue tasted faintly of bourbon and mint.

She pushed into him, her breasts against his chest. He was hard, instantly. Both of her arms had gone around him, and Lord have mercy, if he just took five or six steps forward, leading her like he'd wanted to on the dance floor just an hour earlier, he could have her on the bed.

Not that he would do that. Somewhere in the back of his mind, he knew that wouldn't be right for her, and some small reserve of grace and will kept his feet in place.

One more second of this and he wouldn't have any more will left. "Hang on."

Molly blinked. Her pupils were dilated in the dim light. Or was it the kiss that had done it? God knew he felt like he was over the limit and he'd only had one beer, hours ago.

She touched her bottom lip. "What the hell?"

Colin immediately wanted to try nibbling on the tip of her finger, chasing it to her lips again, restarting what he'd just paused.

But he hadn't thought any of this through. He hadn't thought about a damn thing since he'd heard Tinker's voice and watched the crushed look cross Molly's face. It was a good thing the guy had a warrant, because Colin had to arrest him for something better than just being a cruel, stupid jackass, which wasn't against the law yet. Sadly.

He cleared his throat and tried to push oxygen back into his extremities by sheer force of will. He stepped away from her body, hoping she hadn't noticed just exactly *how* turned on he'd gotten.

Say something. Anything. "Have you been to the old folly since you've been back?"

"No."

Her voice was breathy, and Colin was struck with the urge to make it even more so. He jammed his hands back in his pockets so that he wouldn't touch her again.

"Let's go."

She brought her hands in front of her belly, running the tips of her fingers against each other. He wanted to catch a hand and press it to his lips, biting softly on each knuckle.

She nodded.

Hope was so foreign to Colin that it almost felt like he was getting a cold. Right in the middle of his chest.

Hope for what?

Colin wouldn't let himself name whatever it was.

He just let it flood through him, a rising tide that came in fast.

CHAPTER TWENTY-ONE

W as this what it felt like to lucid dream?

All Molly knew was that she'd been trying to get out of the room, and then she'd suddenly been smack-dab in the middle of kissing a man who had a starring role in her most recent humiliation.

Kissing him *hard*.

Seconds later, it seemed, she was settled deeply into the leather seat of a gold-colored muscle car, and Colin was next to her, his arm so close to hers that she could feel the heat radiating from his body.

"What –" She started to ask a question, and then, as he took the curve going past the marina, she forgot entirely what she was going to say. *Awesome. Great conversationalist.*

"Sorry?" Colin's voice was almost as low as the rev of the powerful engine.

"Um. What...what kind of car is this?" She didn't give one single rat's ass. She couldn't tell a Dodge from a Chrysler (or were they the same?).

"Nineteen seventy Chevelle Super Sport four-five-four." Pride filled his voice.

"Ah."

"It's fast." They reached the straight section of the road and he punched the gas, making the engine roar. She was pressed backwards into her leather seat, the thrumming of the car rumbling through her.

"Feel that?" He glanced at her, and as they passed through a streetlight's glare, she could see he wore a small smile. Everything south of her bellybutton tightened in awareness. She tucked her hands under her thighs.

"You want the seat warmer on?"

"*God*, no." Her nether regions would spontaneously combust if they got any hotter.

He laughed, low in his throat.

His driving was fast and precise. Molly got the feeling from the way he handled the wheel that he liked speed – maybe loved it – but wasn't driving fast to impress her.

On the contrary, it felt as if he was driving safely. Slowing exactly enough for the curves so that she wasn't thrown against her door (or against him). Speeding up until the white lines were a blur, and slowing again and lowering his lights when an old pickup truck rattled by in the opposite direction.

"There's no one out tonight." All she could come up with was the tiniest of small talk, apparently.

"Never is. You've forgotten what Darling Bay is like."

What was she *doing*? Riding in a strange car with a man who had just kissed her after arresting a man who had insulted her.

Maybe it was appropriate they were going to see the folly.

Colin turned left on the old fire road that led out to Stine's Cove. It was more rutted than she remembered, and he took it slowly now. "You mind if I put the top down? You're really not cold?"

She would never be cold again, probably. "Do it."

With a sound barely louder than a purr, the top opened to the night sky, folding back upon itself. The windows lowered.

"Oh, my." Overhead, a million stars shone as if just for them. "Oh, *my*," she said again. Inanely.

"You forget when you're in town, how bright they are out here on a clear night."

In town? She'd noticed every night since she came back to Darling Bay how dazzlingly the stars shone. And that was in town, around the "light pollution," such as it was. Sure, the stars had been bright out at sea, but out there the sky was so vast and enormous that the night sky had looked like a heavy blanket of ink poked with bright holes.

Out here, the stars danced more than they did at sea. They seemed brighter somehow. She could probably read a book with small print, just by the light of the stars and the bright half-moon. Not that she'd want to hold a book, not when his hand was so close to hers – she wanted to touch him, to put her hand under his on top of the gear stick. But she wasn't quite brave enough. The car purred throatily as it rumbled down the hard-packed dirt road, the stars dangling so low overhead she imagined reaching up to grab one. She would tuck it in her pocket next to the plastic badge.

At the end of the fire road was a small parking lot. To the right, there was nothing but a walkway that wound its way along the edge of the cliff that looked over Stine's Cove, the destination she and Adele had ended up at earlier in the day. Straight ahead was the wooden marker for the trail that led down to the beach. And to the left, surprisingly, ran what looked like a private driveway. A mailbox stood at the end, and a power line trailed away to the west. She didn't remember that from the old days. "Someone lives out here now?"

"Yep," Colin said. "But we'll try not to let them know we're here." He killed the motor and turned off the headlights, and then there was no noise except for the ticking of the cooling engine and the roar of the surf below. Nerves prickled her, running from her scalp to her fingertips.

The car's doors slammed closed heavily, solid thuds. They walked to the trail marker.

"I don't remember that, either." She pointed to the "Private Property" sign. "Are we going to get in trouble?"

"I know a guy," Colin said. "I can get us out of any trouble we fall into."

"Okay, you sound like a mobster."

He held out his hand. "No swimming with the sharks, I promise."

Molly, her heart in her throat, took his hand and followed him down the trail. It was just wide enough for the two of them walking side by side, although the recent El Niño rains had washed out parts of it. For these sections, Colin was careful to go first, pointing where she should put her feet. The stars and moon gave just enough light – Molly could make out the side of his jaw. Then, recklessly staring at him and not at her feet, she stumbled a little and swore.

He tightened his grip on her hand. "I've got you."

Overhead, the willows made an arch, their bare branches tangling. If they'd been clothed in leaves, the path would be pitch dark. As it was, it was like walking through a narrow, downward-sloping cathedral. Molly caught and held her breath as she looked up. "It's gorgeous."

Colin nodded, and put a brief hand on her waist as he guided her around another rut. "Careful here, make sure you go slow."

But Molly was better at running down trails to the beach than following direct orders (now, anyway). She released Colin's hand and darted around him. With a laugh that came from high in her chest, she picked up her pace, hearing his footsteps fall behind her.

It felt enchanted – the moonlight streaming through the bare branches, their shadows chasing each other. Molly remembered the fork in the path and took the left one, scrambling around the last big rock.

Then they were on the long, low dune, and the folly rose in front of them like a fairy castle.

Molly stopped and stood in place, her hands at her mouth.

Colin stood a breath behind her.

"Look at it." She stretched an arm to point, as if there were any way he could miss it. It was a rotunda, two stories high. It had been built, if she remembered correctly, from ironwork left over from building the rails into Darling Bay at the end of the nineteenth century. There had never been walls – both round rooms stood wide open to the salty ocean air. The folly's second story was held up by lace ironwork that reminded her of New Orleans in its ornateness. Or maybe it was more like the pattern of surf, as it traced itself along the water's edge. The wind picked up, and a sweet, mysterious tinkling could be heard over the waves breaking a hundred yards down the sand.

"Oh, it's even prettier than it ever was."

"I think so, too."

But it seemed as if he was looking at her, not at the folly.

Hurriedly, Molly said, "What's making that tinkling?"

"Let's go see." Colin smiled at her, and his eyes were warm in the moonlight. She had a sudden urge to lunge at him, to kiss him the same way he'd launched himself at her in the door of her room, but then heat hit her cheeks. For all she knew, he was regretting what he'd done.

No. Better to explore. Safer to ignore whatever – this – was between them.

"Oh, look." She stepped up onto the step that led to the open lower level. "It's halfway swept by the wind. I would have expected the ocean to have buried it by now."

"Not quite yet, looks like."

"And those!" She pointed upwards, to the many pieces of wire that were tied to the decorative holes in the ironwork. At the end of each was a piece of weathered, rounded glass, and as the wind moved through the wires, they hit each other, clinking musically. "It's like a beaded curtain, only prettier." She looked down at the floor, at its wide wooden beams. "Someone must have replaced these, don't you think?"

"Probably."

She looked through the open walls to the south. On a rise stood a small, dark house. The shape of it was black against the lighter sky, and two trees tall enough to be cedars stood at its eastern side, growing straight as if the house took the brunt of the ocean wind. "I don't remember that house, either." She squinted, but it was just too hard to see the details. "It looks old, though. Did I just forget it?"

"It was a falling-down shack for most of the last century. Just got fixed up in the last ten years or so."

"Who lives there?"

"A crotchety old guy, the same dude who works on this place."

She moved to the middle of the round floor and reached to touch the pillar, the one that went up and through to the upper level. A wood-and-iron circular staircase led up through the hole in the floor above. "Do you think it's safe?"

"I do, actually. The floor's pretty newly redone up there, too." He gestured. "Ladies first."

The metal was cold and slightly damp from the night air, but the steps felt sturdy under her feet. The second level had the same lace wrought iron and had a waist-high balustrade. Down the beach, the waves were pounding, the break in the surf bright white in the moonlight.

Colin stood next to her. He put his wide hands on the metal and leaned forward. "One night I was out here and the sea was bright green. The water was just lit up with it, halfway to the horizon."

"Oh..."

"Yeah. A friend told me it was phytoplankton bioluminescence."

"I saw it once, on a ship near Bali." Molly had been stunned by the eerie, silent beauty of it. She'd been surrounded by gasping couples clasping either each other or drinks with umbrellas from the Holiday Deck bar. She'd stood alone, trying to impress upon her memory the look of the waves moving in color.

"Then you know. It felt like –" He broke off.

"Like what?"

"Eh, it's silly to say." He cleared his throat. "But it felt like magic."

Molly looked at his profile in the moonlight.

She was an inch from being in serious trouble.

CHAPTER TWENTY-TWO

She was *this* close. She could fall for a guy like this.

And she had absolutely *no* intention of falling for a guy who was as bossy as they came. The boss of a group of mostly men, who had the capability of bossing the whole town.

That was the reason she told herself, anyway. The voice that told her she wasn't brave enough to do so was the same voice she was used to squashing.

So she lightened the mood, for her own sake. "I suppose you don't want me to laugh at you."

The corner of his mouth twitched. "I really, *really* don't. I don't think big, tough guys are supposed to say things about magic. Next I'll be talking about fairies and invisible people that wear, I don't know, little green hats."

"Leprechauns?"

He snapped his fingers and his smile was soft. "Those are the ones."

"But it *is* magic, I can't disagree with you on that." She leaned forward and smelled the night. "There's nothing better than this air, is there? When I was a kid in Nashville, I used to dream about this smell. You can't describe it. It's like if electricity were softened. If you could touch current and, you know, not have it kill you. That's the way I feel when I'm here. Like I'm plugged into something amazing."

"That's a great way to describe it."

"My mom loved it out here." Molly had forgotten that completely. Till that exact moment. She had a sudden stunning memory that fell into her head in one piece – she and her two sisters up here, lying on the floor where the hole for the staircase came up, gazing down below as their mother and father danced to a song they sang in low tones to each other. "I can't believe I'd forgotten this so completely." Except for that one concert when she'd kissed the boy with the corn-nut breath, she hadn't thought she had any other memories of the place. What had the song been, that her parents had sung to each other? Something Mama had written, probably. She'd had a million of those tunes, carried around in her body, ready to sing at any moment. The original Songbird.

"It's a special place." He ran his hand along the metal. "Full of memories. My mom loved it here, too. We used to have picnics here. My dad called it his third favorite folly."

Molly reached to set a piece of glass swinging on its wire. "I don't think I even know what a folly *is*, really."

"A folly's a building that's built for no purpose other than just to be beautiful. It's useless."

"So he had two other favorite ones? Where?"

Colin blew out a breath. "In his house. His wife and daughter."

"Oh, damn." Molly stilled the glass with her hand, stopping its tinkle.

"My mother was known for being the prettiest girl in the county. You've seen my sister. He didn't think they were worth much, though, and he didn't mind saying it."

Shock jolted through her gut. "That's pretty harsh."

"He was, yeah."

"I'm sorry."

"I actually don't know why I'm talking about him." Colin sounded startled. "It's okay. He's good and dead, and I'm fine with that."

Molly recognized bravado when she heard it. She turned her back on the surf and looked upwards. The open metalwork overhead made lace of the sky, and starlight sparkled through. "You know, my mother told me that once there was a grand piano up here." She pictured people standing near a piano under the open sky, holding martinis and glasses of wine, as below couples whirled as her parents once had. "That can't be true. Can it?"

"This floor has been rebuilt a few times. Once was in nineteen thirty-seven, after the piano crashed through the salt-rotten wood to the level below. Luckily no one was below when it happened." Colin reached out as she had to touch a piece of glass hanging from a wire, sending it tinkling against its neighbors. "This is salvaged piano wire, and this old glass is from a couple of old windows that didn't even make it through five seasons."

"All of this took someone so much work. So much *love* was put into it. And it takes work now, to keep the sand mostly out, to rebuild it. Who does it all?"

He didn't need to answer – his face gave it away.

"I knew it." Molly pointed to the house. "*You're* the crotchety old guy."

"Not quite sure what a crotchet it, but I think I might be it." There was something new in his voice – happiness. That was it. When Colin looked up at the house, he was happy. It felt good – right – to hear him like that.

"Why do you do it?"

"Because."

"Because why?" she pushed.

"Because my mother loved it here most of all."

And he'd loved his mother. She laughed. "You're a big softie."

He shot her a look then. His eyes were so dark she couldn't read them. "I am, huh?" He stepped forward just as a gust off the water caught Molly from behind.

She sucked in a breath, unsure what would happen next. She didn't know what she *wanted* to happen, but she wanted something to. That much was true. Her heart pounded. Fear? Excitement? Did they feel the same?

Colin reached for her right hand, and then took her left, too. He held both of her hands wrapped in his big ones, and stood in front of her, stock still. He was only inches from her. The wind blew her hair forward, slapping against her cheeks. She was grateful for the relative darkness.

"I'm not soft." His voice was amused. The double entendre was intentional and direct. But he wasn't going to close the distance between them. She could feel that he was giving her that.

He'd made the first move.

Now Colin was waiting for her. It was up to Molly to make the next one.

She should break this off. She should stop it in its tracks. She didn't need to be involved with anyone, and certainly not the sheriff. She didn't *want* to think of anyone except herself in the next few months.

But this man did something to her.

He drew her like no one else ever had.

Colin's eyes held hers, and it felt like a touch, a stroke.

That was the problem.

In her mind, over the pounding of the surf behind them, she heard what the man at the bar had said. *The fat one.* Oh, God, was that why Colin was out here?

Because he was sorry for her?

Because he wanted to make her feel better?

He was that kind of guy – Molly knew that from working with Nikki and the treats he'd quietly left them on the table outside. Once it hadn't been cookies or coffee – it had been a thick, warm fawn-brown coat Nikki had laughed. *He's always telling me I'm going to freeze to death, but I just don't like wearing jackets. We live in California! It's cold, but if a sweatshirt is good enough for the surfers, it should be good enough for me.* Molly had noticed she'd shrugged it on as she'd left, pulling the arms of the jacket around like a hug. *He's so bossy.* But her face had been pleased. Happy.

Bossy.

He liked to make women feel better about themselves.

Had the kiss at her room been a pity kiss? A be-nice-to-the-chubby-girl kiss? Oh, God, that couldn't be it – she could *feel* the heat between them. Panic rose in her chest anyway. Her jaw tightened painfully. She retrieved her hands, dropping his gaze. "Well, okay."

"Molly –"

Then, before she even knew what she was doing, she was running down the spiral staircase so fast she slipped on the last two steps. She tried to regain her balance, wheeling her arms and grabbing at the railing, but the metal was so cold and wet she found no purchase. The panic flared higher.

She fell, landing on her knees and her left wrist. She was up on her feet so quickly she felt light-headed – maybe he hadn't seen, hadn't heard her land like the freaking elephant she was.

Colin's tread was heavy and rapid on the stairs behind her. "Are you okay?"

"Fine." Molly brushed her wet, dirty hands against her jeans. It didn't matter what she looked like, after all. "I'm fine. I do it all the time." She wasn't fine – that was a lie. Tears pricked at the back of her eyelids, and they weren't tears of pain, even though her wrist was screaming and her right knee felt warm, like it might be bleeding.

They were tears of anger. At herself.

She didn't *care* what other people thought of her. She loved herself as she was.

Or that's what she'd been working on for most of her life. God, she'd thought she'd gotten so much better at it, until this exact moment.

She gulped, an audible noise. Just another embarrassing thing about herself to feel badly about. Was she actually on the verge of a panic attack? Here? Now?

Awesome.

"I'd like to go home." And as she said it, she realized she didn't know where she meant by that. Home couldn't be just a room in an old hotel. Home wasn't any of the cabins on any of the cruise liners. Home wasn't Nashville, not anymore. Home wasn't Darling Bay. Maybe home was her sisters, but they'd been so far-flung for so long she didn't believe that, either. She stopped the sob where it started in her chest, pushing it back down, choking with the effort. She was being ridiculous, and she couldn't make herself *stop*.

"Let's go up to my house. We can put ice on your bruises. You hit hard enough you must have got some good ones."

Hard enough. Was that a veiled reference to her weight? How she'd hit the ground?

No, no – now she was just being ridiculous. It had been a terrible night. That was all there was to it. She needed to go to sleep and start over fresh tomorrow.

"Molly?"

"Can you take me back to the hotel?"

Colin stood in front of her. He put his hands behind his back, as if he knew she was on the very edge of getting so spooked she'd run as far and as fast as she could from this exact moment, which was pretty close to the truth. "I can. I can *absolutely* do that, and if it's what you want, I'm totally, one hundred per cent happy to do that."

Molly bit the inside of her mouth.

"But," he continued, "my house is closer than the hotel is. I have ice, and more importantly, I have bourbon. And a view."

She closed her eyes. Bourbon did sound good. Except...

"I swear to God I won't try anything. Not one single thing."

Of course he wouldn't. Because he wasn't attracted to her. Or maybe he was – how could she trust herself to know the difference between attraction and pity? The silly tears wanted to start again, and now they were just because she was feeling sorry for herself.

Which was so dumb it was almost unbearable.

Molly had decided a long time ago that she would be honest with herself and those around her. That she'd cut off this kind of feeling before it even got started. She was strong and healthy and just right as she was, and if those around her couldn't take it, then to hell with them.

It took bravery to be truthful.

She touched the badge in her pocket. It helped, just enough. "I would like some bourbon, and it seems like going up to your place would get me that a little quicker. Does that trail lead up to your house? Or do we have to go back the way we came in?"

"That one goes up."

"Let's go."

Strong. She was strong. She didn't worry about what other people thought of her.

I don't care.

I don't care!

I don't care that the hottest man I've met in ten years is following me up a trail while looking at my ass. At least it's dark.

It wasn't true. She'd been truthful with him, but she wasn't being the same with herself, she knew it.

She cared. So much.

CHAPTER TWENTY-THREE

Colin hadn't been so confused by a woman since his girlfriend in fourth grade, the one who'd wanted to French kiss him, except her version had involved no tongues – like he'd expected it to – but the actual French language. To this day, just hearing a simple *S'il vous plaît* could bring back the smell of her raspberry lip gloss.

Molly had agreed to bourbon and that was enough.

He'd screwed something up, maybe by kissing her earlier at the hotel. He shouldn't have done it – he knew that now. She was a move-slow kind of girl. A woman who made him weak in the knees the way she did deserved to be wooed, and he'd blown that.

He'd thought he'd been recovering a little bit in her graces, by showing her the folly – his pride and joy – but then he'd gone and scared her off by just holding her hands and looking at her.

She wasn't attracted to him.

That was fine. (It wasn't fine.)

But, God, what about that heat between them when he'd kissed her earlier?

Molly was climbing the trail quickly, even though he could tell that her right knee was stiffening. She'd knocked it good. At the top of the path where it widened, he passed her as he dug out his keys. Sudden nerves hit him right in the belly, and he realized that he wanted a drink as much as she probably did.

"This way. Watch out there, I need to put pavers in here but I haven't gotten around to everything I need to do yet. Is it too dark?" He pulled out a pocket Maglite in the same instant as she shook her head.

"The moon is still bright enough. Oh, my God." She stopped. She looked up at the old, two-story house. "This is gorgeous."

"Don't get your hopes up, it's not that great inside. Come on in." He unlocked the door, hoping to hell that he'd at least washed the dishes before leaving the house.

"Are you kidding me?" She passed him and headed right for what he loved most about the house – the living room that opened up to a solid glass wall. "The view must be amazing during the day."

If this had been a date, he would have told her truthfully what was going through his mind: that it *was* a great view. With the lamps on, all he could see in the glass was her.

And she was incredible.

But this wasn't a date, and he'd already overstepped, and he'd be damned if he was going to do it again. "Yeah. It is."

"Is that a deck?"

"Go on." He gestured. "I'll bring out your drink and your ice pack."

She let herself out, and Colin went into the kitchen. He stared at his blurred reflection in the stainless-steel door of the refrigerator. *Get it together, McMurtry.*

He poured two bourbons, neat, and made an ice pack. He wrapped a dish towel around the plastic bag. He put them on a tray and grabbed the biggest, thickest blanket he had from the back of his sofa.

"Here," he said.

Molly had propped her head on her fists and was leaning forward against the balcony, watching the line of waves break on the beach below. "Thank you." She took the blanket and wrapped it around her.

"If you're too cold we can go inside."

"Why would we do that, when we can see this? Why would you ever spend any of your time at all inside?" She sat on the low swing that ran along the edge of the deck that had no railing, and no obstruction to the view. "That sound. I miss that the most."

"I love the crashing waves."

She shook her head. "Not even that. It's deeper than that. The roar *under* the waves. That's what I heard at sea, every day for years."

"You sound like a proper sailor."

"Oh, yeah, that's me. Stuck in my office or my cabin most hours of the day." She gazed over the railing again. "But I could still hear this. *Feel* this."

It was true, this was the best part of the house – he'd added the redwood deck himself two years before. "I built it The deck." He wanted to groan in embarrassment – could he toot his own horn any more? – but kept himself from doing so. Barely.

"Wow." She shot him a look he couldn't decipher. "A builder and a cop. You must get all the girls."

As far as he could remember, he hadn't invited a woman out here since he'd finished construction.

"I'm just teasing," she said gently, and he felt like an even bigger idiot.

"Cheers," he said lamely, clinking his glass against hers, spilling liquid he knew would dry sticky on his hand.

"Thanks."

Then silence fell as they watched the black ocean and its lines of brilliant-white breakers. The stars sparkled overhead, draped like shining spider webs, glittering and winking. It was late now, and the moon would be lumbering out of the sky soon.

"You're not..." he trailed off. He felt like apologizing, but he didn't know what for. Sure as hell not for kissing her earlier, although he did wish he hadn't spooked her so much. "Sorry that you fell," he ended lamely. What were these nerves doing? And how could he get rid of them? Wasn't there a button he could push that would remind him that he was thirty-two years old and usually smooth with women, a button that would give him the next words to say?

"Look, this is weird. You want to just admit it?" Molly took a long sip of her drink and then pulled up her legs, carefully balancing the ice pack on her knee.

"So weird."

"You kissed me."

Colin cleared his throat. He felt himself stir, at both the memory and the way she said the word *kissed*. "I did."

"I feel badly that you did that."

God, this was going to be so much worse than he'd thought it could be. "Molly, I'm –"

"No, let me finish, if you don't mind. I just want to say this, and it's hard to say, and I'd rather just get it over with." Then she squealed. "What is *that*?"

"Jesus, what?"

"*Is that the kitten?*"

Asiago had come through the open sliding door, padding silently. She stood at Molly's foot and looked up. She made the most pitiful mew, almost inaudible, as if Colin never fed her. "That's her."

"I was right?" Molly scooped up the cat and held her against her chest. Lucky kitten.

He nodded. "She's a girl. And a handful, I have to tell you. The other day she got herself stuck at the top of the shower stall. She eats all day. And then she poops all night."

"She's *huge*." Molly stroked the kitten's head with one finger.

"What's it been, a month?"

"More."

He knew exactly how long it had been since Molly Darling came back to town. He just didn't want to admit it to her.

"I can't believe you kept her."

He shrugged. "John Skinner said they were overrun with kittens at the shelter. He wasn't sure they could get her adopted." It was a line Colin himself had used on citizens when they brought baby animals to the sheriff's office. *Sure, thanks, we'll have to hope it gets adopted, not looking too good right now, but we can try.* It was always funny how quickly they took the animal back, giving in to the pleading look in their kids' eyes. "I'm a sucker, that's all."

Molly's smile made every second of scooping Asiago's box completely worthwhile. "You're amazing, you big brute."

His heart stuttered and stalled in – well – if he had to name it, he'd call it happiness.

Total joy.

He leaned forward and rubbed Asiago's ear. He was rewarded with a headbutt and a purr audible even over the waves. "We're pals."

"Hey, look."

He pulled his hand back and tried to keep his face even. "Yeah?"

"I've seen you with Nikki. I know you hate that she's working with me, and it's kind of you to be so worried about her."

"It's not that I don't –"

She interrupted him again. "And you're so nice to her. It's lovely to see. I get that you're a great guy. But you honestly don't have to do this for me."

"Do what?"

"Pretend to flirt with me."

"Sorry?"

"You know." She shook her head and focused her attention on the kitten. "The...pity kiss."

"Excuse me?" Did she really think he'd kissed her to be *nice*?

"I'm a big girl." She gave a hollow laugh. "I guess that's the point. I'm fine with how I am. Exactly like this."

"You think that kiss was because of what Scott Tinker said?" It felt like he'd been dropped out of an airplane and landed on his head. Surely he hadn't heard her right.

She tilted her head. "We're both adults. We can talk like adults."

"That's so *not* what it was about."

"You didn't have to kiss me, you know. I figure you want to get me on your side so I can help talk Nikki into getting another job, is that right?"

"*What?*" Now he felt like the airplane that had dropped him was buzzing him, and he couldn't quite hear what she was saying over the roar in his ears.

"Or to leave her boyfriend or something. But I'm saying that you can just talk to me. I'm on your side. I think Nikki could be doing better, too. God knows she's smart as hell and –"

"You honestly think I kissed you because of my sister?"

She looked startled. "Well, yeah. Either that or because of that guy in the bar. You want to make me feel better? Honestly, I'm just fine." She stood and handed him Asiago. Then she moved to the steps that led down to the bluff. She sat on the top one, her back to him.

He placed the cat inside the house and slid the door shut, his heart racing.

If it wasn't so insulting, it could have been actually funny. "Wow."

"What?"

"You're for real." He followed her, and then stood three steps below where she sat. His back was to the ocean. Their eyes were level. If he reached out he could touch her.

But he wouldn't.

"I think so." She looked into her glass. "I've only had a few sips. Still sober."

"Honey, I don't kiss girls because of anything about my sister. And I sure as hell don't kiss them *out of pity*." He gripped the glass tighter to keep his hands off her. The way she was looking at him, all open and sweet and soft and gorgeous – he wasn't going to make it much longer without touching her and then she'd be upset and they'd have to start all over again.

"Seriously, it's fine. I'm fine."

He had a sudden hunch, and he knew enough about intuition from his days working beats to follow it. "Is this some kind of a daddy thing?" He might as well ask.

The night couldn't get much worse, after all.

CHAPTER TWENTY-FOUR

*E*xcuse me?" Heat snapped in Molly's eyes, and Colin watched her set her drink carefully down on the step next to her.

"I seriously mean no offence." He didn't, that was true. "My sister has all sorts of crap packaged up when it comes to men. She knew she was a folly to our dad."

Molly's mouth made an O.

"So, what, your dad didn't think you were good enough?"

Molly cleared her throat. She seemed to be weighing whether or not he deserved an answer.

Colin jammed the hand that wasn't holding his drink into his pocket and crossed his fingers.

Finally, she seemed to accept that he was truly looking for an honest answer. "Dad always thought I was perfect. He just thought if I worked a little harder, I could be even *more* perfect, you know?"

"How?" Colin couldn't think of a single thing to improve the woman in front of him. Her eyes, her face, her body – she could be on the front of a magazine and he'd buy it, even if it was about knitting. Her laugh made his blood feel carbonated.

She looked at him in surprise. "Looks-wise. You know."

He didn't. "No."

"I was the one who needed to lose weight."

"Bullshit." It was a kneejerk answer, and the only one.

"Do you think my sisters were too skinny?"

"I never thought about it."

"But you thought about my weight."

It was a trap. He'd fallen into it. It wasn't a *good* trap, and she'd dug it in the wrong place. "Only because I was a human being when your band was big." He'd seen the covers of *People* and *US Magazine*.

She shrugged and took a quick sip of her bourbon. "There you go. Every tabloid trumpeted my weight. What they guessed I was up to. Or down to, if they happened to grab nothing but a good angle."

"That's a dumb thing to say."

"Sorry?" One eyebrow arched, and he wanted to reach out with his thumb to smooth it back down.

"You believe what's on the front of those things? Yesterday when I was buying gum at the market, I read that Angelina Jolie's getting a sex change."

Molly made a pissed-off sound between her teeth. "I don't know how they get away with it. Most of it isn't even embellished or exaggerated. It's all just flat-out lies."

"So you're saying that they're full of shit." He arched an eyebrow.

"God. I know." She rubbed her cheeks. "I *should* know that, I should know that in my *bones*, but when you read those headlines when you're eighteen and nineteen, it screws with your head, you know? It was hard. The band broke up in two thousand and five, right before social media really became a thing. I can't imagine how young women – young people – deal with it today. The worst I got was being cut out of the video for "A Secret Made for Keeping"."

"They cut you out? But you were the lead singer, right? The voice."

"You wouldn't know it in that video. They usually put me behind something, or behind one of the other girls, but for that one, they cut out every image of me. I didn't even know it till the video-release party. I was the voice, all right. And that was all. But whatever. It's okay. I'm over it now."

"Yeah?" She clearly wasn't.

"Most days. Then there are the bad days, but I'm not unique in that. Every woman in America –"

"I thought you were hot then," he jumped in. "And I think you're hotter now." That was the stripped-down truth, unvarnished.

"Mmm." Her cheeks lit pink, and then the tip of her nose went the same shade. He wondered how far down her blush went.

"So with all due respect, fuck your old man. Maybe he had good intentions, but he was just plain wrong."

Molly stared at him.

"What?"

She reached forward and touched his wrist with one finger, lightly. His blood fizzed. "You make it sound so easy. I should just let it go."

"You loved your dad, and I'm sure he loved you."

"He did. That's never been in question."

"Must be nice." The tone was too automatic, too bitter, and it was out before he could stop it.

"What's the story with your dad?"

"Eh. Not worth it."

"What?" She traced the vein on the back of his hand, and he swayed towards her in the starlit dark. "You pushed me into talking about my *deep pain*," but she said it lightly and continued with a small smile, "don't you owe me the same?"

"My dad was a son of a bitch, plain and simple."

"Tell me."

Other women had said this to him before, but they'd always, all of them, had a different look on their faces. They'd known something about his father and they'd wanted gossip, or at least that's what it had seemed like to him.

Molly appeared different. Her face was still so open.

"What do you know?" He was stalling.

"He was the sheriff before you. And your sister told me he killed himself. That's literally all I know."

He sighed and moved to sit next to her. Their knees brushed, and she didn't pull away. "When I was a kid, I wanted to be a police officer, so I could be like him. I remember that, remember looking up to him. For a little while, anyway. I remember how shiny his badge was, and how heavy his gun felt."

"He let you hold his gun?"

"Grow up in a family like mine, and yeah. I learned to shoot before I learned to ride a bike."

"Were you happy?"

"As a kid?"

She nodded.

"I think so. Yeah. For a while, anyway. By the time my sister got big enough to be going to school with me, things changed. I don't know who changed first, my mom or my dad, but he started drinking more. The yelling started." Colin paused. He cleared his throat and considered whether or not he wanted to continue.

Strangely, he wanted to tell Molly more. "They fought a lot. I guess they'd always done that. That's what they did in my dad's family – his brother and him fought physically their whole lives. If my dad hadn't ended up a cop, he would have gone to jail with that half of the family. They were always in and out of prison, still are. But the first time I saw a bruise on my mom's face was when I was going into seventh grade. I didn't know nothin" from nothin" – I knew I was starting to notice girls, but I was confused about everything that happened when I was out of the house – so it took a lot for me to notice what was going on at home. But that black eye – she couldn't hide it."

"He hit her."

"Maybe he always had. But he got sloppy about it. Hit her in front of me, and then, eventually, in front of Nikki, too. I wanted to kill him." He held up his hand and considered it. "The first time he hit me, I was trying to protect her. He threw me against a wall and I landed on my hand. Broke this thumb. Still crooked, see?"

She looked but only briefly, keeping her eyes on his face. She caught his hand as it dropped to his lap and held it, touching his thumb lightly with her own. Then she kissed the pad of it. Once. Softly.

Warmth flooded Colin's torso at the sheer intimacy of it. Had *anyone* ever kissed him like that? He blinked, trying to remember what he'd been about to say. "So. Yeah. I went from wanting to be him, to wanting to be stronger than him. I knew I'd be a police officer, and then some day, I'd arrest him and take his job. I'd be the sheriff and he'd rot in jail for hurting my mother."

"Did he ever hurt Nikki?"

Colin remembered watching her say something cheeky, laughing, knowing she was Daddy's favorite, and then watching her hit the floor. She'd looked up that time, obviously stunned. *What happened?* The worst part of that night had been their mother's face as she'd picked

Nikki up. *Nothing, sweetheart. You fell.* "Yeah, he did." Colin felt a jolt right through to the top of his head. "You're around her, around Nikki. More than I am right now. If you ever see anything on her, you'll tell me, right?"

Molly's eyes got bigger. "What do you mean?"

"If Todd is hurting her, I want to know. Promise me you'll tell me if you see any evidence of that. Or if she tells you anything."

"He *hurts* her?"

Colin didn't have anything to go on, except his gut. And his gut was usually right. "Promise me. Don't tell anyone else, just come straight to me." He probably couldn't get away with killing the guy, but maybe he could come close enough. "Promise?"

"I-I promise. God. Of course. And then your mom...did she get out?"

"Yeah."

"How?"

"A stroke."

"Oh, God. I'm so sorry."

"She was just forty-five." The coroner had said the blood clot could have just been in her body, waiting. Maybe the stroke had been coming for a long time, even as young as she'd been.

Colin would always blame the myriad times her neck had been snapped back.

"Jesus."

"He lost it then."

"Is that when..."

"No. That took another year. He got caught drinking on the job, and back then, it was something you could get away with a little easier. He was sent to treatment, two months, all on the taxpayer's dime. He came back, and not much changed. He arrested a woman on a DUI once, and while he was just joking around in the jail, he blew a higher BAC than she had." Colin had been in the jail that night, booking a kid on a vandalism charge. He was about to be promoted to sergeant. He'd been getting closer and closer to taking his father's job. He'd been only twenty-five. He'd watched his father, the big man, blow into the machine and then show the woman he'd arrested his higher reading, delighted with himself. Colin had told him to knock it off. *Or what? You'll tell who on me? You gonna report me to myself?*

"Holy crap."

"Yeah."

Molly didn't say anything. Another woman might have leaned forward. Might have kissed him. Might have told him he could do it, assured him that she was safe to talk to, that it was okay to let it all out.

Instead, Molly just watched him. One of her hands rested lightly on his knee. She didn't clutch him – she didn't touch him reassuringly. She just waited. Open.

Sudden, horrifying tears clogged his throat. Jesus H. Christ, he hadn't cried for seven years. He wasn't going to start now. He waited, catching a breath high in his chest and holding it, a trick he'd learned early on.

Molly's gaze stayed clear, her breathing steady and slow. Her neck was long, and he could see her pulse beating steadily in her throat. Her hand on his knee was warm.

"It was my birthday. I was about to get promoted. He was going to have to be the guy to promote me. I knew he didn't want to – I thought the gunshot was a truck backfiring on the other side of the station. Didn't even cross my mind that it could be anything else till I heard Nikki scream. She'd stopped by to drop off a cake for me and the guys. A pineapple upside-down cake, my favorite. *Used* to be my favorite. She dropped it all over the floor." He paused. He'd forgotten till this very moment about that damn cake. The paramedics had tromped through it, and then the coroner. "That's funny. The janitor at the department just switched to some pineapple air fragrance in the bathrooms. It's been making me sick. I didn't put that together till right now." He caught Molly's hand in his. "Isn't that funny?"

"No." She squeezed his fingers. "It's not."

"Anyway." Colin tried to scrape up the memory of a smile from somewhere. "You may have guessed the punch line. Eventually, I kept getting promoted until I got his job."

She kissed him.

It wasn't a hot kiss. It wasn't even a sad kiss.

It was just her lips against his.

She was with him.

Molly was *with* him, next to him.

His body felt so weak from telling the story that he wondered if his legs would hold him if he stood. And yet he felt strong enough to move a mountain with nothing but his hands to do the digging.

Then he realized something and dragged his head away from her.

He groaned.

"What?"

"That." Colin touched Molly's bottom lip. "*That* was a pity kiss, wasn't it?"

"Mmm." A half-smile curved her mouth. "Maybe?"

"Okay. I admit it. I kissed you out of pity, too. At the hotel. I wanted to make you feel better."

Molly sat straighter. "*I knew it.* You are a total and complete –"

"But then I lost control of it."

"– jackass," she continued weakly. "What?"

"A pity kiss would have been like this." His heart thumped in his chest so loudly he wondered if she'd hear it. She didn't pull away as he dropped his mouth to hers. He kissed her chastely, close-mouthed, and it almost killed him to pull away again. "That's what a helpful kiss would have been."

"Jackass," she repeated. There was no heat in it, not like the waves of it rising in the two inches left between their bodies.

"But that kiss at the hotel wasn't a nice-guy kiss, was it?"

"What?"

"Admit it. You felt what you did to me."

She gasped, a soft pop of noise that had him just as hard again.

"That's when I knew I'd lost control and that I'd just shot myself in the foot with my helpful attempt at making you feel better. There was no pity about it. Not a second's worth. And you know what?"

"What?" she said again, softer this time.

"I sure as hell don't feel bad for you now."

"Jesus holy Christoballs," Molly muttered.

And then she kissed him.

For real.

Finally.

CHAPTER TWENTY-FIVE

Molly lost any shred of self-control she'd ever managed to pull around herself. She launched herself at Colin, and he caught her. His mouth was as hot as his words, as hot as his voice had been.

The kiss was everything she'd ever missed when she was alone on a ship full of people being together with the ones they loved the most. The kiss was fever and intensity and light and the swooping feeling of dropping off a cliff, only to be raised up again.

The kiss was flight.

And if she didn't fly into a place where she could drop some of these clothes, she would burst into flame, self-immolating cliffside on Colin's back porch. She managed to pull away from the kiss long enough to say, "You have a reputation to think of, don't you?"

His eyes were dark, and he blinked in confusion. "What?"

"I'm sure there's some local or state law against having a naked woman on your lawn?"

"Yeah. Yeah, there sure is." He grinned.

"But you wouldn't get in trouble if we were inside, say."

"Nope."

"So it would actually be the right thing to do if you led me inside. Like, to your bed."

Colin gulped so audibly she couldn't help giggling.

"Yeah." He took her hand and turned, speaking over his shoulder. "I could maybe do that. Lead you, I mean."

She followed him. "In a pitying way, I hope."

"I've got nothing but pity for you, babe."

Molly grinned and found the steps didn't hurt at all, going back into the house. Her knee seemed to have spontaneously healed itself, maybe from the heat that flooded from the middle of her body and radiated from all directions. "I hope it's good pity. And by that I mean hard. And big."

He stopped in his tracks so quickly she ran into him.

And he was on her then, still in the kitchen. He stripped her, making short work of her sweaters. He unclasped her bra expertly with one hand and threw it into the living room, never lifting his mouth from hers. Molly worked to catch her breath. She'd apparently dropped it outside, along with any propriety she might have had left.

"Holy crap," he said against her lips. "Holy *damn*." He stepped away to look at her, and Molly shivered under his gaze. Naked from the waist up, she straightened. Her nipples tightened into buds, and his eyes darkened again.

"You're goddamn beautiful," he said.

"You haven't even seen the important half yet."

Colin was so startled he just blinked. Then he gave a whoop of laughter and pulled his shirt over his head with one hand. "Let's fix that."

"My hero," Molly said, grinning. She stepped out of her shoes, and he undid the buttons of her jeans, helping her shimmy out of them.

Then Molly was in the middle of his kitchen wearing nothing but a scrap of black lace underwear.

"It's kind of cold in here." Molly stretched her arms overhead and enjoyed every second of watching Colin's eyes widen. "Isn't there somewhere a little warmer we could go?"

"Oh, yeah. This way, gorgeous."

And something in his voice, the way the word "gorgeous" rolled out of his mouth, erased the last little shred of doubt Molly held about his intentions.

He led the way, and she followed, close on his heels.

He flipped on the lamp next to the bed. The bed was huge, covered in a dark-blue coverlet. A low bookcase ran along one wall, and the other wall was mostly glass. Molly had a sudden urge to cover herself. And to be a good guest. "The ocean view must be amazing in the mornings," she said politely.

"It's pretty fucking amazing right now."

She felt something like joy burbling up inside her. "That's just pity again, I know it."

He moved Asiago from her place on the bed and quickly put her in the hallway. "Sorry, buddy. I'll make it up to you."

Then Colin stood in front of Molly and took her hand. He placed it on the front of his jeans. "Is this pity?"

"That is –" Molly lost her breath again. "That is not pitiful. No, it is not."

He backed her up until her knees hit the side of his bed.

She sat. "Maybe I can help you with this problem."

"It's a big problem." Colin's voice was deeper now.

"I can see that." She took a moment to trail her fingers over his stomach, feeling the muscles at his sides and how they flexed as she touched them lightly. So lightly.

She heard his breath hitch in his chest as she reached for his belt buckle. As she undid it and then reached for his fly, he stepped out of his boots.

She unbuttoned him. Nothing but black briefs in the way. Molly felt his hardness through the fabric, feeling the girth of him.

"I'm impressed."

"Oh." Colin sounded strangled. "Good to know. It's still pity, you know."

"I see that. A very wide piece of pity."

"Mmm."

"Pity I'd like to taste."

"*Jesus*, woman." He shucked his jeans, underwear and socks, and covered her body with his in one fluid motion. He was on top of her, his mouth on hers again, hot as sin and twice as convincing.

She felt his hardness against her stomach and shimmied against him. "I'm not naked yet."

"I know." He tugged on the elastic of her panties, then gave a low growl and kissed her harder.

Against his lips, Molly said, "That's not fair."

"I'll show you fair."

Colin moved down her body, leaving his weight on her, trailing his lips along her neck to her collarbone. His hand went to her hip, pulling her up sharply against his heat, before he found his way to her breasts. He kissed her nipple, sucking on it, sending a searing heat straight to her clit. Keeping his mouth where it was, he caressed her other breast, rolling its bud between his fingertips as his mouth continued to wreak its havoc. Then he switched his attention, his mouth and fingers trading places, and Molly bucked her hips against him in a blatant attempt to get him to hurry.

But he seemed to have found all the time in the world. "Stand down, woman. Give me a minute here." He nipped at her breast, and Molly gave a small cry.

"God, you're beautiful."

Molly whispered, "There's that pity again." She arched her back as he trailed his mouth lower.

"Damn straight. I'm feeling *so* sorry for you." His fingers touched her heated vee, one finger moving the fabric to the side. "So sorry. Let me show you how sorry I am." His mouth followed his finger, and she felt his breath against her clit through the fabric that was still in the way.

He stroked her slickness, moving his mouth over her panties, breathing against her. She bucked against his hand, and he pushed her down. "Hey, now, wildcat. Let me have my fun here."

"Off," she managed. "Take them off."

"But they're so pretty." He raised his head and ran his fingers along the lace pattern, dipping his fingers in on the sides, touching her wetness and then retreating again before she got what she wanted, what she needed. "I just want to play with you for a while."

"Because you feel sorry for me."

"Exactly. I'm feeling incredibly sorry for you right now."

Molly's stomach flipped with nerves. "Because why?"

"Because I think you're going to get fucked."

Her voice was just a breath, all she had left. "Oh, yeah? How?"

"How am I going to fuck you? I haven't decided yet." Colin straightened and pressed his weight against her again. He pinned her down and put his mouth next to her ear. "Standing up is nice, but we're already lying down. So I might fuck you like this. Good old missionary. Your legs pushed up around your ears."

She felt his cock bulge against her pussy, protected only by the thin black fabric. She pressed back, tilting her pelvis so that he choked, groaning against her ear. "You don't mind if I make noise?"

Colin thrust himself forward, sounding like he agreed. "Jesus, Molly. What are you doing to me?"

"Do you – *please* tell me you have a condom."

He reached sideways into the nightstand drawer. He ripped off the wrapper and rolled the condom on. Molly tried to help but found that her fine motor skills seemed to be affected by the nerves shooting through her body.

When it was on, Colin moved to lie on his side. His hand cupped her cheek. "Are you sure? Because we can still stop."

"Very polite of you to ask." Molly kissed him, hard. He tasted of salt and heat. Then she put both hands against his chest and rolled him onto his back on the enormous bed. In a motion that felt practically acrobatic, she slung off the panties at the same time as she straddled him. "But I don't feel like stopping. Even out of pity, you big brute."

She took him into herself, fully, in one long stroke.

Colin gave a shout and grabbed for her hips, pulling her deeper. Molly took a breath and dropped her forehead to his chest. "Just let me feel you for a second," she said. "Please."

He stilled, and she could feel his cock getting even bigger – hotter – inside her. "Molly," he said, the word sounding tight.

She lifted her head and met his gaze.

His eyes were black heat, and he searched her face. What was he looking for? Was he checking to see if she was okay?

Because she was better than okay. She felt like she could have flown if she'd wanted to, but she *didn't* want to – she just wanted this. Him inside her.

"You're incredible. I want to just look at you for the next ten years, is that okay?"

Was it okay? Hell, yes. It was okay.

She moved.

Slowly at first. Her hips rocked slightly, and she pushed him deeper inside her.

Then she rocked a little higher. His hands stayed on her hips, but he let her set the rhythm. She was so wet, so slick, and he was so hard – she felt powerful and gorgeous, and most of all, strong. Colin bit his lower lip, and sweat beaded at his hairline. His gaze intensified as his eyes narrowed, still focused on her, only on her. He was trying so hard to control himself, she could tell, and that made it hotter and sweeter.

More now, *more*. She moved faster, pulling off him until she was right to the very edge of him, and then she slammed her hips forward, taking him again in one hard plunge. Colin's hips lifted, rocking with her every move. She was in charge of the pace, but he met each thrust with force, and she knew she couldn't take much more of him – he was deeper in her than any man had ever been, and she'd never felt this before – that with every thrust he pushed more air out of her lungs, and what if she died of having no breath by the end, and she didn't care – she didn't want anything in the whole world except this man, under her, inside her, so far inside that she didn't know where she ended and he began. The orgasm curled inside her body, and pushing her clit against his pubic bone, hard and then harder, stroking herself more with every thrust, her pussy tightened until she wondered in an abstract way if she could actually hurt him by being too tight, and then everything that had been tight inside her exploded, and she came with a roar that she didn't recognize as her own until she realized his voice had joined hers and they were both coming, both bursting into flame together, which made the fire blaze higher and she couldn't breathe until he kissed her and then she could pull oxygen again from the air instead of where she'd been getting it – from him, from *him*, from Colin.

She fell forward, pressing her face into the space between his neck and the pillow, inhaling their commingled scent. Her heart was beating so fast she was surprised it didn't just stop in protest.

Jesus.

What had this guy done to her?

Colin's arms tightened around her, and she rose with him as his chest lifted with each breath.

She closed her eyes, squinching them hard, trying to remember who she was when she had clothes on, when she wasn't in this man's arms, when she didn't feel as amazing as she did right now.

Molly felt invincible. She was stronger, braver, better than she'd ever been, and his arms around her made her even more indomitable. Strength tingled in her fingertips, running through her veins like a river.

She lifted her face and grinned at him. "Now, *that* was a pity fuck."

CHAPTER TWENTY-SIX

S he was gone in the morning.

That was the crazy thing.

Colin had gone to sleep holding her tight. Usually he didn't like to sleep right up next to someone, but her body had been just right (God, in so many ways) and they'd *fit* each other. He'd wrapped himself around her after they'd laughed for what felt like an hour, and she'd given this deep, full-body sigh.

"You have to stay here," he'd said.

"I do?"

"You have to stay right here in my arms. Right where you are." He'd kissed the side of her head.

"Hmmph. Is that an order?" Her voice had sounded tight, suddenly.

He'd made his words lighter. "It's the law. You can't do anything but stay here and sleep well."

"And what if I don't? You'll arrest me?"

Colin had nodded slowly. "Yep. You're doomed unless you do as I say."

She'd moved position so that she was resting on his shoulder, and he'd kissed her forehead. She'd made the cutest snerfling noise, and then she'd wriggled against him, pressing harder into his body. The last thing he remembered was wondering if she took cream in her coffee and if he had bacon to go with the eggs he'd fix her in the morning.

Then he'd woken up to an empty bed.

Colin had always been a light sleeper, and it had gotten worse with his job. So many years of working nights meant that even now that he didn't have to work dogwatch, he still usually woke at any small noise. Hyper-vigilance was a bitch. He'd had a cat for years – Sammy Joe, he still missed her grumpy yowls – and just the sound of the cat leaping off his bed to the hardwood floor used to wake him. That tiny click of nails had been enough to jolt him awake.

But Molly getting up, putting on her clothes and leaving, that hadn't stirred him.

And where had she *gone*? He checked every room, not that he had many in the small house. He checked each deck – he used to date a woman who liked to meditate naked out there (it had been her best trait).

The decks were all empty.

Molly didn't have a car. Had she taken his from where they'd left it, at the overlook above the folly? That would be fine, if she'd needed it. He had a spare truck he used to transport building supplies. But she should have asked, if only to keep him from worrying.

Without even taking the time to shower, he pulled on last night's clothes. He remembered the feeling of her fingers at his fly. *Just find her.* There was no time to fantasize about the goddess who had ended up in his bed last night. Better to find that goddess and make sure she was okay.

In the old pickup, he drove to the outlook. The Chevelle was still there.

Damn it.

Now he was worried.

A woman left a man's bed without saying goodbye if she had to get home to someone else *or* if she didn't really want to be there in the first place.

Colin was pretty damn sure she didn't have a man in town, though he couldn't be positive, of course. She'd been back more than six weeks. That was long enough to form attachments. Something spiny sprouted thorns in his chest. What if she *was* dating someone else? He held the steering wheel so tightly his fingers cramped.

Surely he couldn't be jealous. He'd always thought it was the weakest of all emotions. No point to it, just a waste of time and energy.

Unless you were thinking about Molly Darling kissing someone else.

That kind of jealousy might be stupid but it wasn't a waste. No, it was spurring him on, making his foot press harder on the accelerator.

He sped into town, watching the sides of the road carefully. Why didn't he have her damn cell-phone number? He called the Golden Spike but no one answered, which was just as well. What would he have said to Nate if he'd picked up? *Hey, I slept with your girlfriend's sister, and now I can't find her.* That wouldn't fly, no way in hell.

He called Nikki next, keeping his phone low in his lap, putting it on speaker – if any of his constituents saw him using a phone as he drove, he'd get voted right out. Citizens nowadays tended to like a sheriff who followed both the letter and the spirit of the law.

"Hey. Have you seen Molly this morning?"

"Molly?"

"You know the one." Colin palmed the wheel and took the corner smoothly. "I'm worried."

"You're worried about *Molly*? The person you've barely spoken to since she hired me? What am I missing? Were you on a date and she pulled a runner?"

Colin didn't say anything. He considered hanging up. He'd check Molly's hotel room next, but it wasn't like he'd have any way of verifying if she was inside or not, not unless he clued Adele in. Freaking sisters.

"You *were*? I was *kidding*."

"Never mind."

"Did she stay the *night* with you or something?"

It was too embarrassing to even answer.

He heard his sister laugh uproariously. "And now she's in the wind? What did you *do*? You've always snored, but has it really gotten so bad that you'd chase away a perfectly nice girl?"

"Forget it. She probably just went on a walk." What if that was it? What if she'd walked down the cliff to the folly? He hadn't actually looked down there. "You working at the café today?"

"You suddenly the employment police? No, wait. You've always been that."

"Whatever. Just text me if you see her."

"Oh, I see. You're the Molly police."

"And you're annoying." He hung up to the sound of her laughter.

God. What if Molly had fallen from the cliff's edge?

He had a sudden image of her, standing at the edge where they'd stood together, her dark hair blowing back, her chin up as she smelled the air. Then in his mind's eye, she toppled, falling, wheeling until she hit the rocks below.

How many calls had he been on like that in his career? Seven? Eight? The worst had been a young German tourist. His blond hair had turned red, and his new wife had been hysterical. He'd never forgotten that, the idea that somewhere in Germany there was a woman who associated Northern California with unbearable tragedy, not a happy honeymoon.

He was almost at the café. One quick check, and he'd find out if she'd made it home. Even if he had to jimmy the lock on her door himself.

This was not good. After a man got laid as spectacularly as he had, he should have a grin stuck on his face for at least the next forty-eight hours. He shouldn't have this sinking feeling.

But then he saw her.

In front of the grocery store, there she was, just walking. All in one perfect piece. She was wearing a different shirt – a red button-down plaid shirt that made her look like a cowgirl – and a denim skirt. Cowboy boots. Her hair was pulled back into a ponytail, and it still looked wet. She'd had time to shower, then, and get herself looking cute as hell. The relief that she wasn't smashed on the rocks next to the folly was strong, as strong as the physical urge to yank the truck over and park badly, diagonal to the curb, which he did. His own parking enforcement – Polly White took her job exceedingly seriously – wouldn't let him get away with this if he was caught. She'd write the sheriff a ticket without thinking twice. But he didn't give a crap.

Colin placed himself in Molly's walking path. She had her head down and was looking at her phone.

"Hey."

She looked up, appearing startled. "Hey, yourself."

"Coffee, huh?" He knew he didn't sound friendly as he gestured to her coffee cup, and he didn't care. What she'd done was rude. Discourteous. And Jesus, he didn't know how worried he'd been until he saw her looking as pretty as a daisy and just as unconcerned.

"I usually get it from Nate at the bar, but there was no one around, and I was feeling lazy. The market coffee is pretty good, it turns out. You'd think with the three coffee makers I put in a café, I could use one of those, but I'm reluctant to get a single stain on anything before we open. Silly, huh?"

"Where did you go?"

"Back to town." She looked down at her body as if to check that she was where she thought she was. "Right here."

Colin straightened, and if he had been on the job, this was where he would put a hand on his hip, just resting on the butt of his gun, never a threat, only a reminder. "And how did you get back to town?"

Molly frowned. "Didn't you get my note?"

"Seeing as how I have all these questions, I'd go with no." Lord, he sounded like an ass.

"I left it on the counter in the kitchen. In front of, ironically, the coffee maker. I thought for sure that would be the first place you'd look."

Funny. The first place he'd looked was in his own bed. "Didn't see it. And you haven't answered my question of how you got back here."

Her frown got deeper. "Am I being interrogated?"

"I'd appreciate it if you just answered the question."

"Fine. I grabbed a ride."

"As in, you hitchhiked?" Irritation rankled. She didn't have to check with him first. She owed him nothing. He had no right to be irritated about a damn thing, and yet he was.

"Thumb out and everything. I haven't done that in years. My sisters and I used to hike down Mount Millson and hitch back up to the car when we were done, and it always felt like we were an inch away from getting murdered. But a hundred per cent of the time, the people who picked us up were nice. Just like this morning! I met a guy who's a strawberry farmer in the spring and a beach bum in Hawaii in the fall."

Colin had a whole string of new images in his mind, and he didn't like any of them. Molly dead in all manner of ways, stabbing, gunshot. He'd seen too many awful ways of dying. "Well, that was stupid."

"Thanks." Molly's bright expression vanished, and it didn't look in danger of coming back anytime soon. "That's always what a girl wants to hear from the guy whose bed she recently climbed out of."

"I was worried."

"So you get to say what I do? How many hitchhikers have been killed in your county, anyway? More than ten?"

He kept his mouth closed tightly.

"That many, huh?"

"Yeah, well, you got lucky."

Molly took a long sip of her coffee while considering him. Colin had the distinct feeling he was coming up short, and that was a feeling he really didn't like.

"No," she finally said. "*You* got lucky."

He snorted. He couldn't help it. "I did. You're right. That I did. Why didn't you just wake me?"

Her thumb played with the plastic top of the coffee cup. "I don't know. You were sleeping so peacefully, and I didn't want to disturb you. I couldn't sleep, and then I got to thinking about the thermometer for the walk-in, and I just wanted to get back to work."

"Yep, that's what all the girls say."

She laughed, and Colin felt like the sun had come out, even though it was still hiding in the fog. "Come out to breakfast with me."

"No, thanks. I really do have work to do."

"Just put it off."

"I'm good."

Why the hell was it so important that she do what he wanted? Colin was annoyed at himself, and if their places were reversed, he'd blow himself off, too. But he couldn't stop pushing. One more time. "You have to eat." He tried to soften it. "Right?"

"You know, I've got this pretty human trait of not wanting to do anything I'm told I have to do." Any trace of humor was gone completely from her voice. "So I'll see you later."

Colin stepped out of her path as she moved forward resolutely. The way she said *see you later* could have easily been substituted with *fuck off.*

And he deserved it.

He watched the prettiest girl in town unlock the front door of the café and let herself in.

He was a complete and utter idiot.

CHAPTER TWENTY-SEVEN

Molly got three steps into the café before her knees started shaking. She went behind the counter, set down her coffee cup carefully, and pressed her hands flat against the wood.

Big talk. That's all it was. Bravado.

Had she wanted to have breakfast with him? Of course. She wanted to go get bagels with him. She wanted to find out if he preferred regular or fluffy cream cheese. (It had to be regular, right?)

Had she wanted to stay in bed with him? Of course she had. He'd pulled her into his arms, spooning her perfectly, his heat exactly right to keep her warm, the feeling of his breath in her hair making her want to stay there for the next thirty or forty years.

And then he'd told her to stay.

Which was exactly why she had run.

Darling Bay, if she were to make a real go of this, was a place she had to stand on her own two feet. She'd been trying for so long to get her life right, screwing it up over and over again. When she was in the band, every move she'd made had been carefully ordered by her father or Adele. After the band broke up, her boyfriend at the time, a class-A jerk, had insisted that she join the gym with him to get in shape. He'd signed her up for nutrition class. When she'd expressed interest in the topic, he'd talked her into going to school. And when she'd graduated with her degree, he'd dumped her for a Pilates instructor who had boobs the size and shape of Texas grapefruits. Her next boyfriend took her on her first cruise where she'd been delighted to chat with the onboard nutritionist (and then to cry on her shoulder when she caught her boyfriend in their stateroom with a redhead from Argentina). Rick, Molly's last boyfriend, the one who took all her money in the protein-shake scheme, had been the worst. Drunks were said to have to hit bottom before coming up, and Rick had been her lowest point. She'd let a man make her think she was worth nothing. He'd said terrible things to her, and she'd *believed* them.

She'd never let that happen again.

No matter how nice it was to wake up next to a man who smelled like sex and the ocean air.

The order Colin had given her to stay, though. It was a sweet order, she knew. It was along the lines of *You have to have another piece of cake, I insist.* Or *Sit right there, you'll get the best view.*

But behind it were echoes she couldn't quiet. Adele, telling her she had to sing louder and strand straighter. Her first serious boyfriend telling her she had to go to college. The press, telling her and her sisters to smile, to stand there, to move or to *not* move. And the loudest echo of all, she knew, was her father's voice the one time he'd said, "Honey, you just have to lose a *little* weight." It had been right after the music video that didn't have a single shot of her in it. The pain she'd felt, the pain she was sure had been obvious on her face. "Adele and Lana have it easy, they got your mother's metabolism." Her father had patted his own gut when he'd said it. "You're like me, though. We can't eat one damn biscuit without putting two around our bellies, right, sweet girl? You have to *show* them you can."

He'd loved her. That had been evident in everything her father had ever done for her. And because of that, she'd changed to please him. Always strong and sturdy, she'd almost stopped eating. It had been when she'd gotten so thin that she'd been cold all the time, even when they were touring in places like Miami and Naples, that the media had started speculating on an eating disorder. *Middle Songbird Not Eating, Should Her Family Intervene? Molly Darling Shows All the Signs of Bulimia.*

She didn't. Her teeth were strong and unstained. She'd never made herself vomit, not even once. (She'd *thought* about it, though. That much was true. Maybe that's why it had hurt.)

Molly had just done what she was told. The "nutritionist" her father had hired (Molly had found out later that Becca had been a publicist who read a lot of fashion and diet magazines) told her to eat an apple for breakfast, a banana for lunch, and a healthy meal of chicken and broccoli for dinner. Nothing else.

And Molly had done it.

She'd lost the weight.

She'd always been so good at following orders.

Until she hadn't been.

So at Colin's house, she hadn't let herself slip off to sleep. She'd curled into his shoulder. She'd given it a good hour after he'd started breathing heavily and steadily. She'd murmured something under her breath about the bathroom, and had slipped out of his arms as quietly as possible. She hadn't even known her own plan until she got outside, under those stars.

Get out. Get back to town. Get away.

The strawberry farmer who picked her up had been astonished. "I don't think I've ever picked up a hitchhiker out here. When I drive up to Humboldt, they're everywhere trying to work in the fields. And not the strawberry fields, if you know what I mean. More like those illegal *green* fields I can't help but be jealous of. Strawberries, they're good. Not as green, cash-wise, you feel me? But out here, I can't figure out where you're coming from."

If he spent any time in Darling Bay, he'd eventually see her at the café, so it didn't do to lie. "I'm reopening the Golden Spike Café. But my car broke down in San Francisco, and I'm hitching back. I got dropped about a mile from here." If he spent any time in Darling Bay, he'd also know who the sheriff was, and where he lived.

"Once, up in Humboldt again, I picked up a hitchhiker who had two ocelots. On leashes! You know they make little squeaks?"

Molly hadn't, and it hadn't taken much encouragement to get the strawberry farmer to talk about ocelots all the way to town. She'd laughed in the right places, but her mind had stayed firmly on one thing: Colin.

She didn't know what had happened to her last night.

Okay, she knew exactly what had happened, physically. She'd gotten laid. And gorgeously. She'd been kissed and touched by a man who lit every one of her nerve endings on fire. She wanted it to happen again.

And at the same time, she wanted to run.

Colin was a cop. Nothing wrong with cops, of course, but the two she'd dated in the past had shared one very strong, very annoying characteristic. They liked to tell people what to do. Maybe they got used to it on the job. They *had* to tell people what to do to be safe. They had power behind their words. They expected to be listened to, and people did what they said or they risked literal imprisonment.

She'd known that feeling, once, a long time ago. When she'd finally shed the weight, the tabloids had started to listen to her, instead of just chasing her. Even news outlets had wanted to know the girls' stand on topics of the day. Adele didn't like talking into microphones unless she was singing, and Lana was as willing to drop an f-bomb as she was a smile, so talking had fallen to Molly.

It had been her only place of bravery. Her voice had had power. When the CIA admitted there had never been an imminent threat from weapons of mass destruction in Iraq, Molly had gone on the talk-show circuit, raising awareness for the soldiers who were coming back from a useless war with PTSD, which had been seriously ignored until then.

She'd been one of the first singers to talk publicly about the studies that proved autism wasn't caused by vaccinations.

She'd talked about global warming before it was an accepted fact.

The year they'd broken up, Hurricane Katrina had just hit the south. When the levee broke, Molly was one of the first people to publicly call out the government for not doing enough. Her sisters had gone to help, giving out water and food in the makeshift refugee camps. Molly had flown, alone, to New York, to be on *The View*. Meredith Vieira had asked if she was actually blaming an entire presidency for the mass loss of life.

I am.

But Bush had nothing to do with the weather.

He had everything to do with the slow response of the National Guard. He has everything to do with the level of poverty this community is currently living in.

Some might argue with you.

I don't care. Her voice had been strong. Right.

Then Barbara Walters had asked, *You have opinions about a lot of things, and I happen to agree with you on this one. But what about your personal life? There's been talk your recent weight fluctuations have been the result of a failed gastric-bypass procedure. How do you answer that?*

And on national TV viewed by millions, Molly had realized people didn't care about what was right. What was necessary. They cared about how people looked. Fury had filled her throat like cement, and she could only choke. The anger had risen until tears came to her eyes – they had *not* been tears of embarrassment, they'd been tears of rage, but since she couldn't speak, she couldn't make that clear.

She had lost her voice.

And then she'd panicked.

Molly had just got up and run. Unfortunately, she'd been still attached to a mic through the back of her shirt, so she'd only got three paces until she was jerked short. She'd given a small scream and tore out the microphone, ripping the shirt in the process. Then she'd run straight out, through the cameras (which had swiveled to follow her), through the studio warren and right out of the building.

Barbara Walters had just been doing her job. Molly's job was to sing with her sisters, to be the voice of the group, to talk about politics when asked to do so, and to talk about make-up and clothes when asked about those instead.

But Barbara Walters' face, one perfect eyebrow flying upwards in reaction to Molly's rudeness, got played around the world. Smoothly, Babs had said, *Well, it seems our guest has more important questions to answer elsewhere.* She'd smiled as if she'd been in on a joke. The women of *The View* had tittered.

How many times had Molly seen that clip?

Her voice had had a hell of a lot less power after that. The band broke up shortly thereafter when their father died. They'd all lost their voices, and their way. Molly took away one thing: she wouldn't be *forced* into situations. She wouldn't be pushed.

The way Colin had told her to stay.

And this morning, the way he'd pushed her to eat with him.

Overbearing. Arrogant. Authoritarian and officious.

But she couldn't stop thinking about his bold mouth, and the way he'd used it on her. She'd had talented lovers, of course. Men who knew what they were doing, and she herself liked to think she was no slouch in the creativity department.

Colin hadn't required creativity, though. He'd practically required a fire extinguisher to put out the flames he'd started in her body.

"Hey!" Nikki popped her head in from the kitchen.

Molly jumped. "Whoa! I didn't hear you come in."

"How could you possibly have missed it? It sounds like I'm opening a car with a can opener. We really need to get the handyman to look at that." Nikki pulled back her blonde hair with a band. "What were you thinking about here?"

Molly shook her head. "Nothing."

"Huh. Because you're all pink. No, kind of red, actually. You don't want to tell me what you're lost in thought about?"

"Just...getting the inspector in here. She should be coming by today, and –"

"You weren't daydreaming about my brother?"

Molly groaned. "He called you."

Nikki bounced past Molly, giving her a quick, one-armed hug as she went. "I'll start working on the menu again. And yeah, he was worried."

"Did he tell you . . .?"

"Anything? No."

Relief washed through her like a cool wave. "Okay."

"But I've figured it all out."

No, she hadn't. "Okay."

"You want to hear my theory?" Nikki opened the lid of the box where they'd been keeping their menu notes.

"Not really."

"You and he had one hot night of passion."

Molly covered her ears. "Stop."

Nikki waited until Molly gave up and dropped her hands. "Y'all had fun, naked fun, et cetera, and then you woke up early and decided you were freaking out about sleeping with a cop because he has a big head and a bigger mouth and is used to telling people what to do, and you want to be your own person and a cop just isn't your kind of guy."

Molly tried but knew she failed to hide her surprise. "Not exactly."

"Okay, then you never went to sleep at all."

She slid into one of the tables and touched the newly refinished top. It still smelled like the wood stain and polyurethane they'd used. "I think I'm officially scared of you."

"Do you know Norma? From the bar?"

"I've met her a couple of times." Molly's eyes narrowed. "Did she teach you fortune-telling? Is that how you knew?"

Nikki smiled and winked. "I'll never tell."

"Tell me."

"Okay. I'm weak. Nah, I guessed."

"How?"

Nikki pointed at her own neck. "You have a hickey right here."

"I *do*?"

"And my brother called me looking for you, so obviously whatever happened between you two was important or he wouldn't have done that. And you're new in town, and you've told me about your old bossy boyfriends."

"I'm sorry."

"What are you sorry for?"

"I dunno."

"For sleeping with my brother?"

"Maybe." Molly's voice was small, and shame crept up her arms in thin prickles. She felt the smooth, newly sanded underside of the table.

"Why? It's high time he settled down, anyway."

"What?"

"You." Nikki danced her pointer finger in a circular motion in the air and then pointed at Molly. "You're just right for him. You'll take some of the bossy upittyness out of him. And you'll make him remember that love isn't a guaranteed crisis that has to be fixed immediately."

"It wasn't even a date. It was an accident. Like a car crash, but more painful." Her ankle throbbed as she thought about her thumping fall the night before.

"A good one." Nikki nodded, hard. "And you know what? I approve. I haven't approved of one single other girlfriend, but you, yes. You'll do."

The prickles on Molly's arms turned to heated embarrassment. "Stop. I can barely look at you. How many interviews did you manage to set up for this morning?"

"All business, huh, boss?" Nikki winked. "I get you. No problem." She rolled up her sleeves, took a list from her pocket and sat down opposite Molly. "We have six this morning and two this afternoon."

Molly took a deep breath and held it. She could do this. She could make this place work, and she could do it on her own. Alone. No matter how much he affected her, she could push the feelings back, stuff them under the virtual mattress of her mind. Which led *immediately* to imagining his mattress, which had been firm but giving.

And it had given, and given, and given again . . .

"Tell me about them."

CHAPTER TWENTY-EIGHT

Nikki had made up a spreadsheet and a roster for each of them. "See, take your notes here and here, and here I left places for scores."

"Like a game?"

"*Totally.* Look, I put down a column for experience, for enthusiasm, and for looks."

Molly winced. "Do we need that?"

"Think of it as aesthetics."

"Same thing. It seems mean."

Nikki shook her head. "No. It's necessary. For a while Mrs. Lamprey was working at Caprese, you know, the fancy place?"

Molly nodded.

"And she just had this *funk* about her. Like she bathed, maybe, but only once a week and maybe she was one of those who didn't believe in soap. You know those people?"

Molly felt compelled to stand up for Mrs. Lamprey, whom she'd never met. "You can't say that. What if she was just environmentally sensitive?"

"Bull hockey. Those people are nuts."

Molly had met a woman on board one of the cruises who broke out in full-body hives if she touched anything with lavender oil, and she'd seen the doctor treating her after an ill-advised massage. "Not always."

"Okay, fine. Must be hard to live that way. *Boy*, they can be annoying, though. Right?"

Nikki had rough edges, but there was something so refreshing and real about her that Molly couldn't help smiling. "I'm not even going to agree with you."

"Fine. The box is still there to fill in, and you should think about whether you want to use it when you meet Nancy Klondike."

She winced. "Tell me."

"She doesn't believe in toothpaste."

Molly flopped back in her chair and enjoyed the way the solid furniture was made. A lesser chair wouldn't stand up to a flop like that. "Now you're just pulling my leg."

Nikki shook her head. "I'm telling you. The one tooth she has left isn't that pretty. But it's big, so it has that going for it."

"Is there anyone coming in you'd recommend?"

"Oh!" Nikki said brightly. "Lots of them!"

Molly drank six cups of coffee while they did the interviews. After each candidate left, she went to the bathroom and looked at her face in the mirror. Every time, the hickey was still there. Each time, her hands shook a little more. At the long wooden table, talking to the applicants, she kept her hands firmly in her lap or playing with the pen to hide the tremors.

It wasn't just tiredness, though she hid her yawns behind the sample menu she went over with each person.

It was thinking about him.

"Molly? What do you think?"

"Sorry!" She jolted back to attention. "What was the question?"

Clois Knesick, their last interview of the day, wore a tight blue halter top and a tighter electric-blue skirt. "I was wondering if I could bring my dog with me to work."

"Oh." Molly touched the Health and Safety Code she'd left on the table top. "No."

Clois straightened. She tugged at a bra strap. "But he's wonderful. He's a teacup cocker spaniel. I bet you've never even heard of one of those!"

"I haven't, no."

"And he's completely silent. No one would ever know he was there."

"This is a restaurant, though. We can't have animals in the food-preparation area. I'm afraid that's just the law." Molly fervently hoped she was right about that.

"But what about service dogs?"

"*Is* he a service dog?"

"We got rejected, but that was because they didn't understand the gravity of my post-traumatic stress disorder." Clois's eyes started to fill with tears.

Nikki leaned forward and slid a napkin across the table. "And the nature is . . .?"

She was just being nosy – Molly knew it – and she kicked Nikki's ankle lightly. PTSD was a legally protected and valid medical condition.

"Oh." Clois wiped her eyes so emphatically that her green eyeliner smudged down to the tops of her cheekbones. "I failed out of physical education."

Molly waited a beat for more information, for the trauma, but none came. Clois looked at least twenty-seven. "That was your major in college?" Failing out of your major would probably be traumatic, sure.

"No, I mean in high school. I loved it, but the section I failed was volleyball, and I never really got over it." Clois's eyeliner appeared to be magical, sliding almost all of a piece down to her jawline. "I ran backwards, see, to get the ball, and I turned around and ran into a pole and cracked my cheekbone and I *almost* had to have plastic surgery." She pushed at her cheek, and green eyeliner came away on her fingertips.

"So..." Molly didn't have a follow-up. "Okay."

"Bet you didn't even know I had him in my purse."

"What?"

"Doodle!" Clois grabbed her small bag from where it sat on the floor. "Surprise!" A tiny curly mop exploded out of Clois's bag, springing into the air. "Doodle, give everyone a kiss!"

The dog scrambled across the table top and leaped into Molly's lap before jumping at her chin. "Wow! No! I did not. He's cute, yes siree." Fur flew in the air and up her nose. "I love dogs."

Clois beamed. "I knew you did. I could tell."

Molly firmly pushed the dog back towards Clois. "Thank you. We'll be in touch."

"I can't wait. I have *so* many ideas about how we can renovate the place so it doesn't look so much like an old diner." Clois made an itsy-bitsy-spider move with her fingers. "You know, like marble countertops. And waterfalls! Once I was in Vegas, and there was this bathroom that was a big waterfall, and the guys just peed onto the wall. It might be harder to do that in the women's room, though."

"Thank you so much. Thanks." Molly stood and held the door open. "Thanks. Okay. See you. Thanks again." Maybe if she thanked her profusely enough, Clois wouldn't notice she was getting the hook.

"And maybe like a meat-cutting station! Like those Brazilian places have, you know? Trays of meat? I love those things. And singers. I sing, did you know that? Have you thought of starting a band to entertain here? Oh, my *God*, of course you have. You're a Darling. I *have* to sing for you." Clois angled her combat boot so that the door stayed open. "Can I sing for you?"

"*Now?*"

Nikki moved forward and pretended to trip over Clois's boot. "Oh! Watch out. I'm so clumsy." Deftly, she pulled the door shut and locked it against the sound of Clois singing the Star Spangled Banner on the sidewalk at the top of her lungs.

Molly and Nikki stared at each other.

"*Was so gallantly streaming!*" Clois's face plastered itself against the glass. The dog appeared to be tucked somehow between her breasts, loyally yowling along.

Molly lunged at the pull for the café curtain, snapping it sharply down.

"No," said Nikki.

"Agreed. No, no, no, over my mother's blessed body." Molly slid back into her chair and looked at the list. "But who?"

"Let's start at the top."

"Phillip, no. Cynthia, no way. Lucky might be good, and I liked Aubrey for busboy."

Nikki nodded and scribbled.

"And Cesar. I want him," Molly said. "He has the experience, and I loved his laugh. Seems smart."

"Ooh, good. He's dreamy, isn't he?" Nikki made a check mark on a sheet. "Yum. I went on a date with him once."

"You did? Okay, that's fine. I won't hire him."

"No! You should."

"Todd won't mind? You said he was jealous of the way the bus driver honked at you."

Nikki tucked her chin and kept her eyes on the paper. "Whatever. Doesn't mean I can't look at a hot guy, right?"

"You're right." Molly lightly bit the end of her pencil. She considered taking another swig of coffee to prop open her tired eyes, but decided against it. The jitters were finally wearing off. "What was the date with Cesar like?"

"Mmmm." Nikki rubbed at her cheeks and held out her fingertips, as if checking for stray eyeliner. "You know. That perfect date where everything goes just right. He kisses you, and it's everything you ever wanted."

Molly remembered the feeling of Colin's fingers just under her jawline.

"It was my typical mistake. I slept with him on the first date. Our bodies just *fit*."

A yawning pit opened in Molly's stomach. "What happened?"

"Nothing." She shrugged. "I thought he was amazing. And I thought *he* thought *I* was amazing. But he never called."

"Did you call him?"

"Please. Do I look like the kind of girl who wouldn't call a guy? Of course I did. And I texted him twice, which is one more than my normal rules allow. And nothing."

"We are *so* not hiring him."

Nikki smoothed the hair at her temples, tucking it back to make sure her curls were still captured in the rubber band. "Come on. Did you pick up on even a frisson of thrill between us?"

Molly shook her head.

"Water under the bridge. I'm happy with Todd."

"Bullshit." The voice came from behind them.

Molly jumped at the sound of Colin's voice. Truth be told, every single little part of her jolted. "Lord, if McMurtrys keep sneaking into my business through the back door, I'm going to charge you in advance for the heart attack I'm planning to have."

"Never scared a woman to death yet."

Molly wasn't so sure about that. He was capable of stopping a girl's heart just by the look of him in blue. She'd seen him in his uniform before, yes. But that was when she'd merely thought he was good-looking. Now that she knew what was under that uniform, he was a walking myocardial infarction. "Yeah, well, I don't have health insurance and I can't afford the ambulance ride."

"I know people at the fire department," he said. "I'll get you the friends-and-family discount."

Today kept getting more surprising. "That's a thing?"

"No," he said.

Nikki groaned and tugged on her cardigan. "A'ight, kids. I don't feel like watching you two flirt. I think you're adorable and all, don't get me wrong. But *ew*."

"Don't run off on my account. I'm here on business." Colin set down the thin metal box he was holding and flipped the top. "Official, restaurant-type business."

"If that's some kind of kinky fantasy you two have going, I'm *so* out of here. See you at eight, Molly?"

Molly nodded. "Thanks for today. We'll make the phone calls tomorrow."

Nikki nodded and was gone.

"What's your real plan here?"

"I told you." He took out a pen and clicked it open. He jabbed at the paper now clipped to the box. "Official."

"This isn't about me walking away from you this morning?"

"If you mean about you running away from my house in the middle of the night to catch a ride with some would-be slasher, no. This isn't about that or the fact that you ran away from me on the street like you were scared of me." A crease formed between his eyebrows. "Jesus. You weren't, were you?"

Molly bit her bottom lip.

She was terrified, but probably not in the way he meant.

CHAPTER TWENTY-NINE

Colin hadn't even thought about the possibility. "You *were* scared of me?"

"No," she said. But her eyes weren't convincing, darting up and to the left, like she was searching there for the answer. If he knew one thing, he knew when people were lying. And Molly was. He just didn't know why.

"Talk to me."

"You're overreacting." Her tone was curt, and her gaze was now clear. "What are you doing here, anyway?"

She was making her voice light, Colin could tell. And her body language was obvious and readable, too. She wanted to cross her arms, and she kept almost doing it, then shaking them out and letting them hang at her sides. She didn't want to be seen as defensive. She wanted to come across as open. The way she kept trying to square her hips but failed, turning sideways again and again, was textbook.

"Just a quick inspection, it's not a big deal."

Her control over her body language went out the window. Crossing her arms tightly, she frowned. "You're not Code Compliance. That's June. I talked to her on the phone last week. We had an appointment today, and she was going to walk me through anything that I needed to fix."

He nodded. "She's out."

"I'll wait, then."

"She's giving birth."

"How long can that take?"

"To twins."

"Are you making this up?"

"Yes." Colin wanted to taste those lips that had intoxicated him so badly last night. "I'm making up a story that could easily be fact-checked about an employee whose water broke at her desk yesterday."

"Oh, God, you're serious."

He shrugged, and tried to push down the feeling of disappointment that was so strong he could almost taste it, yellow and bitter, at the back of his tongue. "I'm Code Compliance until we hire a temp. June's taking four months off."

"Shit."

"Oh, *come* on. Am I really that bad? Was it something I did last night? Molly, you've got to tell me."

She kept her lips shut and shook her head.

"Did I hurt you?"

She shook her head harder.

"Because you're freaking me out. I did have to come here today, yes. It's one of the million things I have to get done, but no matter how much I had to do, I would have come to see you. I screwed something up last night and I'd do anything to figure out what it was. All I can think is that I did the wrong thing, either physically, which makes me feel sick, or verbally, and I don't know which is worse."

Molly slumped, sticking her hands into her black apron. "I swear. It was me. All me."

"The old it's-me-not-you line?"

She didn't meet his eyes, and reached for a rag from a pile of clean ones. She wetted it under the sink and then sprayed cleaner on it. "It's not a line."

Colin clicked his pen again. "Okay." Damn, his feelings hadn't been this hurt since he was sixteen and Sally Williams told her best friend who told *his* best friend that he kissed like a fish flopping to death on a deck. He'd worked on his kissing since then. A lot. And last night, he'd kissed Molly. The way their mouths had met had made him feel, at those moments, like she was the best kisser in the whole world and that he wasn't that bad, either, but maybe his tongue still flopped like a moray eel. "Let's get this done."

Molly nodded, her lips pulled in tight.

As if she was scared he might try to kiss her again.

Yeah, that wasn't going to happen. He knew when he was being rejected, even if he didn't know why. "You're going to use the wood stove your uncle put in, right? Let's check the flue first, and I'll check the chimney outside before I leave."

She looked miserable. "Okay. Do you want some coffee? I can make some more. We finally broke the coffee machine in earlier."

Her expression didn't make him feel any better. "No thanks." He pointed with the pen to the industrial sink. "Where's your hand-washing sink?"

"That's it."

"It's too close to the dishwasher."

"What?"

"Ware-washing sinks have to be separated from hand-washing sinks by a six-inch-high metal splashguard or twenty-four-inch separation." He flipped the pages in front of him and jabbed at the line he needed. "See? Right here."

Molly just nodded. "I'll get it fixed."

They went over everything, step by step. He had to admit, she'd done a great job, the sink notwithstanding. Every time he questioned something, she had an answer, and better than that, a reason. New on-demand hot-water heater. New hand dryers in the bathroom. New gutters on the roof, and two new industrial disposals, both in the kitchen and at the coffee station in front. The food-prep area had been gutted, ripped apart, cleaned to within an inch of its very old life, and put back together.

Stainless steel shone from every surface. The corner where Hugh Darling had put his foot through the dry rot and needed the fire department to come pull him out had been ripped out and rebuilt. The whole place smelled of sawdust and epoxy and stainless-steel polish. She didn't have the treated wood in stock yet to run the wood-fired stove to prove its safety, but she still had time for that. The regular stove worked, as did the grill. She must have spent hundreds of hours in here already. She mentioned two local contractors, one electrician, and a plumber – all of them trusted in the community – and he couldn't fault her on a damn thing except the sink separator.

It all looked great.

And both of them were acting like someone had died.

"Front-door lock?"

"Double strength, per code," she said. "Not that someone couldn't just smash a pane of glass and turn the locks, though."

"Locks are made to keep honest people out." He checked off the right box. "Capacity sign?"

"Fire Administration is having a hard time figuring out how many people should be allowed in here. They said they'd talk about it at their next meeting and get back to me. The grand opening is in a week. I hate to ask this, but..." She trailed off and tugged at the lobe of her right ear.

He'd had his tongue right there last night. Nibbling on that lobe had made her giggle and then groan. "Go ahead."

"Do you know anyone over there? Could you find out when they'll make that decision? Because I keep worrying that we fill up to capacity and that I'll need to hire a bouncer." She smiled, obviously kidding, but Colin pictured himself in that role. Standing at the door, counting heads, making sure she – the café – stayed safe.

"Yeah. I'll make a couple of calls."

She met his eyes for the first time in the last hour. "Thank you."

You're the prettiest girl I've ever seen in my life. You're the kind of woman I could fall in love with. Instead, Colin just said, "Can I have the copy of your filled-out T-seventy-eight? That's the last thing I need before your final inspection."

Molly set down the stack of napkins next to the cash register. "What?"

"T-seventy-eight. Your copy, the section of it you didn't mail."

"I don't know what that is."

"That should have been the first thing June gave you in your packet."

"I didn't get any packet."

Impossible. "No, you have it somewhere. It's with the guide you've been using to get everything up to code. Should be the last page – it's perforated. Maybe you didn't read it all the way through?"

Her hackles went up – he could almost see them rise. This was now officially the most awkward inspection in the history of the world. "If I had a guide, I would have read it cover to cover. I have no guide. I have no packet."

It wasn't that he didn't believe her, he simply didn't understand. "What have you been referring to, then? When you've been doing all this?"

"The internet. And the California Health and Safety Code. I bought it online."

"Well, hell. That T-seventy-eight should have been mailed to the state two weeks before the opening."

"You're kidding me right now."

"I wish I was."

"Why didn't June give it to me? She never mentioned it."

Colin leaned against the counter, rubbing his forehead. A headache was coming from his lack of sleep, and if he didn't get an aspirin or two within the next five minutes, it was going to be a doozy. "Two aliens in her belly. Last week she forgot how to make an egg sandwich and put yoghurt in with her eggs instead of mayonnaise. She lost her car keys three times, and every time they ended up being in the pocket she'd already checked. Look, what about this? You meet me at my office." He had aspirin, a big department-issued industrial-sized bottle, in his top drawer. He could down three with a Coke and maybe start to feel better before he went home to the bed that was still gloriously unmade. "I've got T-seventy-eights there. You can fill one out, and I'll scan and email it to a guy I know at the state."

She jutted out her chin, and something about the obvious tough-guy routine she was putting on made his heart ache. "Can you call your person at the fire department, too?"

"Yes." He would do whatever she wanted, whatever it took to bring light back into her eyes. He just had no idea what that was. "Do you want to ride over there with me?" She would say no.

And she did. "No, thanks."

What he hadn't predicted was the way she would look at him when she said it. Like she wanted something she couldn't – would never – ask for.

The sheer, open *want* in her eyes matched how he felt.

And as he shoved the keys into the ignition of the patrol car, he decided he'd give his left arm – he'd cut it off himself with a blunt kitchen knife – to be able to give her whatever that was.

CHAPTER THIRTY

Her sister. She needed to talk to her sister, if only for a moment. To get her bearings.

Molly raced into the bar. Norma, in her normal blue muumuu, was sitting on the floor, laying out tarot cards in front of the jukebox.

"Hey, honey! Before you ask, I'm not drunk! Not yet, anyway. But I need to know exactly what kind of music the building wants to hear today, and I realized this would be a great way to do it."

"Where's my sister?"

Norma flapped a hand. "Maybe upstairs in the apartment?"

"Thanks."

"I wouldn't go up there if I were you."

Molly froze. "Why?"

"She and Nate had that look in their eyes. Again."

"Oh, no."

"Oh, *yes*. Lovemaking is a sweet, sweet thing, and we can't hope to stop what the universe has put into motion." Norma tucked a card into her back pocket, as if she were hiding it from herself, and peered at Molly. "Looks like you got some yourself, am I right?"

Molly gave a small squeak she couldn't quite contain.

"Oh, honey. I'm glad. You've got to get you some more of that."

"I can't."

"Why not?" Norma's face was open and accepting. "Making love is just hanging out with another celestial being at the elemental level. And by elemental I mean naked as the day you were born. And by hanging out I mean fucking –"

"Oh, my *God*. I know what you mean."

"So why do you look so panicked?"

"I don't *know*." That's why she'd run to see her sister. Adele was good at figuring things out. At fixing them when they were screwed up.

Molly had none of that skill.

"Eh." Norma looked like some kind of saloon deity with her dress spread out on the floor around her like holy robes, the ropes of necklaces she wore clinking slightly every time she moved. "Come here."

"I have to –" Molly pointed out towards the street.

"Just touch this deck. One second. That's all I need."

Molly jerked forward and tapped the deck with her fingers.

"Good. Now let's see." Norma turned over the top card. "Just one. That's all it takes when it comes to matters of the heart. Ah. That's lovely, that is." She held it up. "See? Isn't that wonderful?"

"I have no idea." But Norma looked so comfortable on the floor that something inside Molly relaxed. "What is it?"

"The Ace of Cups. A new relationship, a strong one. You're going to find the thing you're looking for."

"The T-seventy-eight?"

Norma tilted her head. "It usually points more to love than a highway. You'll find what you're meant to, have faith in that." Then she raised her hands, pressing the palms together at her heart. She bowed her head, before flapping both hands at Molly. "Scoot now. Go find whatever it is you're looking for."

The only thing Molly had been looking for was her sister. But now her heart was lighter. Her very limbs felt warmer.

"It'll be okay, honey."

"Thank you." And then, feeling like an idiot but doing it anyway, Molly bowed back.

As she went out the front door, Norma called one last thing. "When your sister gets done loving her man on the elemental level, I'll tell her you were looking for her!"

CHAPTER THIRTY-ONE

At the Darling Bay Sheriff's Office, Molly knocked on the glass window.

"I'm here to see Sheriff McMurtry," she said to the elderly woman who wore a crooked plastic name tag that said VOLUNTEER.

"Do you have an appointment?"

"Yes," she said. She kind of did, right?

"Name?"

"Molly Darling."

The elderly woman dropped the book she'd been holding. "Oh, my stars. You *are*." She pointed to the door to the right and pressed a button. The door buzzed. "Come in, you precious thing, you."

The woman, Sweetie Swensen, escorted her to Colin's office, twittering all the way. "I think you were always everyone's favorite, weren't you? You know, I remember when you girls *first* came to town to visit your uncle. You must have been about a year old, and little Lana wasn't even born yet. Your mother took you girls to church, and the pastor had to ask her to leave because you wouldn't stop screaming like you'd been dipped in Lucifer's hot oil."

Of course she had. Molly had always been the one to embarrass herself if anyone was going to. Always the one who tripped going up on stage. Always the one to get the words wrong. Always the one Dad had notes for after a show. Adele did everything right. Lana did everything wrong but somehow got away with it, every time. Molly was the one who always needed help.

She sighed. "That sounds like me."

Sweetie rapped on the closed door. "Sheriff? A Darling girl is here to see you." She opened the door and peeked inside. "And she is *darling*, I have to say." She tittered. "A little joke, oh, mercy. You must hear it all the time."

"Always funny," lied Molly and mustered up her brightest leaving-the-stage smile.

"Hi." Colin pulled the door open all the way. He was still in uniform, but he wasn't wearing his gun at his hip and something about his face made him look a little more tired. "Come on in. Thanks, Sweetie." He closed the door quickly, ignoring whatever it was the woman had started to say. "Oh, my God. She exhausts me. She's like an eighty-year-old Energizer Bunny, and her batteries never, ever wear out."

"The perfect person to have at a front desk." Molly looked around. The room was smaller than she'd thought a sheriff's office would be, smaller than a staff cabin on a ship. He had a wooden desk that was covered with paperwork. On the wall was an American flag and what looked like a photo of the whole department, everyone in uniform. At a glance, she spotted him, standing to the left of the group, his hands folded in front of him. Handsome, even in low resolution. The rest of the room was impersonal – a desk chair and two other metal chairs. A dusty rubber fig plant stood next to an empty umbrella stand. The room smelled delicious, though, like fresh copy paper and something spicy – his aftershave?

"True, she's a front-desk ninja. You should see her interrogate people when they come in. Since we put her there, she's managed to get at least four men hooked up on outstanding warrants. She pours tea down their throats until I come in to slap the handcuffs on them."

"Why do they come in if they have warrants?"

"They call in to check to see if they do, and she tells them that they have to come here in person so she can check their ID before giving them the information. Which is true. You can't give that kind of info over the phone. But they just trust her voice, I guess." He pointed at the chair on the far side of his desk. "Have a seat. I've got the packet here. June had a Post-it on her desk asking someone to get it to you, but I guess no one saw it." He sank into his chair and rubbed his eyes. "When people around here are going to catch on to the whole email phenomenon, I'll never know. Probably not in my lifetime."

"You sound tired." Molly had the same fatigue in her own limbs, a weight that felt sleepy and cold at the same time. For a split second, she let herself imagine moving around his desk and sitting in his lap. She wanted to rub away the deep crease between his eyebrows. She wanted to kiss his cheek and then move her mouth to his lips.

"Yeah. I am." He looked at her, and for a moment she wondered if he was having the same thought. His gaze dropped to her lips, and then color rose to the tops of his cheekbones. But all he said was, "Here, take a look, and let me know if you have any questions. Happy to help." He pushed the blue folder of paperwork towards her.

She'd panicked and she'd run away. That's what she did, after all. If she'd do it on camera in front of millions of people, of course she'd run from one man who suddenly made her feel. And want.

She'd ruined any possibility of climbing into his lap, of running her fingers along those cheeks, of sliding her hands down his wide chest. She had no right to imagine unhooking his badge, feeling the edges of that star. Were the points as sharp as they looked? How did it attach to his shift? A pin? Strong magnets?

Business. She was here on business. She flipped through the papers with unseeing eyes. "I'm sorry."

"It's not your fault. June should have gotten hold of you long before now. I can't really apologize for her, though." A smile crept into his expression. "She's wanted to be pregnant as long as I've known her, and I've never seen a person more excited about an impending birth. Or births."

Goddamn. The man was gorgeous, all hard edges and uniform, but when his face went all soft like that, happy about a woman's pregnancy, well, it was enough to melt Molly's very bones.

"Not about that." She slid the folder back onto his desk. She couldn't give a crap about the T-seventy-eight. "I'm sorry I left this morning."

He'd been rocking back and forth in his desk chair, but he stilled. "Oh. That."

"It really was me. It really was *not* you."

"I was worried."

"I left a note," she reminded him.

"Yeah."

"Why are you a cop?"

"To help people." His answer was fast on his lips, but there was something heavy behind the words that she didn't understand.

"And do you?"

Colin shook his head. "Almost never."

Molly was startled. She'd expected a less hopeless answer. "Really? Then why do you stay here?"

"Because I'm hopeful that I will. And honestly, sometimes I do help. A little." He steepled his fingers and looked at them as if searching for the answer. "That has to be enough."

"What about the days when you don't help people?"

"Those are the normal days. I tell people how to do their job. I try to help my deputies investigate cases."

"You order people around."

He tilted his head, and she noticed a tiny gleam of silver at his temple. "I do."

"Do you like that part?"

He leaned forward. "Are you interviewing me?"

"I'm just trying to figure out what you get out of it."

"Out of giving orders?"

"Yeah."

"Not much."

Her toes were cold, as if her blood wasn't moving enough. "Why does anyone order anyone around?"

"Molly, did I do that? Because I don't remember doing it last night, but if I did, I'm incredibly sorry. Something scared you, and I'm beginning to think it was me, and that's the last thing I would want."

"I just want to understand it. What it feels like. Why people do it."

"You've never just barked an order at someone?"

Molly pushed a strand of hair out of her eyes. "Besides telling my sisters to cut something out? I don't think so. It's not the right thing to do, to just tell someone imperiously to do something."

"Try it."

"What?" Something shot through her chest, a quicksilver lightning bolt.

"Give me an order."

"Number one, that sounded like an order, and I don't like that."

"I'm picking up on that about you. Go on." Colin paused. "Please."

"And number two, is this some kind of kinky –"

He laughed, a big, round sound. "Will you do me a favor and just try it?"

"Giving you an order?"

"Just for fun. Like a game."

There was a catch somewhere here, and she knew it, but she couldn't *quite* figure it out.

The look on his face, though.

It was hot.

CHAPTER THIRTY-TWO

*S*uper hot – the way he was looking at her was making her heart race and warming her extremities like he'd turned up the heat in the office without moving. Her toes weren't cold anymore. Nothing was. She was aflame, just from the look in his eyes.

Okay, then. She'd play along.

"Why don't you..." she paused for effect, "get up?"

He leaned back in his chair, linking his hands behind his head. "Nah. That's a question. Not convincing enough."

She narrowed her eyes and lowered her voice. "Get up."

He stood.

"Come here."

He did, standing in front of her.

Oh. Right. It had worked.

And he was too close now. Her bent knees almost touched his straightened ones. "Um..." She swiveled her head, looking around the tiny office. There was a window on the door, one that anyone could look through. "Shut the blinds."

Colin nodded his head once, silently, then, in a move she didn't expect, reached *over* her, and tugged shut the blinds on the door's window.

The right corner of his mouth was quirked, as if he was pleased, as if he was orchestrating this.

Time to take over.

She pushed her chair back and stood. Her breasts brushed his chest, and she caught her breath, but she was busy. Experimenting. She moved to the left, out of his way.

"Sit," she said.

He sat in her chair, his hands resting on his thighs.

She scooted aside a radio and a file folder, then rested her rear on the edge of his desk.

Then, screwing up all her courage, she undid the first button of her shirt.

Colin's smile grew.

"No smiling."

He sucked in his lips and straightened his expression, but his eyes kept shining at her. That was all right. She liked that.

She undid another button and then another, working slowly, until the shirt was open without being parted. Maybe he could catch a glimpse of her bra, maybe he couldn't. She wanted it that way. She wanted to tease him, to play with him.

His eyes darkened.

"Close your eyes."

On a low groan, he did.

"Without opening them, stand up." She waited for him to do so, and then she said, "Come stand in front of me, slowly. Keep your eyes closed."

It only took two steps for him to be knee to knee with her again.

She reached forward and took his hand. She raised it, placing it on the side swell of her breast, over her shirt. He took in a quick breath, and his hand moved, pushing aside the fabric. Molly said sharply, "No." She slapped the back of his hand. He laughed, but the tone of it was strained.

"You can open your eyes." He did, and they widened as she parted her shirt, putting her black lace bra on display. Then she hitched up her denim skirt slowly, an inch at a time, until the edge of her black panties was on display.

"Holy..." his voice trailed off.

Molly felt like she might fly apart. Tension sawed at her insides, deliciously. He was holding so still but she could feel the tremor in him as clearly as if she had her hand on his chest.

She reached forward and took his hand again. "Slowly." She drew his hand to her, placed it on the front of her panties, just under the denim. "Don't move."

"Impossible," he whispered, though his hand stayed still. The heat of his hand made her pulse.

"Now one finger. Just one." She used her own hand to guide his. His forefinger dipped, pulling the fabric to the side. She let him trace her slit. "Softly. Just once."

She watched his face. His lips parted, and his eyes met hers as he moved his finger slowly, *so* slowly.

Molly needed to shift her hips, to move forward, but Jesus, she was already sitting on the edge of his desk. This was insane. And she loved it. "Did you lock the door?"

He nodded.

She lifted his hand to her lips, and slipped the finger that had just touched her into her mouth. She sucked, and without asking, his other hand went to her thigh as he groaned. She swirled her tongue, licking his finger from its base to its very tip. Then, when she could hear in his breathing that he was as crazy as she was, she said, "Kiss me."

He was on her instantly, his body between her legs, one hand behind her head, his fingers wrapped in her hair, cupping her skull so that he could pull her against him as he kissed her hard. His other hand slid up her bare thigh, under the skirt, until it hit the edge of her panties.

"Oh, Jesus. We can't do this here," he groaned against her lips.

"I know." She reached up and put her finger into his mouth, and he sucked it the same way she had sucked his, long and slow, licking it like a lollipop, except this one wouldn't melt, this one she could let him keep licking, and had she *ever* been this turned on in her life? She was so wet and slick that her panties were soaked, she knew it. "How do we stop?"

He smiled into her eyes and gave her finger one last suck. "You're the boss, boss." He pressed against her, and his uniform-clad hardness moved against her panties. "I'll do whatever you tell me to."

Molly's brain seemed to have left the building, dropping right into her core, where she felt like she might explode if she didn't have him inside her soon.

And then the door to the office burst open with a clatter.

"Sheriff McMurtry, sir!"

A man in full uniform stood in the doorway with his hand over his eyes.

"Deputy Hoskins." Colin's voice went from soft to full roar by the time he turned, holding out his arms to ineffectively shield Molly behind him. Molly slid off the desk, bumping him forward as she desperately tugged down her skirt and closed her shirt. "You'd better have a damn fucking good reason to interrupt me –"

Colin was so loud it sounded like his voice was echoing from the officer's radio. *Interrupt me, interrupt me, upt me.*

No, it really *was* echoing.

"Hot mic, sir! You've got an open mic!"

"Jesus." The curse echoed, too. *Jesus, sus, sus, sus, us.* Colin hit something at his waist, then reached around Molly to whack the radio she'd moved on his desk. "How long?" He wasn't echoing anymore.

The deputy didn't drop his hand from his eyes. "A little too long, sir!"

"Thanks, Hoskins. Sorry. Good man." Colin slammed the door shut again. "Well, that'll make something for the city council to talk about, anyway. Wow."

"*You said you locked the door.*"

"I thought I did! It sticks open..."

"Oh, my *God*. How many people listen to that?"

Colin scrubbed his face. "Not that many. Only everyone on the city council. Everyone in the fire department. Oh, and Public Works. The post office has a scanner. The computer store. Sometimes the hardware store puts it on. Everyone in a city vehicle. The school district."

"Stop, stop, *stop.*"

"Is that an order?"

"Oh, my God, I'm so out of here." Molly snapped her fingers. "Give me that form. Give."

"This one?" Colin held it up.

Two seconds from laughing hysterically (or crying), she snatched it away from him. "I'm going to kill you."

"Go to dinner with me tonight instead."

Molly rolled her eyes. "Is *that* an order?"

He shook his head, and his eyes were so soft Molly could almost feel his mouth on hers again. "No. It's a favor I'm asking. I'd really, really like to take you to dinner at Caprese. No strings."

"Call me." Another direct order. It felt good.

"*I don't have your number.* That was the whole reason I couldn't track you down this morning."

"Good point." Molly took the pen out of his pocket, just under his name tag. She wrote it on the back of his hand. "Now you do."

He grinned. "I feel like a teenager. Oh, *damn* it. I'm short a deputy, so I have a patrol shift tonight. Tomorrow? You don't have to come back to my house afterwards. In fact, I won't even ask you to, how's that?"

Molly felt the smile spread across her face. *She* didn't feel like a teen. Back then, she'd been confused and nervous and insecure and then, at twenty, heartbroken over the breakup of the band and the loss of her sisters.

Colin made her feel like a woman.

He continued, "And I won't invite myself to your place. No chance for shenanigans."

"You don't like shenanigans, check." She was still feeling brave. Cheeky.

"Oh, good *God*, woman, I love shenanigans. Particularly yours. But I don't want you to feel pressured."

A thrill ran up her spine. She didn't mind that kind of pressure. No siree, she did not. The corners of her mouth wouldn't stay straight. "Call me," she said again, and winked. Then she fled, her heart hammering more loudly in the hallway than the heels of her old cowboy boots did.

Outside, as Molly walked past the bakery where Josie was putting fresh chocolate-chip muffins in the window's display case, she realized something terrifying. Something huge.

She was dangerously close to falling in love with Colin McMurtry. She was standing on the edge of it, teetering.

He was bossy.

Overbearing.

Cocky.

And it didn't matter. She was falling head over heels, heart-thumpingly and ridiculously in love with the sheriff of the damn county.

And instead of stopping herself, instead of fleeing from real emotion and not being brave, she might be ready to fling herself off the cliff.

With some luck and maybe some trying, they'd learn how to fly on the way down.

CHAPTER THIRTY-THREE

He was supposed to be on patrol, but Colin was just plain distracted. He let a little old lady off with a warning after he pulled her over for failing to signal. She was the one who pointed out she'd been speeding – he hadn't noticed. "Credit for your honesty goes to you, ma'am. Have a good night."

He kept thinking about her.

Molly.

Gorgeous, sweet, amazing Molly who made him feel like he was a superhero.

He wasn't one, he reminded himself. He was just a guy with a company-issued automobile.

Just to kill time, he pasted three cars on the abandoned-vehicle list with the appropriate stickers, and then realized he was on the wrong block of Pine and why the *hell* did so many people own blue Priuses? He spent almost forty minutes peeling the orange stickers off, and he had to convince one irate man that it wouldn't ruin the window's finish. "My tax dollars at work, I see," was the guy's parting shot. If he had a dollar for every time he'd heard that one, he'd, well, he'd be paying more in taxes, that was for sure.

So if it wasn't with *relief* that he heard the 273.5 in progress put out on the radio, it was at least with cheerful acceptance that the last of the guy's stickers was going to remain unpeeled until he'd responded to the domestic violence call.

The old Balmer house was a frequent-flyer place for the sheriff's department to visit. An old commune-turned-flophouse, Mrs. Balmer still lived on the top floor and was seen once a week in town, ordering more canned goods to be delivered to the back door. She let people live rent-free on the bottom two floors as long as the occupants let her dogs (two very tall standard poodles) in and out as they pleased. One week it was all hippie-granola weed smokers passing through on the way north to the growing fields, the next week it was a couple of transients headed south for the winter, strung out on crack and looking for a fix. Fights there varied in intensity, from people whacking each other with sage smudge sticks all the way to the Wild West shoot-out that happened the previous spring in which two people were maimed, one in the arm, one in the buttocks.

This beef, though, appeared to be starring his cousin Bailey, the only McMurtry male beside himself not in prison.

"It's fine!" Bailey yelled as Colin drove up. Bailey's naked upper torso looked disco-tastic in the strobes from the police car's red-and-blue lights. He wore a pair of shorts and one flip-flop. "It's all fine!"

Colin got out and stood next to the car. Bailey wasn't the worst of the family, but he wasn't the best, either. "Where's Angelica, Bailey?"

"She's inside." He lifted his chin in the direction of the house.

"You been drinking tonight?"

Bailey looked at him blearily, swaying a little. "That against the law?"

It was, as a matter of fact, against the law to be intoxicated in public, and if that's what he had to haul Bailey in on tonight to settle everything down, he would. "She made the call, so I just need to talk to her before I leave y'all in peace, okay?"

"I didn't touch her, I swear I didn't. She's a liar."

A shriek came from inside, and then Angelica flew outside wearing only a black robe that was torn at the shoulder. "Get him out of here! Take him! I don't want him!"

"Ah, fuck off." Bailey didn't sound concerned as he lit a cigarette.

Normally Colin would tell him to put it out, but his backup was on the other side of town, and he needed to keep the scene peaceful if at all possible. He showed his palms in a friendly, non-threatening way. "So, what's up, Angelica?"

"What's *up*? His *dick*, that's what! He slept with Caitlyn Gendron, and then he had the *balls* to come try to get back with me!"

Colin couldn't give a crap who either of them had slept with. "You're both staying here right now?"

Bailey flicked his cigarette so forcefully it broke in half. "Since you put my daddy away? Yeah. He lost the house, so I'm homeless, thanks to you." He picked up the still burning half of the cigarette and sucked on it filterless.

Bailey's father, Huffer McMurtry, had his nickname for a reason. Better known for huffing paint than anything else, he'd gone up for burglary with aggravated assault when he robbed a paint warehouse in Kalamas County. And it hadn't been Colin who put him away, although he would have, given half the chance. "So tell me. What's going on tonight?"

"She hit me! Right here!" Bailey pointed at his upper arm, which, apart from a botched tattoo of a mermaid that looked more like a sailor, appeared unhurt.

"Yeah, well, he deserved it! *Caitlyn Gendron?* She doesn't even *like* you!"

"Ah, *shut* up," Bailey said.

"She said your breath smelled like cat food!"

"Go back inside and shut the hell up! Do as I *say!*"

Usually in a heated situation, Colin felt himself go calm. He felt his breathing slow and his heart rate reduce. Later, it always caught up to him, but in the moment, he stayed even-keeled and composed. Now, though, he felt heat flare up his neck. "How about you not order her around, Bailey?" His throat was tight.

His cousin ignored him. "Go inside, Ang! Don't talk to him! Don't you dare say another word."

"Word!" she screamed. "Another word!"

"Shut up, shut up, *shut up!*"

Red coated the insides of Colin's eyelids. In one fast move, he had Bailey face down on the ground, his arm pulled behind him. Gravel dug into the knees of his uniform, and Bailey gave an *oomph.*

Angelica shrieked, "Police brutality! Help!"

Colin lifted his head. "I'm taking him in for being drunk, and so help me, I'll take you, too, and put you in the same cell if you say *one* more word."

She turned and ran into the house, throwing a high-pitched laugh over her shoulder as she went.

Colin heard his words played back in his head, as if he had an open mic again. He felt sick.

He was arresting Bailey for being drunk in public. That's what the report would say.

But he knew, it was really for ordering Angelica around like she didn't matter. *Do as I say.*

And then he'd gone and just done the exact same damn thing.

As he packed Bailey into the back of the patrol car, his cousin kept up a string of curses, coloring the air blue, along with one-liners like, *You're just like your daddy. All about who wears the badge, innit? You're one of us, like he was, too.*

On the way back to the station, Colin clenched his teeth, refusing to take the bait.

He wasn't his father.

He was *not* his father.

Just trash. No-good count-outs, and you know I'm right. I bet the best thing your daddy ever tasted was that bullet, going down his throat.

Colin choked on his need to respond.

He didn't. He didn't respond. Because what was there to say?

He ordered people around.

He arrested his own family for basically being stupid.

How was he better than his father?

Maybe he just plain wasn't.

Colin wondered if he could break his own jaw if his teeth clenched tightly enough. It would kind of be like punching himself out, wouldn't it?

And that might be okay.

CHAPTER THIRTY-FOUR

This isn't going to happen," said Nikki.

"Yes, it is." The happy elation she'd felt leaving the sheriff's office the afternoon before had abandoned Molly by then. A whole morning's work on the old caboose, and they were more behind than ever.

"Come on. We can't get this ready to be the coffee bar by opening day."

"We *can*," said Molly from a kneeling position. "One more try." They were attempting to install an old (but really good – the best her limited funds could buy) espresso machine. "It should fit now."

"I think he put the water line in the wrong place."

Molly shook her head, and they heaved the hulking beast up and onto the counter. "There! Look. It's beautiful." She stood back – well, as far back as she could stand in a space that was three by five. Uncle Hugh had used to sell regular old coffee out of the caboose, and had originally put in the service window. The stainless steel had polished right up with enough elbow grease, and because they weren't going to use it as a sandwich stand like he had, they had plenty of room for everything else – a small cash register, all the cups, sugar, a small fridge for milk. She'd stolen the idea for white twinkle lights from the back of the saloon, and she'd wound them around every part she could on the old train caboose. Even now in mid-afternoon, sunshine was dim through thick fog, and it looked magical, as if somehow it might chug silently away down the trackless street.

"We still have to teach the employees how to make coffee with it. I don't even know how to use it yet." Nikki sounded despondent.

It wasn't like her. Usually Nikki was so cheerful.

Molly flapped a rag at her. "You okay?"

Nikki nodded. "Yeah."

"It feels good, though, this hard work. Doesn't it? I helped a friend of mine shear some of his sheep one year on my vacation time, and I woke up every morning feeling places I'd never felt before. This morning when I stood up, I felt a tiny muscle in my *butt*. You know? You don't think about muscles in your butt until they hurt and then you think about them a lot."

Nikki stretched her arms and then pulled her hair up, piling it loosely on top of her head. "I guess so."

"The side of your neck is so dirty." There were streaks of brown and green and an almost dark black at the base of Nikki's neck, just above the clavicle.

Nikki looked stricken. She dropped her hair and leaned forward so that it covered her neck.

Her hair had been down all day.

"Oh, my *God*."

"It's nothing." Nikki scrubbed the counter next to the machine – a part of the counter she'd scrubbed already three times. "I promise."

"Nikki."

"It's fine."

"That's *not* fine. That is literally the opposite of fine. Show me again."

Nikki wrapped her fingers around a steel bar they planned to hang service rags from. "Please don't do this."

"Don't *do* this? What else did he do to *you*?" Molly couldn't see the bruise now, but she remembered the shape of it. It was seared into her vision as clearly as if she'd been staring into a light. Two fingerprints, one maybe as wide as a thumb. Nikki's head had been slightly turned, but Molly wouldn't have been surprised to see a matching set of bruises on the other side of her neck.

Nikki had worn a collared shirt all week, now that Molly thought about it. And her hair had been left down, even though it must get in the way when they were working hard. How had Molly not noticed?

"What happened?"

"Nothing. I swear. We were just messing around."

Molly stretched out her hand, hoping Nikki would take it, but Nikki had retreated, was as far away as she could be from Molly while still being in the same small metal room. Her arms were folded, her chin tucked, her eyes on her dirty rag.

"Talk to me. Nikki." Molly left her hand in the air, open. "You can talk to me."

"I'm fine."

"Yeah. You're acting fine about it." Molly's heart galloped in her chest. Somehow this pushing felt wrong. Intrusive.

It wasn't polite.

But.

"Nikki, please."

"Back *off.*"

Molly felt her courage shrink, a balloon deflating. She was being so rude. What if it was nothing? Who was she to cast aspersions on Todd? On any part of Nikki's life?

Then she imagined the look of that thumbprint, so dark it was almost black, with a sickly green center.

"No," Molly said quietly. Her head hurt from the sudden rush of blood. "What happened?"

Nikki jutted out her chin. "It's hot. We like to role-play. You know, BDSM?" She said it loudly, as if daring her to ask more.

Jesus, now Molly was prying into someone's *sex* life. She couldn't do this.

Nikki went on, "You do know what BDSM means?" Her voice was ice.

Molly nodded.

"So just drop it."

It was wrong. It felt wrong. Molly would have laid dollars to donuts that Nikki was the kind to swap sex stories over lunch, titillating and hilarious stories of funny noises made while love-making, who fell out of bed, who lasted longer.

But this wasn't bragging.

This was deflecting.

"I don't...I don't believe you." Molly squared her shoulders. "Tell me the truth."

Nikki bared her teeth. "He likes it rough. So do I."

Molly spoke as softly as she could. "Why do I feel like you wouldn't want me to tell your brother about this?"

"About my sex life? *No* brother wants to hear about that, believe me." In the next three seconds, Nikki changed completely. She lost her rigidity and got smaller, balling her hands into fists and pressing them together, as if she were about to enter a ring wearing boxing gloves. As if she knew she would lose. "Please don't."

"Why not?"

Nikki made a choking noise in the back of her throat.

"Because he wouldn't believe you, either?"

"I'm *dealing* with it."

"How?"

A pause. "Counseling."

"As in you're in it?"

"I looked it up."

"You need to get out."

Nikki shook her head. "It's so easy to say that. You sitting there, with your money and your fame and your...your *stature* in this town. You think I could walk into the bank and get a loan against my *name*? Like you did? I can't even get a job except as a glorified janitor."

"I can try to help –"

"Oh, good. Charity. That's what I need."

Molly wanted to apologize, to run away, to pretend this had never happened.

But goddammit. She stuck a hand into her jeans pocket and felt the plastic star poke her. She couldn't look the other way. She took a deep breath. "You tell me or I'll tell your brother. Take your pick."

Nikki stood. "Then we walk. It's too tight in here. I can't breathe."

Outside, Nikki made for the narrow path that ran from the business area down to the sand. Molly followed, carefully staying silent, swallowing the lump of fear in her throat. Was this the wrong thing? She was prying. She was forcing her way into something that wasn't her business.

Nikki wouldn't react like this if it wasn't something bad.

They walked past the old changing rooms that had been renovated into public restrooms years ago. From here they could see Skip's Ice Cream was doing a booming business despite the coolness and overcast skies.

The pathway ended at the boardwalk that wound through the marina down to the water. Nikki strode forward, anger crackling off her skin.

But it wasn't directed at Molly. And even if it was, she'd handle it. *It's okay if Nikki hates me right now.* It was a lie to herself, a brazen one. One she would choose to believe.

They walked out to the end of the rocks, to the big flat one that had been a favorite seagull-baiting spot with kids through the decades. It was deserted. Rain started to spit fitfully, fat drops slapping and stopping again, inaudible in the sound of the waves.

"I don't..." Nikki shook her head and kept her eyes on the whitecaps. "I mean...Shit. What am I trying to say?" She folded her arms, grabbing her elbows.

"It's okay."

Nikki just stared. "It's *not* okay. I know that. I'm not stupid, you know. People probably think I am, the McMurtry girl who didn't even graduate from high school. No place to go but down, you know? But I was smart. I used to be smart. And I know that when Todd...loses his temper, I know I should get out. But it's my fault, too, that's what no one like you can understand. God *knows* my brother wouldn't understand it."

"It's not your fault." Unsure what to do with her hands, Molly kept them in her pockets. She rubbed the badge again, counting the points of it with her thumbnail.

"See? You don't get it. You can't get it. Your boyfriends have always treated you like the princess you are, haven't they? Yeah, they told you you're beautiful and perfect and exactly right, the way you are."

"My ex was verbally abusive."

Nikki stared.

Molly clicked the badge with her nail faster. "So talk, lady."

Blinking rapidly, Nikki said, "I do it on purpose. I aggravate him. He builds up pressure like the old pressure cooker my mom had, you know? If I work him up, he blows faster and we get it over with and then everything's good for a while. Sometimes for a long time."

"It's not your fault."

"*God.* You're not listening to me. Your ex may have been an asshole verbally, but he didn't touch you, did he? I fight *back.* I hit *him.* For everything he does, I try to get my own in back."

"It's still not your fault." Molly used to think she'd driven Rick to his meanness. His anger.

"I just said it was."

"It's not." She knew it was important that it be said. "*It's not your fault.*"

"Promise me you won't tell him."

She didn't have to ask who Nikki was talking about. "Why?"

"Because that won't fix anything – it'll only make it worse. I mean it. I know what I'm talking about."

"You have to get out."

"That's where the money you've been paying me is going."

Raindrops hit Molly's face, but she didn't wipe away the moisture. "Explain, please."

"Suellen Cotter has a room for rent. I've given her two hundred dollars to hold it for me, and I should be able to pay the first and last month's rent by the end of next week, when you pay me."

"I'll give you the money now."

Nikki's response was lightning quick. "No."

"Then I'll give her the money."

"Let me *do* this." The tears that had been staying in place in Nikki's eyes finally spilled over, just as the rain started in earnest. "I need to take care of *myself*. I thought you were the kind of person who might understand that. It doesn't do any good if someone does it for you. You just end up right back where you were."

Molly thought of how she'd literally taken the cell phone out of Adele's hand when her sister had said she was calling a floor refinisher because Molly had looked too exhausted. She'd hung it up over her sister's protestation and handed it back. The only way the café would be hers was if it was *hers*. Not anyone else's. It was the difference between eating candy and protein. One made you feel great for a few minutes before you crashed and felt worse than you had before. The other made you feel good for a few hours and helped you build muscle. "I do understand that. Maybe more than you think I do."

"You know, once my mother went to Kalamas County to report my father for hitting her."

Lord. Molly brushed the rain off her forehead and nodded.

"They said legally she had to report it in the jurisdiction where it had occurred. They couldn't take action. It had to be reported here. To the sheriff. Who was my dad."

"Nikki..."

"When they sent an investigator out to check on her, to talk to Dad, he beat him up."

"He beat up another cop?"

"He thought the investigator was lying, that he was seeing my mother. He almost killed him. But the sheriff can get away with a lot in a small county. Professional courtesy. They told him to stay out of Kalamas for a year and Dad paid the guy's hospital bills." Nikki paused. "She died to get away from him."

"What?"

Nikki rubbed her eyes. "She died of natural causes. A stroke. But I swear to God, she threw that blood clot to get away from him. What am I going to do, huh? I'm younger than she was then. I'm healthy. I don't actually want to die. I want to get *out.*"

"We can –"

"And when shit goes down, it happens in my brother's jurisdiction because of where we live. I won't put him through that."

"That's just stupid." It was rude and Molly didn't care. Something about the salt air was making her brave. "That's fucking ridiculous."

"I know." Nikki turned to face Molly and took her hand. Her fingers were ice. "I promise. I'm getting out. You're helping me, with this job."

Molly hesitated. "You have to be honest with me."

"I will be."

"About everything."

"Yes."

"About whether you're safe going home."

Nikki flipped her hair back and let Molly see the bruising again. It looked even darker and more shocking under the clouds that matched them. "I'm safe for at *least* a month with this one."

"It's not your fault."

Nikki smiled and looked out to sea again. "I think you're wrong. It does feels nice to hear, though."

For a long moment, Molly kept hold of Nikki's hand. It was smaller than either of her sisters' hands. Colder.

But just as strong.

Molly gave a tight squeeze. "You want to help me fix that last window in the caboose?"

Nikki said, "Hell, yes. I do."

"Okay."

They walked back quickly.

Molly, soaked to the skin, barely felt the rain.

CHAPTER THIRTY-FIVE

They worked hard, finishing the caboose.

Somehow, Nikki dug out of Molly that she had a date with her brother that night. "Go. You go get cleaned up. You look terrible." Nikki had winked. "And don't do anything I wouldn't, which means basically don't do fifteen shots and expect to be able to win at pool. Beyond that, you're free to do what you want."

The light was back in Nikki's eyes. Molly was still worried, but she'd pocket it and look at it again later.

She had to get ready for her date.

She showered. She did her make-up so that her eyes looked smudged – thank God for the lesson the girl at the make-up counter had given her the last time she'd paused in the department store. Dark-red lips – were those still in? Eh. Molly smiled at her reflection and then felt silly.

Red lips must always be in.

Her cell rang and she dug it out of her pocket. Maybe it was Colin, confirming tonight. He'd already texted once, earlier. *Can't wait for tonight.*

"Hello?"

It wasn't Colin.

"He broke my arm."

"Nikki? Where are you?"

"He was trying to kill me. It was different this time. He tried to strangle me, and then he forced my arm back and it broke, I think, and I got away –" Nikki's voice was so thin and her words so fast it was hard to understand her.

"Where are you?"

"I took a cab to Kalamas General."

"Nikki! A whole hour away?"

"I want to – oh, God. My brother can't be involved in this. It'll break his heart, and I'm afraid he'd go after Todd and then get in trouble with his job." She broke off in a sob. "Can you come?"

"I'm on my way."

S o Molly helped Nikki lie.

Nikki told the doctor the fight had occurred in Kalamas County in Todd's car, behind the Broken Wagon.

"You'd been drinking there?" The doctor held an iPad, his finger poised to fill in a box. But who knew how much the local sheriff's department would investigate?

Would they go into the Broken Wagon to verify Nikki and Todd had, in fact, been there?

Molly spoke before Nikki could answer. "You said you'd just gotten there, right?"

He shot her a look. "Let her answer, please."

Molly sat up straighter and tried to pretend she wasn't intimidated by his grey eyebrows, which flapped like bat wings, and his starched white coat.

"We hadn't gone in yet," said Nikki.

The deputy arrived, ducking in apologetically through the hospital curtain. "I'm Deputy Todd Viejo. Sorry it took a while, ma'am. Problem with my patrol car starting."

"Todd?"

"My mother calls me Toddy, but she's the only one who can get away with that."

"Of course," said Nikki faintly.

The officer looked at some notes scribbled on his pad. "Ah. Your boyfriend's name is Todd Meyers, did dispatch get that right?"

Nikki nodded.

"Well, then." The officer pulled himself a little taller. His badge was so new it sparkled, and his boots didn't have a scuff. He was thin but handsome in a puppy-dog way. "Let's call him Bad Todd. You can call me Good Todd. Oh. That's not very professional, is it?" He paused. "Screw it, let's do it anyway. Tell me the story."

If Good Todd doubted any part of the story, he didn't push it too hard. He took careful notes as Nikki spoke, and only interrupted her for clarification. "Okay, almost done. Just a few more things, just so I have it right. You were in Bad Todd's car when this happened."

"Yes."

"How did you get to the hospital?"

"A cab."

"Okay. And your last name is McMurtry? Any relation to the sheriff in Darling County?"

"My brother."

Another pause. Molly, sitting in a hard plastic chair next to the bed, crossed her fingers.

"Okay, so your dad was...You might know this already, but since it happened here in Kalamas, we have jurisdiction to make the arrest. Not your brother."

"*Good.*"

"But we could ask for his help, if that would make you feel better."

"Please. Don't. Leave him out of this. Please?"

"Okay."

"Please don't tell him. He'll be so disappointed. Promise me?"

Good Todd shuffled his feet back and forth. "I can promise I won't tell him, if that makes you feel any better. But everyone knows each other in this business, you probably know that already. I can't guarantee he won't find out eventually."

"Do you...have to arrest Todd?" Nikki's voice, normally so strong, quailed. "Can't you just make a report? I thought you could get me a restraining order or something."

Molly shook her head at the deputy. Todd *had* to be arrested. That was the whole point, wasn't it? Was Nikki scared now?

Good Todd just said, "We're going to do both of those things with you, yes, but we have to arrest him, also."

"What if I don't want to press charges?"

Molly leaned forward. "Nikki! You have to!"

"But I've changed my mind. He didn't mean to and –"

Good Todd interrupted her. "California doesn't let you make that decision. Not anymore. Any physical sign of injury in a domestic violence case requires an arrest by the state. You're not the one pressing the charges, the state is. There's nothing you can do to drop them, either. Takes the blame off the victim." He shot her a look. "That's you. Just so we're clear. I have to ask you, though, is it possible you left any mark behind on him?"

"I didn't touch him."

"Good. Because that requirement of arrest on domestic violence doesn't protect anyone based on gender."

Molly sat forward. "Wait a minute. If she fought *back* and scratched his face, say –"

"But I didn't."

"You're saying if she put up a fight at all and left anything physical behind, you'd arrest her, too?"

Good Todd seemed relieved to be looking away from the gorgeous Nikki. "We would have to. State law. Penal code 273.5. It ties our hands. Which is why I'm glad Nikki didn't leave a mark."

Nikki looked at her hands. "But I have in the past."

"Truthfully?" Good Todd glanced at Nikki and then down at his paperwork again. "I'm glad you did in the past. Fuck that guy."

Molly couldn't help her small snort.

"And fuck him if he thinks he can keep getting away with it. He can't. And you won't let him."

Nikki kept her gaze on her hands.

"Right, Nik?" Molly kept her voice soft, but touched with one finger a bruise that was fading on her forearm, just the size of a thumb. "You won't let him?"

Nikki nodded. "I won't let him. *Wait.* That's too easy to say. You don't understand what he's like. He can be so wonderful." She stretched out her fingers, as if seeing them for the first time. She turned them over and looked carefully at her palms. Then she touched the bruise on her forearm.

"He hurts you," said Good Todd.

"Fuck that guy." Nikki's voice was soft and her words slow, but there was conviction underneath it.

"Good girl," said Molly. And in those words, she heard her father's voice, the tone he used when he really meant it. When she'd done something scary, when he was proud of her.

The father Nikki'd had probably hadn't said much like it to her when he was still around.

So Molly said it again. "Good girl."

Nikki mouthed it to herself, as if practicing it. "*Good girl.*"

"Good woman," corrected Deputy Todd.

CHAPTER THIRTY-SIX

There was no way in the world Molly could go on the date that night.

Maybe if Nikki had just told her about it. *He hurt me, I made a report. He'll get arrested soon.* Maybe if Molly'd had no involvement at all, she could have kept it a secret from Colin.

But even then, she doubted it.

Colin would look at her with those dark eyes that seemed to see right inside her to who she really was. He'd hold her gaze. Then she'd open her mouth and say, "Your sister got hurt."

Molly had always been a bad liar.

So as Nikki finished up inside the sheriff's office, as the female officer gave her a stack of pamphlets, Molly texted him.

I'm sorry, something came up.

Disappointment burned like stomach acid.

The reply was almost instant. *Can I help with something?*

He would ask that. Of course. No. *Just a private matter. I'm sorry. Raincheck?*

Sure. Take care.

Such small words. Innocuous.

And how they cut at her as she drove back to Darling Bay with Nikki. *Take care.* It was what you told the cashier at the grocery store when she handed you the receipt. It was what you said to co-workers you didn't really like as they embarked on a journey to new climes. It wasn't what the man you had just realized you'd fallen for said, if he felt the same way at all.

No, God, she was reading too much into it. She was the one breaking the date, after all. His feelings were probably hurt, if only a little bit. That was okay. That would be natural.

Nikki stayed silent for almost the whole ride into Darling Bay.

"You okay?" Molly asked. Stupid. Of course she wasn't.

A nod, seen in a passing headlamp. Darkness had dropped while they were still in the station, and the lights of town blinked dully at them as they came over the final rise. The far half of town was shrouded in a bank of fog that appeared to be devouring houses and shops. The pier was invisible. If Molly wound down her window, she'd hear the foghorn blaring every nine seconds. But it was cold out.

"What street again?"

"Stonecrest." Nikki had had a bit of buoyancy when she'd asked Molly to drive back. *I just want to rest and think.* Her tone had been hopeful even though her head had been down.

Now that tone was as dull as the fog-draped lights in front of them.

Molly turned carefully onto the street, and counted houses until they got to the fourth one from the second stop sign. There was an old, fat, miserable palm tree in the front lawn, shielding the house, just as the female deputy had told them. *No numbers on the outside of the house, so don't bother looking for them. Just look for the diseased palm tree.* The siding was worn, and the whole place looked shabby.

She braked. "I still can't believe we don't have a women's shelter in town."

"Veronica puts people up when they need help. She said I could stay for at least a week."

"Then what?"

"No clue." Nikki pulled up her purse and dug out a piece of chewing gum, which she chomped viciously. "Thanks for the ride."

"We can go get your car tomorrow, if you want. If your arm doesn't hurt too much."

"It's fine. Veronica asked me not to park in the neighborhood anyway."

"You want me to come inside with you?"

"No." Nikki paused with her hand on the door handle. "I'm sorry that I dragged you into this."

"It's no problem."

"Yeah, it is. I know that. I'll call you tomorrow."

"Call me? I'll see you at work, right?" Molly tried to put a smile into her voice. Nikki wasn't looking at her but maybe she'd hear it. "The grand opening's in five days. You're not going to leave me high and dry?"

"I thought..."

"You thought what?"

"That you wouldn't want me at the café. At least until he's arrested. Just in case. Maybe longer."

"Nikki!"

"And you're too nice to tell me to my face."

"You thought I would just *text* you later to fire you?"

Nikki shrugged. "It's fine. I get it."

Molly wanted to grab her by the hand, to take her arm, but thought better of it just in time. The last thing Nikki probably wanted was to be manhandled in any way. "You're my friend."

"Yeah, well, you're a nice person. Sometimes those two things get confused."

"I need you."

"Oh." Nikki looked at her lap, but there was a tiny smile on her face. "Don't tell my brother. Please?"

"Why is it so important?" Molly still didn't understand.

"Because I'm worried he'll react like Dad did. Something terrible will happen and it'll be all my fault. This is the first step, I swear I'm taking it."

Molly's head hurt. "I'll respect your wishes. But promise I'll see you tomorrow at work?"

"Yes." Nikki paused. "Thank you." Then she was out and hurrying up the walkway to the house.

As Molly lit the wood stove to test-fire it one more time, she wondered again if she could have gotten away with not cancelling on him. The kindling she'd found on the hill behind the hotel was still a little wet from the last rain, and it smoked on top of the newspaper she'd balled up underneath.

No. She pictured Colin's face, that wide, serious jaw, the way his eyes lit when he looked at her, belying the severity of his features.

She would have folded and he'd have learned she'd broken the only promise she'd ever made him, which would make it likely to be the last promise he'd ever ask her to make.

A stupid, small, *ridiculous* image swam through her mind's eye. Colin, on his knees, a ring in a black box held between them.

I'm an idiot.

She wasn't worthy of promises asked for.

Molly should have told him.

As she'd walked to the back door of the café, she'd caught sight of her sister in the bar through the side window. Through the old, wavy glass, she'd seen Adele laugh at something a customer had said and then put one hand on Nate's waist.

If anyone had hurt Adele and kept it from Molly? Just the thought of it drew heat into her arms and hands. Molly, who couldn't remember having a violent thought since the time she'd thrown a Barbie doll right at Lana's head for stealing the last of her Halloween candy, felt fierce, hot fury course through her. If Nate (darling, sweet, quiet Nate) had hit Adele? She'd claw his eyes out. No one could hurt one of them without having to answer to the others. Even Lana – who Molly hadn't spoken to in a month or more, who hadn't talked to Adele in, what, almost a year – would come running if she knew one of them needed her.

Adele was the fixer.

Molly was the voice.

Lana was the artist.

They'd all had their roles, yes, but their number-one role, above all else, had been *sister*. She shoved a few more pieces of newsprint into the belly of the stove, and pulled out her cell phone.

Lana answered after six rings. She sounded sleepy. "Tell me you're calling because you're finally figuring out that you hate Darling Bay."

"What would you do if I told you Nate was hurting Adele?"

A thick silence filled the connection between them. Then a rustling. "I'm on my way. I'll get the next flight. Shit goddamn motherfuck *shit.* I'll kill him."

Something caught in the back of Molly's throat – a combination of a sob and a laugh – and she spoke around it. "I was just testing you."

"*What?*"

"He didn't hurt her. He worships the ground she walks on."

"You *ass.* Why would you *do* that?" Fury was clear in Lana's voice, and Molly figured she had thirty seconds or less before Lana hung up on her.

"I just wanted to know what you'd do."

"Jesus Christ." A pause and another rustle. Suspicion lit her next words. "Is someone hurting *you?*"

"No!"

"You swear to me?"

"Yes."

"On Mama's grave?"

It was as solemn a thing as the girls had between them. "On her grave. I swear. I'm fine. A friend of mine here has an abusive partner."

"So you help *her* kill him."

"I'm seriously not into murder, I gotta tell you." It was so good to hear her sister's voice. It felt like drinking cold water after waking up too hot under the covers. "And I have to tell you, I'm dating the sheriff, so it wouldn't look that good."

"You're *what*? As in a lawman? Like with a gun and everything?"

"Yeah."

"I dated one of those once. Except by dating I mean slept with twice. Two very excellent nights of not sleeping. I got to strap on his gun once. Have you done that yet?"

"Lana!"

"Because I have to say, it feels good to have that much power right next to your –"

"I cancelled on him tonight because his sister is the friend I'm helping, and oh, God, it's too confusing to go into. Just come here."

"No."

"But I miss you."

"No." Lana's voice was fainter, as if they were literally getting farther apart as the seconds ticked by.

"But Adele misses you."

A snort was the only answer.

"Fly home." It's what Uncle Hugh had always said to them, it's what Adele had said to Molly almost every time they talked when Adele had been trying to convince her to come to Darling Bay.

"Oh, screw you."

Molly knew it was Lana's way of expressing love. "Where are you, anyway?"

"Chicago. Then to Toronto. Got a gig opening for a new kid."

Lana was better than opening gigs. "It's the grand opening of the café on Thursday night. I wish you could see it. It looks like it used to when we were kids, only even better."

"You're really staying there? This is seriously what you're doing now?"

Lana's unhappiness was clear, even if the line was getting fuzzier. "Yeah. I got a loan that says I'm staying here for the rest of my natural-born life, anyway." She meant it lightly, but wings of panic beat in her chest as she said it.

What if she'd blown it with Colin? What if he found out that she'd helped Nikki hide her abuse from him? What if she lost the thing that was blooming between them? The thing that made her heart soar?

She looked into the still low flames of the wood stove.

A café would have to be good enough.

Funny. It didn't feel as if it would be.

"Eh. No one ever said you had to pay a loan back, did they?"

Molly laughed. "That's *exactly* what they said when I signed the paperwork."

"If you want to run, just let me know. I'm pretty good at hiding."

"I know you are." Molly wrapped her fingers more tightly around the phone, and she shoved another piece of newsprint into the stove. She swallowed a gasp. Colin's face looked at her from the curled edge. He was shaking a Boy Scout's hand, handing him some kind of medal.

"Hey, I have to go, okay? I have sound check in ten."

"I love you. Be safe." The scout's image had already curled and burned. Colin's face scorched at its edge. She grabbed for the paper but the kindling was finally catching and it was burning too hot, too fast.

"Yeah." A click.

Molly blew on the tips of her fingers. The kitchen door made its scraping noise behind her. Then there was a roar. "*What did you do?*"

She spun, dropping her phone on the tiled floor.

"You *promised* me."

CHAPTER THIRTY-SEVEN

Molly looked stricken. And, frankly, terrified. Colin felt a searing pang of regret for scaring her so badly and then he remembered what she'd done. "You don't remember that promise at all?"

"I do." She didn't bend to pick up her phone, and it lay on the floor between them, mute.

God help him, he wanted to kick it right into the wall. He wanted to hear her phone (the one on which she'd texted him to cancel because she'd betrayed his trust) shatter – he wanted to see it fly into little pieces.

But he could kick something later. Now was for figuring out what the hell had happened, how he'd gotten cut out of the whole thing.

"Where is she?"

"She's safe." Molly tugged her shirt lower so that it covered her belly. Her cheeks were pink, probably from standing as close as she was to the wood-fired oven, and she looked prettier than she had any right to.

This was the worst thing ever.

No, scratch that. What had happened this afternoon was the worst thing. (And in his cop mind, he knew it wasn't. It wasn't. The worst thing *hadn't* happened, and he'd do well to remember that, but he'd seen the worst too many times, and it couldn't happen to Nikki. No way in hell.)

"Is she with Veronica?" The way Molly stared at him told him he'd scored a direct hit. "Good. That's fine. I'll go see her there."

"Don't." Her voice was small but clear.

"Oh, yeah? You want to tell me why? Oh, wait, I forgot, *you* have all the information. I don't. I would *love* for you to give me some of it. Jesus."

Molly closed her eyes.

He'd frightened her.

That voice that had just come out of his body – he knew that voice. It was the one he'd heard almost every day growing up.

But he didn't apologize.

Also a trick of his father's. He'd just wait and she'd eventually have to say something.

Sure enough, Molly opened her eyes and laced her fingers together at her stomach. "She doesn't want your help."

"She doesn't get a say in that. I'm the goddamned *sheriff.*"

Again, his father's voice came out of his mouth. Colin felt a burning pain in his gut. So, what, it took the sister he loved most of all to make him into the man he hated more than anyone?

Fine.

The skin around Molly's eyes was white. "Yeah, well, you're not the boss of her."

"Are you five years old right now? Oh, wait, I forgot, you *are* the boss of her. That's right. Okay, boss, tell me what happened."

He watched her inhale. And then, to his surprise, she just said, "No."

Colin blinked. "What?"

"I'm sorry, but no. You'll have to ask her." Her voice gathered strength. "She can tell you herself. If she wants to."

Colin was known for getting what he wanted from people. Good people talked to him because they liked him. They trusted him. Bad guys talked to him because he didn't give them a choice. When he'd been partnered with Shelley Dinario, she'd called it his Black Look of Doom. *No one's immune to it. You could make a mob boss cry.* They'd laughed. There were no mob bosses in Darling Bay. It wasn't even a town a mob boss would visit on vacation. Colin had to make two-bit thugs talk about stealing from the locked cabinet at the church. He made kids cry after they stole and wrecked their dads' tractors. Every once in a while, he got to arrest someone for hurting someone else, and even more infrequently, he got to arrest someone for spousal abuse. Every time he did, he thought of his mother.

Every single time, he did it for her.

"You knew I suspected it."

"Yeah."

Molly was supposed to be quivering. He'd never felt the Black Look of Doom more clearly on his face. His whole *body* was doom.

But she was just looking at him, her expression guarded, steady.

"Answer me."

She turned her back on him, shoving metal tongs into the stove, stirring the mess she'd made.

"Molly," he warned.

She spun. "Or what? You'll hit me?"

Colin lost his breath as clearly as if she'd sailed a fist into his gut. "Are you saying that because that's what he did to her? *Tell* me, goddammit."

"I'm saying that because that's what your dad did. Where do you think she gets the idea that it's okay to be with someone like him? This is the way Nikki's choosing to play it. She gets to make the rules."

"So she lies to a sworn officer of the law?"

"She only lied about where it happened. Nothing else."

"You know what that means if it goes to court? And hear me when I say this, it is *going* to court. It means that everything is in question. If she lies under oath and gets caught, the judge'll throw the whole thing out."

Molly touched her lips. He saw her swallow.

"Then she won't lie."

"Says the expert?" He was being mean. Deliberately. He hated himself for it. But he was so *angry* at her.

"She'll tell the truth – that she didn't want you involved. That's the only reason she went to a different county."

That's what Sheriff Battles had said, too. Colin had been at his desk when he'd got the phone call. The only thing on his mind had been going over a funding projection for the next fiscal year and getting home in time to take a shower before his date with Molly.

Then Sweetie Swensen had told him he had a call on hold from Kalamas. He'd known Randy Battles for fifteen years. The man had been on his oral-board interview back in the day. Randy and his father used to share war stories, until Chuck had thought Randy was eyeing Colin's mother and had ordered him to stay away from his family.

Every time Colin and Randy had worked together on task forces, every time they'd sat together at fundraisers, that particular day had never come up.

It wasn't uncommon for Sweetie to tell him Randy was on hold. He'd been happy to pick up the call. "What's up, buddy?"

"I'm sorry to make this call, Colin, but I think I have to."

Colin had leaned backwards, and kicked his legs up onto his desk. "I got a hot date tonight. Hopefully this won't take long?"

"Might. It's about your sister. She's fine, but she got hurt by that boyfriend of hers. Made a report. Said it happened here, but videotapes of the premises' back parking lot say it didn't. You want a copy of the report?"

"She went to a different *county*?"

"My deputy tried to make the jurisdiction stick for her. Apparently he has a few stars left in his eyes. But my records clerk sent it up to me with a query, and I knew you'd need it."

"Send it over." Colin had pulled his legs back and put them carefully on the floor under his desk, even though he couldn't feel them at all.

He'd read the report closely. Slowly.

He'd stood up and touched his office wall. Once his father, drunk at work, had punched a hole through it, right here. The plaster had been repaired, but if Colin ran his fingers along it, he could still feel where it was raised.

He'd wanted to do the same thing.

Molly had cancelled on him. He understood then why.

And besides Todd Meyers, whom he'd happily shoot in the kneecap, he'd never been angrier at anyone in his life.

Now, as smoke filtered out of the crappy wood stove behind her, he said, "You know why I'm here."

"Because I helped her."

"No." The truth was he was glad that his sister had someone to talk to.

But Molly had someone to talk to, also.

Him.

"Because I didn't tell you, I know." Molly didn't sound sorry at all. "We could go around this for hours, but that doesn't sound fun. I didn't tell you because she didn't want me to. It's as easy as that."

"He ran, you know."

Molly frowned. "What?"

"He must have a tie to someone in the department there. Which, I should point out, he *doesn't* have at my department. So he heard about the warrant, and he's in the wind."

"They didn't get him?"

"They being Kalamas? No, they didn't. I will, though."

"Can you do that?"

"Can I *do* that?" Colin felt a red pressure behind his eyes. "Hell, yes. I'd do it for any of my citizens. And I'd do it for my sister if he'd hurt her while they were in France or Istanbul. Mars. Anywhere. Molly, she's my *sister*."

"I know." Now she looked miserable. "I get that. I promise. If I understand anything, it's about sisters. But Nikki didn't want you –" She cut herself off and covered her lips with her fingers again.

"What the hell aren't you saying?"

She picked up a piece of newsprint and started tearing it into strips. She didn't look at him.

"Molly."

"It's fine. I can take it."

"What?"

"She was worried that you would...that you might hurt him."

"What?"

"You know, like your dad did. With that guy, the deputy he thought was seeing your mom."

His sister had told Molly about that?

Nikki had been *worried* like that? She'd thought he had that potential hiding inside him? Once, a long time ago, he'd made a stupid bar bet with a fellow deputy that he could keep his hand in a bowl of ice water longer than his friend could. It was true – it turned out he could (only longer than Julio by a few seconds, but still, he'd won) though the pain had been more intense than he could have imagined. Sharp splinters of pain, shoved up under his fingernails, shards of agony under his skin.

Knowing Nikki thought – *really* thought – he could turn into their father felt like that. Two hands full of unbearable, shocking pain. And knowing that Molly maybe believed it, too, felt like his whole body had been dropped into an icy lake while wearing a concrete belt.

Molly went on, as if he were still a regular person with a heartbeat, with reason. "I know you can't be mad at her. And you can't find Todd to be mad at him. You have to be angry with someone, and it's fine if I have to be that person."

Colin finally caught half a breath through the pain. "Oh. Really? You think that's my problem here?" He ground his curled fingers into the metal edge of the middle island. "Get this. The Meyers are all from Kalamas County. Todd's brother got popped on domestic violence charges two years ago. The photos were clear, bruises all over his wife's body. But their cousin is the county ID tech. The evidence was misplaced, and by that I mean erased off the server."

Molly's mouth dropped open.

Colin knew his voice was dangerous. He could feel it. "And another cousin? You're gonna *love* this one. He's the DA. The damn District Attorney, do you believe that? The Meyers family doesn't go up on charges in Kalamas County. The DA never thinks there's enough evidence to put them to trial. Ever. I suppose if one was up for murder, he might *have* to prosecute. Maybe we'll find out when Todd kills my sister, huh?"

Molly appeared frozen. Her eyes were horrified.

Colin kept his voice low. He didn't want to hurt her – he had never wanted to hurt a woman. Ever. He was *not* his father. But he wanted her to remember his words. "You're the one who helped Todd get away with it. If she gets hurt worse, it will be on you. Completely on you."

"I didn't know. Colin, I had no idea."

He coughed. The smoke was getting thick. The oven still didn't work, wasn't fixed. He could close her down right now. Her eyes darted to the flickering kindling that was still sputtering. Two weeks, that's how long a violation-with-hazard called for. She'd have to get it fixed, and get approval. Her grand opening wouldn't happen.

He *should* shut her down. June in Compliance would do it in a heartbeat.

But he wouldn't. Not out of spite.

He was *not* Chuck McMurtry.

"Put the fire out. Get it fixed – *really* fixed – within fourteen days. If I hear you've fired it up even once during business hours, I'll find a reason to cite you and close you down for a month."

"Colin –"

"The very worst part? You want to know what that is?"

"What?"

In that single word, her voice was so sad it broke his heart to hear it. That is, it would have if he'd still had a heart to break, but a man trapped at the bottom of a lake of ice had no heartbeat at all. Not a single thump.

"I was falling in love with you."

She gave a small sound, the edge of a sob. "Colin –"

"I thought I could trust you. Such a small thing. So easily earned, you know? A guy picks me up off the side of the road when my car breaks down, and I'll trust him forever. I gave you that trust, and you broke it –" He had to stop and breathe so that his own voice didn't break in that dead giveaway. "And now I'm taking it back. You can't have it." He took a moment to look her up and down. Then, very deliberately, he said, "You don't deserve it."

He waited a beat to see what she'd say.

She didn't say a word. Her eyes said it all, but he refused to listen to what they were telling him.

"I thought you were the brave one," he said. Jesus, he was *taunting* her. What kind of an asshole was he? "The voice of your sisters."

"I am," she managed, just barely.

"Bullshit. If you'd been brave, you would have gone against what she wanted. You would have told me what was happening, the way you promised."

"Oh, my God." Her breath was heavy. Loud. "You are such a *bully*."

Colin didn't move a muscle, but the word knocked him sideways.

"*This* is what you do when you don't get your way?"

"No, I don't –" How had she just turned this upside down?

He heard her breath catch in her voice. "I understand that I screwed up. But I also told you I didn't like doing what I was told. You were right about Nikki. And you're right – I'm not very brave." Her voice broke. "But you don't get to boss me around. No one does. I sure as *hell* am not your mother. *I* am not trash. I worked through this with one guy already. I'm not going to do it again. If you're going to act like your extended family, if you're going to act as low as your father was, *get out*."

The way she was pulling air into her lungs as if oxygen was the thing that gave her strength and purpose, just like the fire that was finally catching behind her – she was marvelous. Gorgeous.

And he was just a McMurtry.

He was the wrong person from a long line of people used to being nothing but wrong.

Trash.

Like his father. She was absolutely goddamn right.

Funny, though. He'd told her she didn't deserve his trust. As Colin left, the heavy door thudding closed behind him, he had the feeling like he didn't deserve one damn thing, either. Ever again.

The thought made him want to howl.

Instead, he floored the Chevelle's gas pedal, and roared out of the parking lot, then out of the marina area, then out of Darling Bay as fast as a man could make a 450-pony engine go. Maybe if he drove fast enough into the dark he could outrun the thing that made him feel most sick.

Himself.

CHAPTER THIRTY-EIGHT

Someday Molly would live in a house. In that house, she'd have an entry hall and then a room or two, and *then* a bedroom so when people knocked on the front door it didn't sound like they were standing inside her brain.

Her sister's voice floated through the hotel door. "Are you okay? You're usually up by now! What's going on?"

Molly opened the drawer of the side table. The hotel had always provided ear plugs for its customers who didn't want to hear the bands playing late into the night in the saloon, and she knew there was still a plastic-wrapped pair or two at the back of the drawer. With her ears blocked, the knocking became more like a counterpoint to her jagged thoughts.

She should have told him. He'd been right. He'd been a jerk about it, yes. But he'd been right. She'd been wrong, *so* wrong, and so had Nikki. Nikki, though, had the excuse of wanting to protect her brother from pain. Molly didn't even have that.

She'd just wanted to help Nikki. She'd wanted to do something good for a woman who'd been helping her, who'd been listening to her. Molly had ignored that voice in the back of her head that had said to call Colin. To *text* him at the very least. How long would that have taken? *Your sister is hurt. Meet us at Kalamas Sheriff's Office.* Molly groaned. Her breath was hot against the sheet over her face but she didn't tug it off. At least with the ear plugs in, her own voice was louder and better drowned out her sister's. So she groaned to herself again.

She could even admit the truth: she'd wanted to impress Colin. Not that she'd gone through it all in her head clearly – she hadn't – but she'd had a brief vision of herself greeting him in a sterile police department hallway. *Your sister will be fine. I've been with her. We've got it handled, but we're glad you're here.* He'd kiss her, gratefully. He'd embrace his sister. She wouldn't be a *hero*, exactly, but she would have been helpful.

She used to be helpful. A long time ago.

What an idiot. Instead, she'd contributed to a man going on the run. She'd assisted him in getting away. Todd Meyers wasn't behind bars because of *her.*

"I will let myself in, see if I don't!" Adele's voice was muffled, soft at the edges. It was only because Molly knew her so well that she understood what the words were at all. But Adele wouldn't be able to open the door. On Molly's way up the walkway from the café the night before (after Colin had dropped the bomb on her, after she'd carefully put out the puny fire in the oven, after she'd had a quick and violent attack of tears, after she'd swallowed them back along with the taste of soot and grief), she'd made a brief detour into the saloon. It had been almost closing time, and Adele had been nowhere around. Nate was behind the bar and had given her a friendly wave. She'd made a show of grabbing a can of Coke from the back room, holding it up and cheerfully calling, "Pay you later, okay?"

Nate hadn't noticed that she'd palmed the master key when she'd grabbed the soda.

So now, Molly waited. Eventually, her sister went away.

A little later, the pounding got louder and stronger. Nate's voice filtered thickly through her earplugs. "Your sister is worried! Molly!"

She didn't respond.

"Just give me a sign you're alive, or I swear to God I'll get the fire department over here to bust this open. If there's anything Tox Ellis loves to do, it's use his tools."

Molly threw a pair of balled-up socks at the door.

Nate went away.

Another hour went by.

A softer knocking.

Molly knew it wasn't Colin.

She took out an earplug, listening, waiting.

For one second, she dared to hope.

"Molly?" Nikki's voice was loud but shaken. "Are we working today? Should I do the stuff on my list? You're freaking me out. What happened?"

A pause.

"Did Todd get to you?" Terror laced Nikki's words.

Molly sat up. She stood and opened the door, just a crack. "I'm fine."

"What is *wrong*?"

"Nothing. I just need a day off." Or a year. Maybe a lifetime.

Moving more quickly than Molly would have predicted, Nikki slipped inside. "Talk to me."

"I just think..."

"Are we still opening in four days?"

God, wouldn't that be great? If they put it off? Forever? "I saw your brother. He said the oven isn't working right, and that it's a hazard."

"Oh, that *asshole*. I'm going to kill him. He shut us *down* because you helped me?"

"No."

Nikki frowned. "No, he didn't shut us down? What's going on, then?"

"How do you feel?"

Nikki touched her arm cast self-consciously. "Like I fell off a horse. But I'm not the one hiding. Talk to me."

"I just think I'm not up for working."

"Today?"

"Ever." It was suddenly true. Lana's voice came back to her. *If you want to run, just let me know. I'm pretty good at hiding.* She slid back under the covers. It was only out of courtesy that she didn't pull the blanket over her face. Yet.

"Are you crazy?"

"Maybe." Molly could run. Get the hell out. She'd have bad credit for the rest of her life, but you couldn't get blood from a turnip, right?

Shit. The Golden Spike. Adele had co-signed on the loan for the café. They'd come after the saloon if Molly left town.

Tears rose, and she pushed them back as hard as she could. If she started crying, she would never, ever stop. The room would fill with salt water, and she'd drown.

But after she drowned and died, she'd have to eventually drag herself back to life and stand up. She'd have to take a shower and walk down to the café and work with Nikki on all the last-minute things they still had to do (so many, even more now that they couldn't offer pizza for a while).

"What else did my brother say to you?"

Molly shook her head.

Obviously guessing, Nikki said, "Something about Kalamas County being a bad place to file the report."

"You *knew?*"

"Of course. If my brother got hold of Todd, he'd go down for years. I figure a failed report in Kalamas plus a restraining order might be all I need. I have to get away from him, that's all. I don't need him to be behind bars. I just have to turn off the juice. *Make* myself stay away from him." Nikki bit her bottom lip.

"But you will. Stay away from him. Right?"

She shrugged. "I'm going to try. Love is really stupid."

"I know."

Nikki didn't look surprised. She sat on the edge of the bed and touched Molly's knee. "What are you going to do?"

"You think I can get a restraining order against myself?"

"Girl. If you could, I'd have been the first in line a long time ago."

"Colin really loves you." His name was painful in Molly's mouth.

Nikki sighed. "I know. It's awful. And I see the way he looks at you. He loves you, too."

The air in the room got thin. "No."

"He does."

"He said he didn't." Molly's chest hurt, as if her heart wanted to get out, to run away without the rest of her body. Could she live without her heart? Manage the café and talk to people and serve coffee and smile at babies, all the time without anything to pump her blood? She'd figure out another way to get her blood pumping through her body. Maybe Amazon sold a machine for it.

If she didn't have a heart, she wouldn't think of Colin.

She'd called him trash.

And his raised voice had triggered anxiety she'd thought she'd put behind her.

It was the lowest moment she could remember.

I was falling in love with you.

I was falling in love with you. All night, as she'd struggled through sleep, she'd heard his voice as if someone had put it on repeat. *Thought you were the brave one.*

"Then he's an idiot, too." Nikki closed her eyes as if thinking.

Molly waited, daring to hold the smallest whisper of hope. Maybe Nikki would have the answer. The way Molly could fix this. She knew Colin, after all, better than anyone else.

But all Nikki finally said was, "Yeah. Maybe we're all idiots."

CHAPTER THIRTY-NINE

Four days later, the grand opening was a smash. The Golden Spike Café was swamped. They opened their doors at four o'clock in the afternoon, and by five, there was a line halfway down the block.

Molly broke a sweat in the first hour and her hairline never quite dried after that.

A TV crew from a network affiliate down the coast arrived right after Molly noticed she had ketchup already smeared on her black apron. A man with a lot of thick white hair and teeth to match shoved a microphone in her face. "Molly Darling, how does it feel to be starting a new venture in this tiny town? Following in your big sister's footsteps? Worried about failure?"

She felt herself turn red.

"Oh, come on, have I ever been scared of failure before?" Of course she was terrified. That's all she'd ever been. But he didn't need to know that.

"Can you show us the back of your shirt?"

That, she could do. She was proud of their new shirts, which were also for sale to the public. On the front was a sketch of the Coffee Caboose. On the back was printed: *Get Nailed at the Golden Spike.*

The reporter gave a hearty, fake-sounding laugh as she turned back around. "Ah, that's great. Hey, you look like you've lost weight – quite a lot. Can you tell us how much?"

Molly shouldn't have been so surprised. Reporters always hit harder if their punch came out of nowhere. "Would you like to hear about our grand opening specials on the menu?"

"Any tips for our heavier watchers? Have you got any diet secrets on your new menu?"

Once, on a red carpet for the launch of their fourth album, a reporter had flat-out said, "What do you weigh?" And Molly had lied. Instead of retorting something appropriate like, "Mind your own business" or an even more satisfying, "Why don't you fame whores objectify women less?" she'd just mumbled a figure that she hadn't seen since she was sixteen. They'd run it on national television with a big caption that said, *Really, Molly?*

Now, still in the bright light of his cameraman's spotlight, Molly stuttered, "I...I..."

An image of Colin flashed in her mind. His voice replayed in her head. *You're incredible. I want to just look at you for the next ten years, is that okay?*

She leaned in to the microphone. "Diet tips? I recommend hot sex, a lot of it. As much of it as you can get with a man who thinks you're perfect the exact way you are now, not the way you *could* be if you lost weight." She pushed past the reporter, ignoring his pleas for another sound bite as good as that one had been.

"Who's it with, Molly? That sex? Can we have a name?"

No, they could *not*. "Whoever you've got, buddy!" It felt good. To just walk away from them. To not have her career riding on something they said, something the press could just make up.

At six o'clock, she climbed up on a just-vacated table (after carefully covering it with a paper kids' menu) and announced they were moving to standing-room only. Tables were carried to the back parking lot by the busboys and eager-to-help customers and it turned from a dinner party into a cocktail party.

It was a roaring success.

The locavore mac'n'cheese that Molly was serving (made with flax seeds, organic cheese, and the liberal addition of fresh, locally sourced broccoli) was a smash. She cut pieces of it and served it in Dixie cups. Her server, Boris, new to running the espresso machine, had it mastered in the first hour and was turning out mochas and lattes with floral foam decorations by the time they closed. The fresh-caught salmon crudités were a huge hit.

They ran out of macaroni at the same time they ran out of cheese.

The coffee was gone, both regular and decaf.

The milk cartons were empty.

They eighty-sixed champagne after Molly raided the Golden Spike for their last six bottles.

When there was literally nothing more to serve anyone except water, Molly stood on a chair. She raised her hands.

The town (because by now most of the town had squeezed in, defying Nikki's half-hearted attempts to keep the crowd at the legal fire-code limit) settled down, their faces turned up to look at her. Lord. Molly had forgotten she used to have stage fright, but there it was, large as life. That sick dread in her stomach, the faintness in the back of her neck.

Brave. She was brave.

What a lie.

"Thank you! Thank you so much for coming." Her voice shook. Molly tried to keep herself from searching the room for Colin, but it was impossible, just as it had been all night. He wasn't there. He probably never would be. She hadn't even seen so much as his patrol car since he'd told her she'd lost his trust. Since she'd kicked him out of the café for being a bully.

Since she'd kicked him out for being right about what she should have done, and hadn't.

A tremor shook her legs. Exhaustion threatened to take her down, knees first. "It means the world to me. To us." She smiled her brightest and hoped her lips didn't tremble. She thought with longing of her bed and how good it would feel when she was able to cry underneath the covers again. "I'd make a big speech, but honestly, I'm too overwhelmed. For now, I'll just say thank you again. I'll do my best to serve you all the way my Uncle Hugh used to: good food with maybe a *few* more healthy additives –"

Norma gave a huge groan. Everyone laughed.

"Don't worry, I'm keeping bacon on the menu, and I'll put it in everything I possibly can, just like he did. This weekend we'll have our first barbecued oysters, so make sure you come back for those. I'm reinstating the jalapeño quesadillas with added kale that you'll hardly notice, and you'll be happy to know the shake machine should be here next week." She waited for the cheer to die down. "The wood-fired pizza oven needs a little work, but soon enough we'll be serving you crispy crusts, both regular and gluten-free." She paused. "What, no cheer for the gluten-free part?" More laughter. "Come visit the Coffee Caboose – it'll be open at six in the morning. And from this Darling girl to Darling Bay, thank you all so much."

She stepped down carefully. The grand opening was almost over, and she hadn't died. Maybe she wanted to, but she probably wouldn't.

Now, she just had to get the customers out of here. Then she and Nikki and Boris and Jackson and Chris would clean up and get ready for the order that would arrive in the morning and let them do it all over again.

Tomorrow stretched ahead of her like eternity.

So many tomorrows to get through without Colin.

Bastard. Molly wasn't sure if she was cursing him or herself.

"Wait, wait!" Adele rushed forward, excusing herself as she moved through the crowd, carrying her guitar. "Nate and I have a gift for you."

"What?" Molly looked at Nikki, who grinned, as if she was in on it.

Great. This night needed to end, not be extended.

Adele sat on the chair Molly had just stepped down from, and Nate – also holding a guitar – stood tall beside her.

"We're doing a little unplugged set because I don't think we could fit all y'all in here along with even the smallest amp, so forgive us," said Adele, charming as always. "It's just a short song we wrote for my sister here, and I hope you like it."

The TV crew moved forward eagerly. Of course they did. It would play great on *Entertainment Tonight* or someone else they could package and resell it to. The crowd, so chatty just a few seconds before, quieted, moving back into a semi-circle.

Nate played a simple opening chord progression. Adele joined him, and then they both sang.

One's in the nest
One's just flown home,
And one's still in the storm.
But when she's back
We'll hold her tight
And keep her safe and warm.

Songbird brave
Songbird strong
Songbird back where you belong.

Songbird in flight
Songbird at night
One should be flying home.
Two in the nest,
These two won't rest
Till three are tucked in tight.

Adele's sweet voice held the last note and it floated over the crowd like a benediction. Molly didn't know she was crying until she brushed away the wetness on her cheeks. The applause was a solid thing, pushing against her skin in a way she'd totally forgotten about. They were clapping for Adele and Nate, and so was Molly, but it was more than that. Darling Bay was applauding the story of the Songbirds, *their* Songbirds. No cheering from any stage in the whole wide world had ever sounded exactly like this. It was like her sister had played in front of a family reunion – it was that warm, that bright.

Songbird brave
Songbird strong
Songbird loved where you belong.

It felt like home, and it was the best way possible to end the exhausting, stupendous, heartbreakingly Colin-less night.

CHAPTER FORTY

A n hour later, at eleven o'clock, Molly was finally completely alone. She'd managed – barely – to chase away well-meaning helpers. "That's why I have amazing staff. We've got it." Norma wanted to wash dishes, but Molly didn't want to have to explain the industrial dishwasher. Adele offered to refill condiments – Nikki was already doing it. Boris had the side work almost done and Jackson was finished cleaning the stove and prep areas. All that was left to do was cleaning the floors, and Molly wanted to do that herself. Alone.

She propped open both the front and rear doors to get the ocean breeze to blow through. The salty night air brought back the evening just a week before, when she'd been with Colin. The air had been cool and damp, like this, when they'd been exploring the folly.

Beautiful and useless, the folly was haunting her.

What would it be like to be that? Like Colin's mother, prettiest in the county? Like Nikki?

The metaphor ended at beautiful, though. Nikki wasn't useless. On the contrary, she seemed to be able to do anything she put her mind to. The heating element on the coffee carafe had burned out the day before, and before Molly could call their handyman back, Nikki'd had it taken apart. She'd identified the part that needed replacing and she'd gotten it from the hardware store and installed it before Molly had even really understood what had been broken in the first place. Nikki had fixed a hinge on the walk-in freezer. She'd figured out what was lacking in the leek soup recipe (it had been vinegar). Molly would bet Nikki got her ingenuity from her mother, who'd managed to keep two kids (mostly) safe and sane around a dangerous man.

Was anything *really* useless? Even an empty shell of a building could be inspiring – showing the hope someone had had long ago. The café had been useless for years as it rotted. Tonight it had brought together a community.

Molly took out the mop bucket and ran scalding-hot water into it. How many times had she mopped this place since she'd arrived almost two months before? And how many times had she done it when she worked that summer for Uncle Hugh? It was hard work. It always had been. Back in the day, the café's floors had always been sticky *and* crunchy by the end of a night. Spilled drinks, a beach's worth of sand tracked by closing time every evening. But it was something to put right. To make good again. Molly had always liked the task.

And tonight was special.

The long-accumulated grime from the café's dormant years was gone. This was fresh dirt. It came up easily. She felt good about this.

A stab of pain hit her in the solar plexus as she remembered Colin's face as he'd touched her in his bed. As he'd grinned at her in his office. She gripped the mop tighter and scrubbed at a place where it looked as if a whole cup of hot chocolate had spilled and then been tromped through.

Singing. That would help. The tune Adele had written was still in her mind.

Songbird brave
Songbird strong
Songbird loved where you belong.

She caught a glimpse of herself in the new stainless steel of the double refrigerator. *Lovely.* Hopefully, she hadn't looked that bad when she'd talked to the TV people. Her hair was sticking straight up. Sweat and tears had dried on her face so that she looked like she'd been caught in a downpour after running a muddy race. She laughed, but the fact that her reflection looked so sad made her want to cry all over again.

Molly jabbed the mop back into the bucket as hard as she could.

She would get over this.

Get over him – get over being *seen* by him, being loved by him, being with the man who felt like home.

A sob caught her mid-hope and she scrubbed at another tenacious stain next to the host's podium.

As she worked, she hummed the song her sister and Nate had sung. *Songbird brave, songbird strong...*Brave and strong. She'd thought she could find that here. Ha.

When the whole place was spotless and everything was put away, Molly took out a beer from the fridge. The café didn't have its beer and wine license yet, but Nate had brought over some provisions earlier. This bottle was the only soldier left standing.

She popped off the cap and took it through the dining room. She sat in the doorway on the lintel. The night air cooled her heated face, and she held the bottle to her cheek to help. The Homeless Petes, both of them wobbly on their feet, wandered past. The saloon was still open, but the doors were shut to the cold, and the jukebox had fallen silent. If she held her breath, she could almost hear the waves pounding on the beach.

And Molly sang the last verse that had just come to her, thirty seconds before.

I'm not brave
I'm not strong
I'm not loved, I don't belong...

It was a good thing no one was around to hear her.

CHAPTER FORTY-ONE

Colin woke with a headache that felt like he'd been drinking shots of rum all night on an empty stomach, instead of doing what he'd actually done, which was sit on his back porch with his damn guitar, strumming chords that didn't sound good with each other, trying not to think of the woman he was in love with, the one he wouldn't be able to trust ever again.

He made a pot of coffee and a plan to drink the whole thing before he left for the department. He had a meeting at ten and was interviewing two hopeful new rookies at noon. But then he might pull some vacation hours and come back home.

There had to be something to do to take his mind off Molly.

He fed Asiago.

He stroked her, wondering if her purr was getting louder or if that was just his imagination.

He cleaned the box.

Seven minutes later, he was out of things to do again.

Maybe he'd clean his guns. Then maybe he'd go murder some tin cans on the back forty behind the house. He was far enough outside city limits that no one would complain, and besides, who was going to whine about the sheriff plinking the hell out of some tomato cans?

His front door banged open, and he put a hand to his gunless hip. But a burglar, even one as inept as the Darling Bay burglars tended to be, would never make as much noise as this one did.

Colin felt hope flood his veins for one second, hot and bright.

Then his sister yelled, "You're *such* an asshole!"

His chin sank to his chest, and he exhaled, willing his heart to stop racing. "You want coffee?"

"Of course I do." Nikki barreled into the kitchen wearing a black T-shirt that read *The Golden Spike Café*.

"Get a cup."

When she turned to reach in the cupboard for a mug, he read the back of her shirt. *Get Nailed at the Golden Spike.*

"Classy shirt."

She turned, mug full, her expression as dark as her coffee. "Where's your computer?"

He jerked a thumb towards the couch. "Why?"

She opened the laptop and poked at the keys. "Come here."

"What's wrong with you? Let me see your face. Did he get to you?"

"Jesus." Nikki hiked her casted arm up, waving it at him. "I'm fine. I haven't seen him. That's not why I'm here."

"Of course not."

She spun the computer to face him. "Hit play."

"TMZ? I'm not as into Kardashian gossip as you are." But it wasn't a Kim or a Kourtney. It was a Darling Songbird. *His* songbird. Colin's heart dropped to his stomach.

"*Play.*"

He hit the button.

A man spoke over the images, his voice amped up and amused. *Two of the three Darling Songbirds are reunited! In the small beach town in Northern California that bears their family name, it seems they might have hit the skids a little harder than anyone had predicted until now. An affiliate of ours gave us this footage from just hours ago. The oldest Darling, Adele, and her new bartender lovebird, gave an impromptu concert at the newly reopened Golden Spike Café.*

The camera showed Adele and Nate singing to each other, smiling into each other's eyes in front of a good-sized crowd of people.

"That's definitely more than room capacity."

"Shut up," Nikki growled. "Watch."

The angle switched, and Molly smiled shyly at the reporter.

You look like you've lost weight – quite a lot. The clip broke for a second. *Diet secrets?*

Oh, God, they couldn't do this to her.

But then she answered. *I recommend hot sex. A lot of it.*

Can we have a name?

Whoever! Her voice was thin, and patently, ridiculously false-sounding.

"What the –?"

"Keep watching."

The after party was what caught our eye. Molly Darling, looking road worn and – what's that in her hand? Yep, she's drinking solo again, singing by herself on the sidewalk.

"She's not on the sidewalk. She's in the doorway." Colin leaned closer to the screen. Molly looked exhausted. Even in the low light, he could make out dark circles under her eyes, circles that matched the ones he'd seen in the mirror when he woke up.

"Just watch."

Is she high on something? Or just too sozzled to notice our camera? We can't tell, but we can tell she's one thing for sure: heartbroken.

Molly's voice was heard singing thinly:

I'm not brave
I'm not strong

Colin's heart froze in his chest.

I'm not loved, I don't belong

A grainy close-up followed – the camera had obviously been far away enough that she'd had no idea it was there. It was a miracle they'd caught her voice at all, and the distance didn't do it any favors. Her expression looked like she was a second away from bawling.

Just about the way he felt at that moment, too.

As the clip ended and an ad for a health spa began, he slammed the computer shut. "What the hell is this?"

"You have to ask me that?" Nikki jabbed a finger into his chest.

It hurt. "Excuse me?" All of it hurt.

"You've broken her heart, you selfish bastard."

"Oh, come on. You're surprised? I'm like Dad, right? Just say it if you're going to say it. I already know it, after all." He stood and put himself on the other side of the living room from her. Outside the glass, the sky was a clear pale blue all the way out to the horizon, but a line of seagulls was headed inland, flying in low. The weather was coming in, a big storm by the low-pressure feeling he had in his head. The folly was out of sight, below the cliff to the east. Maybe it would be such a big storm it would take the old building all the way out. Once and for all. Rip it apart, girder by lacy girder. "If anything, she broke mine."

"I don't think you have one to break. Not anymore. Not after what you did to her."

"What I did? She broke a promise she made to me. A promise about *your* safety, by the way."

"What about her safety?"

The question didn't make sense, and it rattled in his head as if the words were just beach stones she'd thrown at him. "*What?*"

"Did you bully her? Is that why you think you're Dad?"

"Did she tell you I did?"

"She didn't have to. I know you. You walked in, you yelled at her about helping me, which was none of your damn business, actually."

"My business? Hell, *yes*, it was. You went out of your way to make it my business when you lied to Kalamas County. The charge will never stick. Did you think of that at all?"

Nikki raised her fists, shaking them in the air. For a second, *she* looked like their dad, and the strangeness of it startled him worse than anything else.

Apples. So close to the tree.

She made a strangled sound and lowered her arms. "Of course I thought of that! You think I'm helpless, like Mom was. You have me pegged, and you've had me that way since I was what, seventeen?"

"Since the first time you got arrested for being drunk in public by *our father*, yes."

"Yeah, well, that was just a publicity stunt he put on for his next election."

Chuck McMurtry was so tough on crime he would arrest his own daughter. Yeah, that stunt had worked, too, if only to remind people where the McMurtrys were in the social stratosphere: Chuck had turned himself around. He was working on straightening out his kids, even if he had to put them in jail himself. The rest of the clan were drunk-in-public trash, always had been.

What the public didn't know was how Chuck had been sober-in-private trash, too. "You can't see it the same way I do, I know. You're his daughter, and he had to be hard on you."

"So I could get used to it? And I did." She pointed to her arm. "Do you really still think that I learned this just from watching him hit Mom?"

Colin shook his head. "He only hit you that one time, though." Their father had whaled on him and their mother. But only once had he hit Nikki. The time their mother had helped her up, telling her she'd just fallen.

"You idiot. He hit me all the time." Her voice was soft, but it had the effect of a scream.

"No. No – I would have protected you..." It was an explosion of the soul.

"Oh, Colin. You couldn't have. You were just a kid. You were too young, and too busy being out of the house and getting away from him. I never blamed you for that."

"Nikki – I didn't know. Jesus, Nik–"

"We all have our demons, that's the thing. All of us. What did you tell Molly when you last saw her?"

Colin's head felt like it was going to split open like a ripe watermelon struck by a .45 hollow point. "That I couldn't trust her."

"Do you actually believe that?"

He pictured Molly's face. Her open, trusting, gorgeous, happy face. Of course he didn't. He shook his head. Molly was so trustworthy she'd protected his sister. *From him.* "I can't trust myself." They felt like the truest words he'd ever spoken.

Nikki fell onto his couch cushions with a sigh as big as the waves that blew into Stine's Cove. "Oh, my God. You're my brother and I'll stick up for you, but you are as big an idiot about her as I've been about Todd."

"Yeah, well, you're trying to get over him."

"I'm going to succeed, thank you very much. I'm getting the last of my stuff out of his place later today."

He turned from the window to face her. "With my help."

Asiago leaped up to sit in Nikki's lap. She stroked the cat with a half-smile. "This little thing is adorable. And yeah, with some officer's help. I don't expect Todd'll be there, but they said to get a citizen standby, is that what it's called?"

"Yeah. And I'll do it."

"Figured you would insist."

"Hell, yes. You'll finally let me take care of you if I have to arrest you myself."

Nikki smiled, and she looked so young in the early-morning sun flooding the couch. He remembered her yellow footie pajamas, the ones with the palm trees on them. He hadn't thought of those for years.

She mewed at the kitten. Then she said, "Have you ever hurt a person? On purpose, I mean, without a reason?"

He looked at his feet. "Yeah."

"Who?"

Molly. But he wouldn't say it. Couldn't admit it. Scott Tinker? He'd twisted that guy's arm a little too roughly – he'd known he had, even if Tinker hadn't said anything about it. Of course, that had been after Tinker had thrown the punch at him.

Come on. He knew he must have been like his father at some point, hurting an innocent person. For fun. He thought harder. "Damien Scandi. I threw him in the cell so hard he tripped and twisted his ankle."

"What had he done?"

Colin scowled. "Broke his four-year-old daughter's arm. Second time."

"So. You hurt a guy who had a habit of abusing his daughter."

It sounded too innocent, too clean, when she put it that way.

"And you didn't mean to hurt him."

That was true. But he hadn't minded Damien yelling in the cell.

"Colin, you don't hurt people. You never have."

"I did, though." He could almost see Molly's face, paling again.

"Did you hit her?"

"No. But, Nik, you have to hear me when I say this." He sank into the couch next to her and kept his eyes forward, out the windows, towards the impending, still invisible storm. "I could hear Dad in my voice."

"Yeah, well. That's where you're better than him."

"What?"

"You can *hear* it. He never did. He always thought he was right, you know?"

That Chuck had. He'd never doubted a word he'd said or a move he'd made in his whole life. No matter what kind of mess he'd created as he'd blown through people's lives, he'd always believed he was more right than anyone else. Colin nodded.

"Then do better. For his sake."

"For *Dad's* sake? You think we owe him one single, solitary damn thing?"

Nikki leaned sideways, putting her head on his shoulder.

Why couldn't Colin remember the last time he'd hugged his sister? Told her he loved her?

"Yeah," she said. "We do owe him."

"For what?"

"For this." She pushed her head more firmly against him.

Quickly, so quickly that he could almost pretend he hadn't done it, he dropped a kiss to the top of her hair.

"So fix it." Asiago purred a rumble on Nikki's lap.

"I don't know how." He rubbed his aching forehead. "Do you have any bright ideas?"

"Not a single one."

"Some use you are to me."

Nikki sighed, but the tension was gone from her voice, the smile back in it. "Just a folly. Pretty and useless."

He was her big brother. He had to tease her. It was the law, and he upheld that law. "Pretty?"

Nikki laughed. "See? I have *this*, thanks to him. I have a brother."

"Yeah. Well." The backs of Colin's eyes hurt. "I have a sister."

In McMurtry-speak, it was the same as *I love you*.

CHAPTER FORTY-TWO

Molly couldn't get the beach folly out of her mind.

It was a trick, she knew, her own brain drawing her as close as she could get to Colin without actually *seeing* him.

But she let herself fall for her brain's trick. She drove herself out to the folly twice, both times hiding her car on a close-by side road. God forbid he should drive home and see her car and think she'd come to see him.

Because she hadn't. That's what she told herself, anyway.

Instead, she sat on the top floor of the folly and hung her legs off the open sides. She threaded her arms through the lacy bars and let the salt spray coat her skin. She breathed it deeply, allowing it to reach her lungs. The air smelled like home more than anywhere in Nashville ever had. It even smelled more like home than any other ocean ever had, and God knew, she'd sailed them all in the last six years.

As she sat and watched the tide pull in one afternoon and retreat the next, as she hoped that Nikki was okay on her own managing the café for the hour or two she took off, she sang that damned song.

The song they'd caught on tape.

It was unconscionable, what the media had done. It shouldn't have come as a surprise, and she knew she was naïve that it had. They'd been *in* the restaurant, after all. They'd asked her direct questions, and she'd answered them cheekily, without considering the sound bite they'd be able to build. She used to know better than that. Worst of all, she'd sung that song, her made-up lyrics to Adele's song. They'd caught it.

I'm not loved, I don't belong.

They'd caught her looking like a drunk, homeless hobo, her legs splayed out in front of her, the neck of the beer bottle slung between her fingers like it was always there, tears running down her cheeks. They must have been in the white van that had been parked in front of the saloon. She hadn't looked. She hadn't *thought*.

And the very worst part was that Colin knew because there was no way in *hell* he hadn't heard about it from someone. Nikki hadn't said anything more than, "Saw the clip. Sorry about that." That was enough. It was good to hear, and Nikki had hugged her hard.

Her sister Adele, though, had been purple with fury. "We'll sue."

"For what?"

"Defamation." Adele had spat out the word as if it had tasted bad.

"Did they actually say anything wrong, though? They just speculated and used my own words. It's been worse, you know that."

Adele had looked over the crowded dining room. "Well. At least it's brought the tourists in, huh?"

"In droves. Whole wild packs of them, all of them wanting coffee and barbecued oysters."

"Good. You're going to be laughing all the way to the bank."

It wasn't that easy. The café, even busy, was expensive to run. She had so much debt to pay off that it felt like she'd still be buried under it when she died of old age. But it was true, any publicity was good for business.

"Have you talked to him?"

"No." Molly hadn't bothered to ask who her sister meant. "And I won't."

"But you're heartsick."

"I'll recover."

The very worst part was knowing that she would. Someday, she'd wake up and not miss him quite as much.

Now, with the ocean breeze polishing her skin, Molly fell backwards on the wooden floor. She looked up through the lace ironwork at the pale-blue winter sky.

The beams that held her up had been refinished by Colin. Honoring the mother he'd loved.

Someday she wouldn't miss him like she did at this very moment, and that day would be even worse than today was – it would mean she wouldn't have this Colin-shaped hole in her heart, and that loss would be worse than this pain.

She *needed* that empty place. It was all she had left of him – that and his silly plastic badge, the one she kept in her pocket. Just in case. She pulled it out and held it tight as she dialed her cell phone.

Adele answered, sounding distracted. "Golden Spike Saloon."

"It's me. I want to do something."

"What?"

"I want to be the voice again. And I need your help."

CHAPTER FORTY-THREE

Two weeks later, *The Jack and Ginger Show* was delighted to hear from her, proving that good things *could* come from bad press. The problem was that the producers insisted that she come to them. "We'll fly you and your sister out to New York, of course. All expenses paid."

"I have my business to take care of. I can't just leave the café. And Adele manages the adjacent saloon. Can't we just do it over the phone? Or send out a film crew to me?"

"We handle these kinds of things every day. We'll have a temporary manager we've used before in Northern California step in. And you have a second-in-command, don't you?"

Molly, who was calling from the small desk she'd put in just off the kitchen, craned her neck to look out on the dining floor. Nikki was balancing three cups of coffee on a tray while laughing with Polly White and at the same time directing a family to the bathrooms. "I have a great one."

"Then it's settled. We think what you and your sister are doing is wonderful, and we can't *wait* to talk to you. It'll be an amazing segment."

A segment. Like a piece of an orange, a thing that could be pulled out and put on a plate, a thing that could be squeezed.

It was okay. They needed the exposure if they were going to make this work.

Molly worried about telling Nikki, how to do it without making her seem like the impetus, which she was, after all. "We're doing an album. Adele and I."

"Just the two of you?" Nikki, wiping down hot plates before stacking them, stared. "What about Lana?"

"She said no." What Lana had actually said was, "Go ahead, you two do what you want to do – you will anyway" before hanging up, but that was, after all, exactly what they'd expected her to say.

"Wow. Why now?"

"It's a fundraiser, actually."

Two lines formed between Nikki's brows, a thin eleven. "We're doing that badly? Have you ever thought about paying a guy to do that dancing sandwich-board thing down at the marina? We get a lot of the tourist traffic, but I know we could always use more, right?"

"Not for the Golden Spike. I want to..." Nerves danced in Molly's stomach. "I want to open a women's shelter. Somehow."

"Oh, Mol." Nikki stayed still. She held a bright-blue plate.

"And I don't want you to feel weird about it. That's why I wanted to talk to you about it first."

"No, of course not." But Nikki's eyes had turned a richer chocolate. They were just like her brother's that way, darkening with emotion.

"You were the inspiration, I admit."

"The poster child for what not to do, right?"

"No. Exactly the opposite. I want to ask you to work with me on it. The media has been non-stop since we opened. This is the right time, I think." Two weeks before, Molly Darling had been almost forgotten, but just that morning, she'd been asked to dance with the stars. (The nerve of that email had made Molly's cheeks overheat. *We've found many of our stars have gained the added bonus of shaping up as a result of the strenuous daily workouts.*)

Meanwhile, Nikki'd been learning to live without Todd. She hadn't seen him once, and Molly was so proud of her. The restraining order was in place, and someone said he'd left for a fishing job up in Alaska. Another someone said he was gone for good. *Finally got tired of being targeted by local law enforcement. Wanted to go somewhere he could be his own man.* Good. He could be his own man in a whole different state. Molly hoped he'd freeze his balls right off, two solid nuggets dropping into the snow. "I'll pay you, of course."

"Don't. I'd never let you pay me for that kind of work." Nikki set the plate down with a tiny clatter. "I'd be honored to volunteer with you."

"We'll work it out."

"How can I help you now?"

There were so many things she wanted to say. *Tell your brother I miss him. Tell him I should never have implied he was trash. Tell him I go to the folly and wait, hoping he never comes with one breath and praying for him to arrive with the next. Tell him I speed past the sheriff's office, hoping he'll pull me over. Tell him I'm furious with him. Tell him I love him. Tell him I wish I'd never moved back to Darling Bay. Tell him I wish...*

But all she managed to say was, "I would take a hug. If you have one to spare."

CHAPTER FORTY-FOUR

Colin had a desk full of important things to do. He always did. There were files on his desk that were so hot they should burst into flame just sitting there. One of his deputies had cheated on his taxes. Another was bankrupt from a gambling addiction. The mayor's son was dealing speed. Darling Bay was, often, darling, but it was also just a town, with real-life problems that balanced out the quirky local color. Colin had critical decisions to make daily. And today he didn't want to make a single one of them.

He called dispatch. "Hey, someone said Leif was out sick today. Who's on crossing-guard duty?"

"No one, yet. I'm working on it."

"I got it." He waved at Sweetie Swensen as he left the building, pulling on his orange vest as he went.

He spent the next hour relishing the simplicity of it.

Wear the orange vest. Wait for kids to approach. Stop the cars with his whistle and one raised arm. He would stop them with his body if he had to. He felt made of stone, and he was pretty sure that he could stop one car flying through an intersection, maybe even two. He'd end up on the pavement, broken into chipped pieces. He'd probably puncture the speeder's tires as well. They wouldn't get far. His last action would be a noble one. (Would Molly come to his funeral? Probably not.)

But the hour passed and all were safe, himself included.

He tucked the orange vest into the pocket behind the seat in his patrol car. He called dispatch to see if he could help clear any calls, but their board, for once, was empty. He thought for the thousandth time about driving to the café, about poking his head in, about apologizing.

How did you apologize for scaring a woman?

Damn it.

He checked his cell phone – no calls, no emails.

He'd get an old-fashioned donut, that's what he'd do. It had been a long time since he'd brought dispatch any goodies. Coffee and pastries were always a good way to make them happy.

The line at the donut shop was so long, and there were at least two city council members sitting at the shop's tables already. He'd have to talk to most everyone in the store.

And today Colin couldn't quite handle the political bullshit. Usually, he could shut down a portion of his mind (the part that wanted to be alone, in quiet) and play the game, but not today. All he could handle was waving kids across intersections. One foot already in the donut shop, he spun on his heel. Guy Mazanti was already in mid-wave, and Colin awkwardly pulled out his cell phone and waggled it in his direction. "Busy," he mouthed, and fled.

Idiot.

What a fucking idiot he was.

Along with the mayor and the fire chief, Colin ran Darling Bay. And he couldn't even handle being in the donut shop?

He drove back towards the department. He waited at the light on Lowry, and it wasn't until the blue car behind eased around him slowly and then passed him that he noticed the light, which had turned green, was going back to red.

Normally, people would honk at the person who wasn't moving at the green. But you didn't honk at a cop car. You eased around it, making sure your every move was legal.

And why was that?

Because people were scared of the cops. Not just the bad guys – the good guys were, too. How many times had little old ladies had panic attacks just because he'd pulled them over? Their hands would shake, and their breath would get short. He would know with one-hundred-per cent certainty that they weren't dangerous escaped felons, but his badge and uniform made them *feel* as if they were. Some young rookies liked that effect they had. They liked making people stutter with fear.

Chuck McMurtry – that had been just about his favorite thing in life, right up there with pot roast and making his beautiful wife and daughter cry.

Colin turned around one more time. He got in line at the donut store. He waved at the council members (four of them, clustered at one table like chickens huddling under an eave in the rain) and made the universal be-right-there sign.

Benny the butcher, behind him in line, said, "Hey, nice sound effects."

"Sorry?"

"I was at the library a couple of weeks ago, and they had the police scanner on. Sounded like you were...exercising?"

Colin just laughed along, though his chest felt tight.

He bought two dozen donuts and a portable box of coffee, the ones the records manager sometimes brought to finance meetings.

Then he strode out with a wide smile and no apology to the city council members he still hadn't chatted with.

In his car again, he pulled over the first mommy van he saw.

Sure enough, the dark-haired woman at the wheel had two little ones in car seats and a kid who looked to be about six riding shotgun. The mother had streaks of grey at her temples and she looked like she hadn't slept in the last three years. "Oh, no. Is it the tags? Because I've been meaning to get the smog check, but every day it seems like it's just impossible..." She put her hands to her face. "God, I'm sorry."

Her hands were shaking.

Her registration tags were, indeed, expired. And he didn't give a shit about them.

Colin said in a clear, firm voice, "You did nothing wrong. Nothing at all." He craned his neck and peered in the side window at the toddlers in their car seats. He grinned at them. "Looks like you're doing great. Seems like you just need a coffee."

"Wha–?"

"Are they allowed to have a d-o-n-u-t?"

She blinked. The kid in the passenger seat piped up, "Yes! We are allowed!"

"Do you know what I spelled, son?"

"No." His eyes were wide, but he didn't look scared. "When grown-ups spell something, we want it."

"Ma'am?"

"Y-yes. Sure."

"Back in a flash." He got a coffee from his car and took the box to the window. "Here. Pick out what you want. I just want you to have a better day than you were having before I stopped you."

Colin pulled over two more mothers, both of whom reacted similarly – with disbelief and then happy laughter. He pulled over a Mexican day laborer who probably didn't have papers. The guy's car was falling apart – if he didn't have a valid driver's license, Colin could legally impound the car for thirty days, after which the storage fees would be too steep for the guy to get his car out of the tow yard. Day laborers tended to buy cars that barely sputtered along and cost under five hundred dollars just for this reason. The man's hands didn't shake, but his jaw was so tight Colin could almost hear his teeth grinding. "Don't worry. *No se preocupe.* Have a coffee. Take a donut. *Gratis.* Have a good day."

He could hear the man's surprised laughter as he walked back to his car.

Colin could do this all day. Maybe he should. Get into the news as the Donut Sheriff. Wait, that didn't sound good. The media would end up mocking the cliché, and he'd probably eventually be accused of poisoning the donuts or something. Yeah, no matter how many donuts he gave away, people would always be scared of the power he wielded.

And no matter how long he spent on the street looking for Molly's car, it wouldn't be a good idea for him to pull her over.

She wouldn't want a donut from him, anyway.

You are a bonafide imbecile, McMurtry.

His inner voice, he realized for the first time, was his father's, with the same depth and inflection.

Fuck.

He rubbed his chest. He'd never known until now that a broken heart could actually produce *pain* in the upper torso. Twice in the last two days he'd hooked himself up to the blood-pressure machine in the cardio room. His blood pressure was fine. So was his pulse. He wasn't clammy, and he didn't have difficulty breathing. He was *not* having a heart attack.

Which, really, was too damn bad. If he'd been having one, he'd have an excuse to stay in bed for a couple of weeks and stare at the ceiling. He could close his eyes and train himself not to imagine her features every time he breathed.

Could he fake a heart attack, maybe? Pay off the ER doc to lie for him?

Could he get a new heart, somehow?

He pulled his sigh up from the bottom of his soul, where all his sighs seemed to be coming from lately.

Colin hated this. Hated love. Hated dashed hope.

Hated himself, pretty much.

As he pulled into his parking space at the department, his cell rang. "Yeah."

"Hey," said his sister. "I have to tell you something."

CHAPTER FORTY-FIVE

W atch the boom!"
Automatically, Molly and Adele swerved in their path to avoid the mic pole that swung in an arc just over their heads. They followed Nina, the assistant floor manager, and dodged a dolly that wheeled past so fast Molly worried for the operator's safety.

Nina turned in the darkness with a quick smile. "Sorry, it's always this crazy. Green room is this way. Watch this bit, don't trip on the cords."

The last time Molly had been backstage on a national television program had been their appearance on *Oprah*, almost twelve years before. The Darling Songbirds had been at their peak popularity. The audience had stood up and refused to sit, roaring with applause and screams. Oprah herself coming out on stage hadn't gotten the same reaction.

That had been a week before their father died, a week before the Songbirds broke up, band-wise and sister-wise. Molly and Lana had blamed Adele for pushing them back onstage too early, but the truth was that by then the sisters had been missing their mother too much for too long. They hadn't been connecting. They'd had hairline fractures already, and the split had been almost instant.

Being on the TV set brought it all back – the debacle on *The View* when Molly had run away from Barbara Walters. Molly's head set up a low, dull throb at the sound and the lights and the *flurry* of everything around her.

They'd been on the *Jack and Ginger* set only once, a year before the band split. Now the show had a bigger stage and more cameras, and it seemed twice as frenetic. Lights shone in every direction, and men were moving furniture around in a perpetual game of arranging fake living rooms. The ceilings were dark and high above. The cold air smelled of perfume and of metal and of the fresh flowers that sat on every stage surface.

The green room was as big as a hotel conference room, and it was packed. Molly felt her sister squeeze her hand in silent encouragement. Guests on that day's show appeared to include a traveling mime troupe from Paris, and the whole skinny group of them appeared to be diving face-first into the fruit arrangements on the heavily laden tables. A mother/daughter duo famous in the world of scrapbooking on Pinterest was showing off a new way to display shadow-boxed photographs. A politician recently embroiled in a DC scandal was having his sweating forehead powdered again.

And then there were Molly and her sister.

Wardrobe put them in quintessential country-girl singer outfits: tight blue jeans, sparkly tank tops studded with Swarovski crystals, and spike heels so high Molly's big toes immediately went numb.

Hair and make-up then performed a miracle of sorts – after blowing out and curling their hair and decorating their faces with twenty or so products, Molly and Adele both looked like they used to when the Darling Songbirds had been a national treasure.

"Oh, my God." Molly leaned in towards the mirror. "What did they do to me?" She touched the tops of her cheekbones. "I look ten years younger." She couldn't decide if she was pleased or horrified.

Adele laughed. "You do. You look like the baby I remember you as." She turned sideways and put her hands on her flat belly.

"Come on, I'm not Lana. And I've *never* been the little one."

"You're both my baby sisters."

Molly held her breath and turned sideways, too, comparing her belly against Adele's. "Don't worry, I'm still the fat one."

"Number one, shut up. Number two, not for long." Adele's cheeks were pink, and it wasn't just the stage make-up.

"What?"

"Yeah...No. Oh, crap." Adele's hands still rested on her belly. "Let's just say I won't be able to fit into these kinds of jeans for much longer."

"You're *pregnant?*"

Adele squeaked and then said, "Damn it! I wasn't going to tell you by myself. We found out yesterday, right before we got on the plane. I *promised* Nate I'd wait so we could tell you together – but that was an impossible promise to keep. I don't even know why I agreed."

Molly flew at her sister, wrapping her in a hug so tight it hurt. She pulled back and looked into her sister's face. In the move their father used to make, she took Adele's cheeks (so soft, still dewy with make-up) and pulled down her forehead to kiss it. "I'd ruffle your hair but they'll kill me if I do. You're going to be the best mother ever."

Adele swallowed. "I'm terrified."

"I think that's normal." Molly held out her hand. "Can I?"

"All you're going to feel is my muffin top over these jeans."

"Please." Molly touched her sister's stomach. "A little baby songbird."

Adele whispered, "I know."

"Oh! You're going to ruin my make-up."

A make-up girl hurried over, brush at the ready, but Molly shook her head. "I won't cry. I promise. Oh, God, I have to pee. I'll be back. I'll meet you in the green room?"

In the bathroom, she leaned her forearms against the cool porcelain sink. She stared at herself, but the face that looked back only unnerved her – it was someone else's. It belonged to a girl she hadn't seen in a long, long time, a girl who at one point had known what she was doing.

Molly wished she had one *single* clue how to do this. Crystalline fear rested at the very tops of her lungs, ready to stop her breath, to close her throat.

Adele was the fixer.

Molly was the voice.

Lana was the artist.

It wasn't true, not anymore. Molly didn't have a voice, she only had fear. And, if she looked deep inside, there was something even worse than the fear – the tiniest sprig of jealousy.

She didn't want to be pregnant, like Adele. She didn't *want* to be her sister – Adele was the best Adele in the world, and Molly, while always emulating her sister's strength whenever she could, had no interest in being like her.

But that love, the love that Adele and Nate shared – the way they looked at each other when they were both tired, the way they leaned on each other behind the bar when they thought no one was looking, the way their hands reached out to touch fingers without words...

She saw their connection, and she pictured Colin.

Colin's eyes, so dark his pupils were almost invisible against the iris.

Colin's fingers brushing hers.

His sudden, surprised bark of laughter. His blow-torch-hot touch. His incredible, talented lips on hers.

The way she felt like she'd finally found home in his arms.

"You love him," she whispered to the Molly in the mirror. That Molly had sparkling, smoky eyes and hair that was shiny and luxe. That Molly looked successful.

"I know," that Molly answered. "I'm working on it."

CHAPTER FORTY-SIX

J ack O'Malley and his co-host Ginger Dodge had become famous for their quick wit and camaraderie on stage. The most watched morning show in the nation, Jack and Ginger were known for spinning from dire story reportage (the father of nine hit by a train, so tragic) right into the fabulous (beloved actress adopts red-headed triplets!).

Nina pulled them out of the green room. "Political scandal section almost done – you girls are up next."

Funny, Molly never used to mind being called "you girls."

"Women," she whispered to herself.

"What?" Adele pushed a long wave of hair over her sparkly shoulder.

"Nothing."

"Here we go!"

On stage, they stood in front of their microphones and ran through a second sound check. Their guitars were amped. Spotlights danced.

Tamika stood on the edge of the darkness. "Five, four..." Then she held up three fingers, then two, then one.

Jack O'Malley's voice carried from the side stage. "And today, we have the unbelievable honor of hosting two-thirds of one of *my* favorite bands of all time, The Darling Songbirds. Known today as the Darling Duet, take it away, girls!"

Molly's heart juddered and then, just like it always had on stage, eased. Time slowed. She held Adele's gaze for what felt like a whole minute but was probably less than a second.

Then they sang.

Hummingbirds migrate at night,
When the sun's asleep they take flight,
They fly low and hard and fast
And when they're home at last,
They know that they're all right.

Molly took the verses, Adele backing her up in harmony on the chorus. The studio was still, and in the darkness beyond the lights, Molly could see the gaffers and dolly operators slow their work. The production managers stopped and watched.

When she needs a place to run
When she knows he has a gun
She runs low and hard and fast,
And when she's home at last,
She'll know her life's begun.

By the time they sang the last line of the last verse, Molly had goosebumps dancing up and down her arms.

It would be a hit. She'd known it about "Remember Me" and she knew it about this one. It would get airtime. It would get them back in rotation, and most importantly, it would raise the money she wanted.

Jack and Ginger seemed giddy as Molly and Adele settled themselves into the couch opposite them.

"That was incredible," said Ginger. "You just blew us away."

Jack shoved back his famously white-and-black hair and shone his gleaming smile at them like a flashlight. "Now I remember why I fell in love with you. But I have to ask, do you miss your sister?"

"Every day," said Adele.

"Is she going to join you eventually?"

"Lana is always with us, even when she can't be on stage with us."

"Awww," cooed Ginger. "So cute. This song will be on a new album, is that right?"

"Yep," said Molly. It was still hard to believe how fast all the agreements had come through. They'd only had time to write the first song on the album so far, but then

Adele had called a friend with an indie label. They'd sung it to him over the phone. He was pulling together a backing band, and next month they were flying to Nashville to lay the first tracks in a big, vacant church. They would sing the songs live and add very little remastering. Post-production would take less than five weeks, and it would be live digitally within a couple of months. The world of music, which used to be as slow as molasses in January, had jumped to light speed. "It's called *Migration*. And y'all just heard the title track right there."

Jack's eyes burned with intensity, but Molly knew from watching the show that he got almost as excited at meeting zoo sloths. "And you have a very," his voice dropped, "*important* message to share, is that right?"

This. This was what was important to get right. The song going well – that was great. But this moment was when Molly had to use her real voice.

"We do." Molly licked her lips and took a breath. "You know we sing pretty, right?"

Jack and Ginger laughed as hard as if she'd told a side-splitting joke. "You do, sure, that you do."

People scurried on the set in the darkness just beyond the lights. They wouldn't hear her – they were too busy doing their job. The audience, sitting in their kitchens and living rooms – they would be busy, too. Feeding kids, getting dressed, shaving, thinking about their day, their worries. Molly had to grab them.

"Well, thanks for that. But you know what's not pretty? A woman with a black eye so bruised she can barely blink. The welts on her arms and legs. The ones she can't hide on her neck."

Jack and Ginger were both appropriately chastened, nodding with grim expressions of deep interest.

"That's who this album is for. There have been country songs about abused women before, yes. It's a popular trope, right up there with beer, bullets and bourbon. But it's glossed over. One song every few years? With the proceeds doing what, exactly?"

Ginger murmured softly, "And *Migration* will be different?"

Molly nodded. "The world doesn't need us dolled up like we are right now, starring in music videos of fake abuse fixed by fake strength. We want to give that strength back to the actual women who've lost their own. Every day, in every town in this great nation, women stay where they aren't safe because they can't afford to leave. And when they finally find the courage to leave, to pack up the kids and run for their very lives, they have no place to go. *Migration* isn't just the name of the album, it's also the name of the non-profit organization we're starting to help abused women get to safety."

Jack nodded. He was a pro at making guests feel important, but his eyes were truly locked on hers. As if this meant something to him. As if it was more than just a sound bite. "And..." He prompted her to continue.

Molly took a breath and thought about the plastic badge she'd tucked in her bra because it wouldn't fit in the skin-tight jeans they'd shoved her into. She thought about Colin's eyes. And she leaped. "Jack, who are you thinking about right now?"

He pulled his head back, looking as startled as if she'd whacked his nose with one of her newly gel-tipped fingernails. "Sorry?"

"You have a look in your eyes. I could be wrong, but I think you have a connection to this topic?"

Jack blinked, and the muscles in his face slumped for a split second. His mask slipped. "My mother."

Ginger looked stunned.

Molly nodded. "Did she get out?"

He shook his head. "She couldn't afford to. By the time I was..." He coughed and cleared his throat. "By the time I could afford to get her out, she'd died of cancer. Truth was, she'd died a long time before that."

"Your father?"

"My stepfather. Stone-cold bastard. I don't know where he's buried, but I can tell you this, it's not next to my mother. I have her safe in a plot I paid for. With our people. Not his." Jack straightened and glanced at the camera. "I can't believe I just told you that."

Ginger put her hand on the sleeve of his jacket, and Molly saw something pass between them. No wonder this show was number one in the ratings.

Molly went on. "People *don't* talk about it. That's the thing. We're scared to. In this day and age where we post pictures of our lunch on Instagram and share feelings on Facebook, it's still somehow taboo to talk about this kind of abuse in the open. Statistics show that bystanders, even if they think something *might* be going on, don't step in to ask questions or to help until they've seen at least eight instances of possible abuse, sometimes more. This album will raise funds to start a national foundation where women – and men, of course, but there are fewer male victims – can register and get confidential help."

"What kind of help?"

"They'll be able to find out about safe houses in their area. They'll learn helpful phrases, the right words to say to their local law enforcement. They can connect – whether online or on the phone – with abuse survivors, people who've been through what they have who can help inspire them to make the first steps."

Ginger glanced at a blue card she held between perfectly manicured fingers. "And in your own hometown of Darling Bay?"

Molly wondered whether to correct her. They weren't from Darling Bay, after all. Their family was, they shared its name, but the girls had been born and raised in Tennessee for the most part, only visiting Darling Bay on school holidays.

But no.

When it came right down to it, Darling Bay *was* home. She felt pride swell inside her. "A friend of mine, a Darling Bay native, recently got out of an abusive relationship. I didn't know how to help, and I have to admit, I did it the wrong way. In helping her, I ended up putting her into a potentially more dangerous situation, because I didn't understand how important every single piece of the puzzle is. Our goal with this album is to help people find out how they can *actually* help. People can have every good intention and still get it wrong. We really want to help them get it right, whether they're the victim or the bystander or the friend."

Jack rubbed the bridge of his nose and made a rueful noise. "I wish you'd been around when I was a kid."

"There's always been help out there. It's just sometimes hard to find. The Migration Foundation will be a national aggregator of places to go for information on all types of abuse, and its main goal will be to help people make themselves safer."

"Well." Jack popped his palms down onto his knees and snapped them back up again. "I sure as hell didn't have any plan to break down on national television." He cleared his throat. Molly could practically feel the country stopped in their tracks, drawn towards him. They were *listening*. "But I *did* have a little plan up my sleeve."

Molly glanced questioningly at Adele, who only shrugged.

"We have a special guest here who would like to help."

"Oh, boy." Molly's stomach flipped.

"You're pals with the sheriff of Darling Bay, do I have that right?"

"What?"

Jack looked at the teleprompter. "Sheriff Colin McMurtry, come on out here and say hello to the two Songbirds!"

The *Jack and Ginger* theme song played triumphantly as Colin walked on stage.

CHAPTER FORTY-SEVEN

C olin figured he was going to throw up.

That would be something. Try to do a good deed at the same time that you attempt to win the woman you love by apologizing in just the right way, but end up hurling on national television.

He stuck a finger to his neck and pulled on the Windsor knot the girl backstage had tied. They'd tried to put him in a bolo tie but he'd flat-out refused. He was going to look like a country bumpkin with an old, out-of-date blue suit because that's exactly who he was. This was the suit he wore to city council meetings and when he had to swear in new deputies. His mother had bought him the dark-blue silk tie when he'd graduated from college. He didn't need fancying (or even worse, countrifying) up.

Molly was sitting next to Adele on a short, low couch, her legs crossed at the knees. Her legs looked amazing in those tight jeans. He hoped all of America could see how gorgeous she was. Adele, next to her, also looked pretty, but he only glanced at her for a moment.

It was Molly his eyes went to. It was Molly his heart tugged him towards.

It had been Molly from the very second she'd come back to town.

He wanted her to stand, to run to him, to throw her arms around him, to kiss him as hard as she had on the one night they'd spent together, but this was national damn television and if he got through this without her cussing him all the way back to California the way he deserved, he'd still be coming out ahead.

Jack O'Malley stood and shook his hand. Another chair rolled in out of nowhere. "Sit, sit, won't you? Yes, next to Molly, that's perfect. We're so glad you're here. Tell us, won't you, what it is you do in Darling Bay?"

"Well, I'm the sheriff."

Laughter rose around him. Was that funny? Up felt down, right felt left, and the only thing he knew for sure was that Molly drew him like a drug he hadn't known he was addicted to.

"You go around arresting people?"

"Sometimes. My deputies usually do that part."

Ginger, whose face was pretty but actually *lacquered*, said, "Our sources tell us that you recently pulled people over and instead of tickets, you gave them donuts?"

He groaned. "I knew that would come back to haunt me."

"Why did you do that?"

"Well, you know. People are scared of the cops."

Ginger inclined her head. "You hold the power, is that right?"

"That's, well, that's the reason I'm here. Yeah, we're the symbols of power." He parted his coat and touched the badge that he'd attached to the breast pocket of his shirt. "This right here. It says a lot about who I am and what I do. But it's really you, the citizens, who have all the power. My job is an elected position. If I fail, I get voted out, and if I fail, I *should* get voted out."

"Have you failed in the past?" She was guiding him.

"Oh, yeah." More laughter. Was he suddenly a comedian? He didn't mean to be.

"How?"

"Recently, in fact. I got a little drunk on duty, but it wasn't on whisky, you'll be happy to know. I got drunk on power. I thought that not only was I the guy to keep my sister safe, I thought I was the *only* man in the whole world who could do it. I was proven wrong by this woman sitting next to me right here. Molly." As he said her name, he dared to look into her eyes, and the sheer shock that resided there made him doubtful this had ever been a good idea. He'd thought it was, and he'd held on to that hope for the long cross-country flight. When he landed, he had sixteen texts from Nikki encouraging him to get it done.

Now, he just wanted to run.

Colin McMurtry was many things, but he'd never been a coward. At least not till now, and he didn't intend to make such a big life change on national television, so he stayed in his chair and kept talking. "Molly stepped in to help my sister in a dire situation. My sister is the one she was talking about, the one in an abusive relationship. You'd think it wouldn't happen to a woman whose brother was the sheriff, right? Or to a woman whose dad was the sheriff before that." He slowed his words down as much as he could. He had to get this right, for so many reasons. "But maybe it's because we were in the business that she knew how to hide it. It took a person *not* in my family to help her. My sister was scared to come to me, scared I'd abuse the power of my badge the same way my father had done in the past. And while I like to think I'm better than him, I'll never know for sure. And that's okay. Molly helped my sister get to safety. We don't have a women's shelter in little old Darling Bay, so she got my sister to the nearest thing we have, a simple room in a simple house. Molly gave her a job, and more than that, she gave my sister a purpose."

Next to him, Molly twisted in her seat and made a noise of protest.

He went on, "I wouldn't be telling y'all this if we didn't know where the guy went. Apparently, he heard that even his friends in the next county couldn't keep a warrant from being issued. He ran to Alaska to work in the fishing trade with his brother. Hey, where's the camera that's on me?"

Jack mutely pointed to a camera lens ten feet away.

Colin looked straight into it. "Todd Meyers, you piece of shit, don't you *dare* come back to town unless you want to argue with me about that warrant, which I'll be thrilled to do. With my bare hands."

Molly laughed out loud, and the sound of it went right to his head.

"*And* it's a good thing we have a three-second delay! With that," continued Jack cheerfully, "do you have something to surprise the girls with?"

"I do have a surprise for the Darling women, yes." He turned in his seat so he could look at them. Molly was biting her bottom lip.

"That folly of mine? It's exactly that, beautiful and useless. I'm in the process of selling it."

Molly's eyes widened and she raised her hand a few inches before letting it drop back into her lap. Colin wanted with all his heart to catch it, to kiss it, but he had to get through this.

"It'll fetch a fair price. Y'all have country music to raise charity funds. I don't have anything but this country boy's heart to bring. I'm going to use the money to help you start the safe house you wanted in our town. It'll be small but it'll be a start." He cleared his throat, suddenly thick with salt. "It'll be the opposite of a folly. It'll be boring on the outside, completely hidden in plain sight, and it'll be useful as hell. Someday, someone like my sister will have someplace to fly away to."

"Colin –"

Ginger spoke, her words clear that their time was almost up. "What a lovely thing to do. In the spirit of that generosity, the network would like to match that donation..."

Colin tuned her out. If he didn't speak to Molly now, he wasn't sure his nerve would come back. Seemed to him he'd left a lot of it behind, when he'd stalked out of the café and out of Molly's life.

He turned to her, turned so far he knew the camera would have a hard time catching his expression, but that was good because there was a fair chance he was going to cry. "Molly, I don't deserve you. I told you that you didn't deserve my trust, and I've never been more wrong about anything in my life." He caught her hand in his – it was cold and small and he wanted to tuck it against his heart. Instead he just held it. She could probably feel his pulse racing under her fingertips. He hoped she could. "Molly, I love you. You're everything I've ever looked for in a partner and about a million times more. Will you forgive me? Asiago learned to meow and I want you to..." Her hand started to tremble in his – or was that his own fingers shaking? "I want you to know that I love you."

"Holy crap."

Colin's heart juddered in his chest. *Holy crap* wasn't exactly what he'd been hoping for.

"I love you, too." She gave a laugh that sounded like a sob. "But I am *not* doing this on national television."

He wanted to kiss her—he *needed* to. How could he possibly wait another second? But Molly was up and disconnecting her mic. He did the same to his, as Jack and Ginger both made hand signs at the camera operators to follow them. He heard Ginger say something he couldn't understand and he heard Adele laugh.

Honestly, Colin didn't give a shit if the whole thing was broadcast on every channel in the world, translated into every language. That would be fine by him. Molly had just said she *loved* him and he could fly, he knew he could.

And he might have to—Molly was running so fast off the stage and around the camera crews that he had to leap a black pile of cables to keep up with her.

A man with a handheld camera dogged his heels, but ahead of Colin, Molly was fast. She yanked open an unmarked door and threw a panicked look at him. "In here."

Colin followed her inside and bolted the lock behind him. They were inside a storeroom of some sort, full of bottles of cleaning liquid and dozens of brooms and stacks of boxes. One bare bulb burned above them. The air smelled acidic and musty.

To Colin, it was heaven.

"Say it again," gasped Molly.

Gladly. Always. "I love you."

"One more time."

"*I love you.*"

"Oh!" Her face was light, and happiness, and everything he'd ever wanted to see.

He went on, "I'm so sorry I was such an ass. You did everything right, and—"

"*I'm* sorry for not keeping my promise to you. I know it turned out okay, but it was the only thing you'd asked of me, and I didn't do it."

Colin wanted nothing from her but the promise of the rest of her days. He'd work up to that—he'd wait at *least* a week before asking her to marry him. Or five days. Maybe three. "You said on stage that..." His courage ran out suddenly, like a clip ran out of bullets.

"I love you."

"God, Molly—"

"I love you." She grinned, and the brilliance of her smile made his knees wobble. "With all my heart."

Behind them, someone unlocked the door with a click. Colin heard it open, and felt, rather than saw, a camera lens aim at them.

He didn't care.

Happiness was a hot air balloon in his chest, and in another minute, he was going to float away and take her up with him. So right there, on national TV, before he drifted into the sky out of sheer joy, Colin kissed the hell out Molly.

And goddamned if she didn't kiss the hell out of him right back.

EPILOGUE

Maybe if Molly jiggled her headset a little more, it would break, and they'd have to get the I.T. guy back in to fix it. Or maybe the power would go out, and the computers would switch off.

Molly would never, *ever* be ready to flip the switch to open Migration's hotline.

It would take bravery she didn't possess. It would take way more than a plastic badge in her pocket, more than a new office four doors down from the Golden Spike Café. It would take more than three new desks, computers and chairs.

It would even take more than the small, sparkling diamond on her left hand, the one that kept freaking her out every time she forgot about it and saw it fresh all over again. Yes, it helped that Colin was standing next to her, that Nikki was at the next desk. She needed *more* than just guts, though. She wasn't sure what. But she was pretty sure she didn't quite have it yet.

Flipping the switch wasn't so much as a *switch* as it was pushing the button that made their phones go live. Pushing that button meant that Migration would be ready to go. That it would be ready to help women who needed it.

It would mean they had all the answers.

And Molly knew they didn't.

She looked up at Colin, who stood next to her. "What if –"

He cut her off. "You'll know what to do."

"But –"

"Just do it. You're fully staffed with volunteers for what, the next two months?"

To Molly's right, Nikki nodded and fiddled with her own new headset. "More like for the next six months. You'll never have to be in here again, if you don't want to be."

Molly stared. "I *want* to be here."

"I know you do. But you've already done so much, bringing in the counselors, training everyone in *all* your free time from the café, and I work with you, so don't deny it's taken over your life."

"Amen," said Colin fervently. Molly knew he was proud of her, and she also knew he wished she was working less. A lot less.

Nikki flapped a binder in her direction. "We're prepared. Every volunteer knows what to do. What to say."

"No one knows what to say all the time."

Colin smiled at her and went into a crouch at her side. "You taught them that, too."

"Oh, crap. So it's time." Terror made her bones feel as weak as tissue paper.

Nikki nodded. "Do it. Flip the switch. No one will call, anyway. What are the odds that the phone will ring even once on the first day?"

Molly put her head on the desk next to the fancy keypad that had myriad transfer capabilities, all of which Molly knew how to use. Theoretically. They'd tested every functionality. But they hadn't needed all the bells and whistles when it really mattered. Not yet. "We advertised. Someone will call."

"Not much, we didn't."

"Excuse me?" Molly thought of the checks she'd been writing from the album sales fund. Big checks. "We advertised in the *New York Times*. The *Washington Post*. We were featured on *HuffPo* and the *Guardian* and they did that segment on the *Today Show*."

Colin squeezed her hand. "It's going to be okay."

"People are going to call. Oh, God."

"Molly? It'll be okay."

His voice was soothing, but not quite soothing enough to make her push the button that pulsed on the screen at her, getting redder and angrier by the moment.

LIVE, it read. It meant that they were live and receiving calls. On the other end of that button, there was a guy named Steve in Eureka who was watching to make sure all connections ran smoothly, that their internet connection was robust, that technical glitches wouldn't put a caller in danger.

Only Molly and her volunteers could accidentally do that. Oh, God. The *LIVE* button seemed to mean more. It could be the difference between life and death for someone someday. This was huge. Enormous.

This was too much.

Colin stood, kissing her cheek as he rose. "You've got this. Do it."

She slid a glance up at him. "Are you bossing me?"

"Would I do that?"

"Because you'd better not be." Riled, she moved her mouse and clicked the *LIVE* button before she changed her mind again. "Holy crap. I did it."

Nikki gave a short whoop. Colin clapped.

Molly leaned back in her new chair. "Oh, man."

The phone rang.

Lord. Molly held her finger over the keypad. "Should I get it?" She looked at Nikki. "Should you?"

Nikki, her eyes wide, pointed at Molly.

Swallowing the deep breath she didn't have time to take, Molly hit the *Answer* button. "Migration, are you in a safe location?" Her voice shook.

"I'm on my cell phone. I've got the kids with me. I saw your ad, and I cut it out, but I didn't think I'd have to call

— we're in the car, and we can't go back, but I don't know where to *go*."

Molly stared at her screen. Apps of all sorts littered the desktop. Five seconds ago, she knew how to use each one. Now her mind was completely blank.

The woman on the other end of the line said, "Hello? Are you there?"

Colin's hand rested on Molly's shoulder, warm and strong, as reassuring as his body was to her at night. He believed she could do this.

Nikki believed she could do this.

And deep down, Molly did, too. "Okay, tell me where you are. We're going to get you some help."

Colin grinned at her and Nikki did a silent happy dance in her chair.

The woman was in Florida, running away from a boyfriend who had hit her with his fists and then walloped their son with a length of wood. While they talked, Molly confirmed they didn't need an ambulance, then pulled up the resource-management guide and directed her on the fastest route to the police department. She told the woman which words to say to the officer inside. She had the woman say them back to her.

"Okay. I'm parked in front of the station." The woman's voice was thin, as if it were a guitar string stretched too tight.

"You're doing the right thing. What he did was *not* okay. It's all right to take care of yourself and your children. Now go in there. While you're in talking to the officer, I'm going to be texting you the directions to the safe house nearest you, okay? All you have to do is click the link, and your phone will guide you there. Does that make sense? I'll send you a bunch of other resources for you to look at when you have time."

The woman was crying now. "Yes."

"I'll stay on the phone with you while you go inside."

"What if I say the wrong thing?"

Molly's heart was thumping so loudly she wondered if Colin and Nikki could hear it. "It's totally okay if you say the wrong thing. We all get scared. Just keep telling the truth about what's going on, okay? That's all that matters."

"Thank you...Okay, we're inside. Thank you again." The line went dead.

Molly stared at the screen. "Oh, my God. What if I screwed that all up?"

Nikki pumped her fist. "You were *perfect*."

"She's right, my love." Colin caught her hand and kissed it. "You just made a damn difference, you know that?"

Molly finally swallowed the lump in her throat that had lodged itself there at the beginning of the call. "I was so scared. But I wasn't a hundredth as scared as she was. How do you get the bravery to *do* that? To go?"

Nikki said, "You don't. Until one day, you just do. Remember what the counselor said? We can help. But we can't make them do anything."

"I hate that," said Colin.

Both Molly and Nikki laughed.

He frowned. "I really do. I wish we could make every woman get help, and –"

The front door opened, and he broke off.

Molly swung her chair around to face the door. They weren't expecting anyone, and it was a tiny call center – it wasn't set up to receive people. Not yet, at least.

The sun glared through the glass, and the woman in the doorway was just a black outline.

Molly stood. "Hello? Can we help you?"

With a thud, the woman dropped a suitcase to the floor. "What's up?"

Molly's heart rose back into her throat. "Lana?"

"I've had a crappy trip. So don't hug me. Don't make a big deal about it."

Don't *hug* her? Don't make a big *deal*?

Yeah, right.

Lana was about to get a lesson in how Molly didn't get bossed around anymore. Molly threw herself at her sister so hard they almost fell over together.

And Lana hugged Molly back every bit as tightly.

ABOUT THE AUTHOR

Rachael Herron is the bestselling author of the novels *The Ones Who Matter Most, Splinters of Light,* and *Pack Up the Moon* (Penguin), the five-book Cypress Hollow series, and the memoir, *A Life in Stitches* (Chronicle). She received her MFA in writing from Mills College, Oakland. She teaches writing extension workshops at both UC Berkeley and Stanford and is a proud member of the NaNoWriMo Writer's Board. She's a New Zealand citizen as well as an American.

Rachael *loves* to hear from readers:
Website: rachaelherron.com
Facebook: Rachael.Herron.Author
Twitter: RachaelHerron
Email: Rachael@rachaelherron.com